Praise for *A Bad Day for Pretty*

"The second novel featuring vigilante Stella Hardesty blends humor and Southern-fried crime-solving, to delicious effect."
—*People*

"Littlefield's rollicking second novel . . . delivers on the promise of her debut. . . . Littlefield wields humor like a whip, but never lets it dilute the whodunit. A force to be reckoned with, Stella is a welcome addition to the world of unorthodox female crime fighters."　　　—*Publishers Weekly* (starred review)

"Fiftyish Stella is a force to be reckoned with in this second outing in an entertaining series."　　　—*Booklist*

"No sophomore slump for Littlefield! Her second novel featuring Stella Hardesty, empowered avenger of abused women, is just as compelling and addictive as her debut. . . . You'll race through the pages of this book and then be sorry to leave Stella and her cohorts behind."　　　—*RT Book Reviews* (4.5 stars)

Also by Sophie Littlefield

A Bad Day for Pretty

A Bad Day for Sorry

Praise for *A Bad Day for Scandal*

"This is the author's third comic novel starring brassy Stella Hardesty. . . . You have to root for a gal who can hunt down murder suspects—and lust after local sheriff Goat Jones—without rumpling her Spanx Hide and Sleek Hi-Rise Panty."
—*AARP The Magazine*

"This caper is more fun than eating cotton candy on a Ferris wheel. Littlefield's zesty dialog and astute observations make this irreverent third series entry (after *A Bad Day for Sorry* and *A Bad Day for Pretty*) fly by. The zaniness evokes Janet Evanovich or Harley Jane Kozak; the story itself, Ben Rehder, who writes so well about good old boys behaving badly."
—*Library Journal*

"If we all had mothers like Stella, this would be a better world. Fans of quirky mysteries straddling the line between tough and funny need to grab a Littlefield pronto." —*Kirkus Reviews*

"Littlefield's eccentric cast of characters grows richer with each book, and Stella continues to dazzle with her wit, charm, and ease with firearms." —*Publishers Weekly*

"Fiftyish Stella . . . continues to carry the day, as always, in this sassy mix of comedy and mystery." —*Booklist*

"Stella Hardesty is a funny and endearing heroine—with just a hint of Dirty Harry thrown in . . . don't miss this gem of a book." —Linda Castillo, *New York Times* bestselling author of *Pray for Silence*

A BAD DAY FOR SCANDAL

· · · · · · · · ·

SOPHIE LITTLEFIELD

Minotaur Books

A Thomas Dunne Book 𝌆 New York

A THOMAS DUNNE BOOK FOR MINOTAUR BOOKS.
An imprint of St. Martin's Publishing Group.

A BAD DAY FOR SCANDAL. Copyright © 2011 by Sophie Littlefield. All rights reserved. Printed in the United States of America. For information, address St. Martin's Press, 175 Fifth Avenue, New York, N.Y. 10010.

www.thomasdunnebooks.com
www.minotaurbooks.com

The Library of Congress has cataloged the hardcover edition as follows:

Littlefield, Sophie.
    A bad day for scandal : a crime novel / Sophie Littlefield.—1st ed.
        p. cm.
    "A Thomas Dunne book."
    ISBN 978-0-312-64837-4
    1. Hardesty, Stella (Fictitious character)—Fiction 2. Middle-aged women—Fiction. 3. Murder—Investigation—Fiction. 4. Missouri—Fiction. I. Title.
    PS3612.I882B326 2011
    813'.6—dc22

                                                                2011005102

ISBN 978-1-250-00227-3 (trade paperback)

First Minotaur Books Paperback Edition: April 2012

10 9 8 7 6 5 4 3 2 1

For Mike.

My brother can turn words into stories
Tears into laughter
And cardboard boxes into spaceships.

Acknowledgments

With thanks to my agent, Barbara Poelle, for all those long conversations in which we talk about the characters as if they're real.

To Toni Plummer, my dear editor, for all the fun we've been having with Stella. To Sarah Melnyk, for that impressive stuff you do; Andy Martin and Matthew Shear, for believing; Olga Grlic, for continuing my cover-magic streak; and Anne, for the top-secret tour. And to my long-lost cousin Bob W., who made several industry events a lot more fun.

To the Pens, the members of SF-RWA, the MurderSheWrites gals, the TPlum Club, my Oakland getaway, and of course Bob and T-wa and Sal and Kristen. Thanks, you guys.

A BAD DAY FOR SCANDAL

Chapter One

believe I'd like to stick my face right smack in the middle of your pie," Sheriff Goat Jones said in his whiskey-over-gravel voice, causing Stella Hardesty to nearly drop the pan she was holding.

Instead, she glanced quickly around the kitchen to make sure they were alone and took a nervous step backwards, tripping over her mutt, Roxy, who was prowling for crumbs that might have fallen from the dinner dishes.

"Easy there," Goat cautioned, his voice going even smokier. Without asking, he took the grasshopper mint pie—which Stella had carefully removed from its bakery box and planted in her mama's old pie tin, to make sure that when the moment came to present her would-be boyfriend with his Saint Patrick's Day dessert, he would be suitably impressed—and set it aside as though it were a plate of stale saltines. "You're as skittish as a filly wantin' broke."

"Oh, my." Stella managed to breathe shakily before Goat backed her into the corner of the countertop and settled his big hands on her hips. He let them slide slowly down to cup her ass, which she had jammed into a Spanx Hide & Sleek Hi-Rise Panty before slipping on the slinky purple faux-wrap dress that her daughter, Noelle, had given her as a surviving-being-held-at-gunpoint-together gift the prior fall. Stella was fairly sure she would enjoy the sensation of Goat's strong fingers kneading her flesh if it hadn't gone numb in its fierce polyester–Lycra prison hours ago.

She tilted up her face and let her eyes flutter closed and waited for what sure looked like it was about to be the third time the sheriff kissed her. She might be a bit long in the tooth to be called a filly—in fact, she would probably be on the glue factory side of midlife, in terms of horse metaphors—but if this law enforcement bad boy wanted to break her, well, sign her right up for being broke.

His hot, soft, gorgeous mouth had just brushed against hers when there was a clomping of heavy, clumsy feet and Todd Groffe's disgusted adolescent voice cleaved through the beautiful moment like a split melon.

"Hey, get a room! There's *kids* here!"

Stella wriggled out of Goat's grasp, yanking at her skirt to make sure it hadn't somehow followed her thoughts and slipped scandalously up her thighs.

"Todd," she said as sternly as she could manage, "the sheriff was just helping me with—"

"I don't guess you need to tell *me* what-all kind a help you was gettin'," Todd snapped, hands fisted on his skinny hips. "Only you might just want to keep things PG in here for Melly and Glory."

On cue, two little blond-pigtailed girls dashed into the room carrying a woven bread basket between them. Dinner rolls bounced and flew from the basket, causing Roxy to abandon her search for scraps under the kitchen table and lope across the room, ears flying. Her powerful tail whipped in delight, and as she skidded to a graceless stop, snout colliding midair with an escaped roll, she managed to take out both little girls at once. They went down in a heap of matching pink jumpers and blond curls and patent-leather Mary Janes, and sent up an impressive wailing duet.

"Now you done it," Todd muttered as he stepped away from the fracas. "I just wash my *hands* of y'all. You're gonna have to deal with *Mom*."

Stella glanced at Goat and saw that his cornflower blue eyes glinted pure mischief. He managed to give her ass a surreptitious little squeeze just as the mother of the three children came dashing into view, which Stella figured was just as well, since her odds for getting any more action seemed slim. Her best bet now was probably to settle everyone's nerves with dessert.

Goat helped serve while Sherilee Groffe got the kids sorted and soothed, and before too long, everyone had an enormous slice of pie in front of them. Saturdays usually meant a visit from Stella's daughter, Noelle, who lived half an hour away in Coffey and often brought her brimming baskets of laundry and stayed for dinner. Saint Pat's Day was merely an excuse to turn laundry-and-pizza night into a party, and Stella had fixed her mother's corned beef and cut out paper shamrocks for the little girls to color. As for Goat, a recent easing of a tense situation in the sheriff's department had given him his first free day in months, an opportunity Stella was not about to let slip by.

"I think me and Joy have something to say," Noelle said as Stella slid into her seat. Twin pink spots stood out on Noelle's smooth porcelain cheeks, and Stella smiled. She hadn't seen the girl so happy in years, and since they'd only recently ironed out a few rough spots in their relationship, she had learned to cherish every moment they were together.

Tonight, Noelle had styled her short fuchsia hair, which she usually gelled into spikes, into a sort of 1940s starlet upswept do. Thick black eyeliner heightened the effect of a screen siren, as did the vintage empire-waisted dress that nearly concealed the trumpet vine tattoos that wound across her shoulders and collarbones. Stella sighed with happiness—her baby girl was looking as fresh and lovely as a ripe peach.

"*I* ain't got nothin' to say," the young woman seated next to Noelle said, blushing. Joy was a new friend—at least, new to Stella. Unlike many of Noelle's friends from the salon where she worked, Joy appeared to have given about as much thought to personal grooming as Todd, and in fact, her plaid flannel shirt and baggy jeans looked like she might have borrowed them from the boy. "And I don't think—"

"We're *gay,*" Noelle blurted, beaming.

Joy colored even further. "Ain't it a little early to be lettin' that cat out of the bag?" she stage-whispered. "I mean, since you and I ain't hardly—"

"Excuse me?" Stella asked, unsure she had heard right. As far as she knew, her daughter had always preferred men—just not nice ones. Noelle had an unfortunate track record of dating the sort of sorry woman-hurting scum that Stella routinely dealt with professionally, but after dumping the last in a line of such losers last fall, Noelle had seen the light and made a vow to be single for the rest of her natural life.

Noelle's grin slipped a little. "What I mean is, we're *about* to be gay. Mama don't need to know the *details,*" she added for Joy's benefit.

"Mrs. Hardesty, I'm real sorry, I sure don't want to make you feel uncomfortable." Joy didn't quite meet Stella's eyes. "I know it must be kind of a surprise. I told Noelle this is the kind of thing most folks like to hear in a private-type setting. I mean, my folks are still kind of getting used to the idea, and I told them I liked girls back in the third grade."

"Oh, dear," Sherilee said. "Todd, take the girls and watch some TV in Stella's bedroom."

"I *know* what *gay* is," Todd retorted.

"What's gay?" one of the twins piped up, taking a giant bite of pie, half of it tumbling onto her jumper.

"It's where a couple a guys or a couple a girls——"

"Not that there's anything wrong with it, of course," Sherilee cut him off firmly.

Stella saw Todd wince in pain as his mother's high-heeled shoe connected with his shin under the table. He sighed heavily and yanked his little sisters out of their chairs and dragged them, complaining loudly, down the hall.

"'Course, I'm *bi*," Joy continued, taking a delicate sip of her coffee, which Stella had liberally spiked with Kahlúa. "I'm only, like, maybe a half or two-thirds or possibly three-quarters gay."

Noelle shook her head in besotted amazement. "And ain't that just a regular wonder, seein' as you *look* gayer than anyone else I know."

"That don't really have all that much to do with it," Joy said. "The face a person shows the world—why, it's like a little window onto the soul. But maybe with curtains or miniblinds or something like that on it. That's what I've learned about myself, anyhow."

"Whipped cream?" Stella asked faintly. She was having trouble keeping up with the conversation, and she wasn't sure she was up for further revelations at the moment, especially after having her make-out session with Goat cut short.

"I do have a strong feeling you're my type," Noelle said,

ignoring Stella and gazing at Joy like she was a cupcake in a bakery window. "I think it's safe to say I'm going to be the pretty one, and you're the, you know. . . . Is it okay to say *butch*? I mean, I'm new at this—is that like an insult or something?"

"How long have you two known each other?" Goat asked politely. He didn't look the least bit ruffled by the strange turn the conversation had taken.

"A little while," Noelle said at the very same moment Joy murmured "Not long." They looked at each other and giggled.

"Well!" Stella said brightly, trying to figure out some new direction to take the conversation. The effort was cut short by the ringing of her cell phone from where Stella had left it on the kitchen counter—Todd had set her up with some new screaming metal band's latest abomination as her ringtone. "Excuse me."

The phone was always on, charged, and at hand, because Stella's side business, though secret, was never closed. Her clients were as likely to need her on weekends and in the dead of night as not. More likely, as a general rule.

"Stella here," she answered, putting the phone to her ear and jogging down the hall to the bathroom, the only place she could be guaranteed a little privacy. As she pushed the door shut and locked it, a voice she hadn't heard in years came on the other end.

"This is Priscilla Porter," the caller said, managing to convey in those few syllables the sort of frosty condescension that implied she was doing Stella a favor merely by talking to her. "It seems I'll be requiring your services."

Chapter Two

Details were not forthcoming. Unlike most of Stella's clients, who tended to sob their way through extensive if meandering and not always sense-making litanies of their trials and woes, Priss didn't seem inclined to spare any extra words.

"The situation is in your area of expertise," she said in a fakey clipped smarty-pants voice that Stella figured she must have picked up by watching that hoochie-looking brunette gal on CNBC, the one who was always talking about business as though she were describing how to jam a stick up your butt.

"I don't guess I know what you're talking about," Stella said, deciding she didn't like Priss any more now than when the gal had taken off for the big city a decade and a half ago at the age of eighteen. News of Priss's successes—college, then business school, then some fancy job in Kansas City, where she evidently made bucketloads of money (though she never saw fit to send any to her poor sickly mother, who died in the same housecoat she'd been wearing to the market for years)—had filtered back to Prosper from time to time. It was generally met with a fair bit of grumbling, either because folks were jealous or just plain irritated, since at one time or another, Priss had managed to alienate nearly every man, woman, and child in town with her priggish, superior ways. "My business is selling sewing machines, if you remember."

"Oh. Yes. Your husband's shop. God rest his soul. So you've managed to keep it profitable?" Priss didn't bother to mask her skepticism.

"It's done very well, actually," Stella lied, seething. In truth, Hardesty Sewing Machine Repair & Sales—which she was now running with the help of her assistant, Chrissy Shaw, allowing her to concentrate more on her sideline business—barely covered its costs and eked out enough extra to keep her in generic laundry detergent and Maybelline mascara and an occasional dinner out at Red Lobster.

"Lovely. So delighted to hear it. I'm looking forward to hearing more about you, Stella, but this is a matter of some urgency, so I wonder if we could continue this conversation here at the farm—I'm staying with Liman."

Stella figured Priss was looking forward to hearing about her about as much as she was looking forward to her next mammogram—but her distaste was overshadowed by surprise that Priss was staying with her brother: Priss hadn't deigned to visit the ramshackle family home in years.

"Look here, Priss, I've got guests. We're in the middle of dessert. I'm using *china,* for heaven's sake."

That last bit was stretching it—Stella didn't own any actual china—but she had taken pains to go through the dishes and pick out the ones on which the fruit-bowl design was least worn.

"Of course. And you know that I am *loath* to interrupt such a special gathering." Priss sighed, even over the phone lines managing to communicate a certain lack of sincerity. "In fact, I'm willing to double your usual rate."

That stopped Stella cold.

Money troubles were a storm cloud that followed her everywhere she went. A small inheritance had helped her pay off her house and car before she sent her husband, Ollie, to an early grave. The wives and girlfriends who started coming to her for help with their own abusive men paid Stella for her services—most of them. But Stella didn't exactly make big dollars. It was difficult to squeeze gobs of cash out of shell-shocked, bruised, worn-down women who often found themselves without any source of income once their no-good men had their attitudes forcibly adjusted by Stella.

And while nobody, neither the newly liberated women nor Stella herself, figured they were any worse for the trade, it generally took a certain amount of getting-back-on-their-feet time before her grateful clients could start up a payment plan.

Adding to Stella's tenuous financial position was a recent hospital stay, courtesy of a case gone dramatically wrong to the tune of a couple of bullets, and a long recuperation during which she was unable to work. Her water heater had developed a difficult personality, likely as not to blast her with a surprise jolt of cold water midshower, and the garage door hadn't worked right since a spate of tornadoes blasted through town last October. Her roof was about to go, damaged by those same tornadoes. She'd recently acquired a dog, and the pretty white fence that kept Roxy from escaping the backyard had set her back more than she'd planned.

The bottom line was that Stella was barely keeping the lights on and food in the fridge, much less fixing everything that was broken. An infusion of cash would be most welcome.

Still, a bitch was a bitch, and Saturday night was Saturday night, and Goat Jones in the chair next to her, rubbing his calf against hers in a manner that suggested it wasn't entirely accidental, and might in fact lead to more rubbing and friction a little later, was an ace in the hole that had to be worth something.

"I doubt you could afford me, Priss," Stella said.

"It's Priscilla now. Nobody calls me Priss anymore—"

"Everybody *here* does," Stella corrected her. "You're just not around to hear us."

"—and I can probably afford a lot more than you think. How does a deposit of, say, five thousand dollars sound to you?"

Stella blinked. She took the phone away from her ear, stared at it, and considered. Five thousand dollars sounded like a hell of a lot of scratch. That might cover the water heater and the garage door and a little fun money to boot. She swallowed hard, put the phone back to her ear, and opened her mouth.

Then she thought of Goat, who had come to dinner in a soft gray sweater that felt like a little baby lamb. Thought about how that sweater might feel against her skin as she tugged it off him in a moment of crazy monkey-love passion.

Thought about driving out in the dark and cold to the old Porter place to get bossed around some more.

"It sounds like you're not keeping up with inflation," she said coldly. "I'll need ten thousand up front, and that buys you a conversation, no promises."

There was a silence on the other line, and then Priss laughed. "My, my, my, Stella Hardesty. So it's true what they say, you've grown yourself a backbone. Fine. I'll have the check waiting. Do see that you get here at your earliest convenience."

Priss hung up without saying good-bye, and Stella slipped the phone thoughtfully into her pocket.

"Darn it all," she announced to her guests. They'd soldiered on through the dessert course without her. The twins—back from their brief television break—were wearing smears of pie on their darling faces, and Todd was well into a second piece. "I have to go help Mindy Jorgenhammer—her alpacas got out."

"*All* of them?" Todd demanded. "That's a shitload of alpacas."

"Todd!" Sherilee exclaimed. "Watch your mouth!"

"I'll help you, Stella," Goat said, pushing back his chair.

"We could all help," Sherilee said uncertainly. She was that particular breed of lady who never failed to offer to lend a hand, despite juggling three children and a mortgage and a pain-in-the-ass no-good ex and a shit-for-pay job in another town.

"Sit, sit," Stella said as cheerily as she could manage. "This happens all the time, and it's just a two-person job. You all would be in the way. And you'd scare them. Very skittish, alpacas. Really, it's best if I go by myself."

She turned to Goat, who was standing at the ready next to his chair. She allowed herself one last appreciative up-and-down view of his fine broad-shouldered form before sighing and grabbing her purse off the breakfront.

Duty called.

"Y'all know where I keep the good stuff," she said a little wistfully. "Just make sure to leave me a little shot of Johnnie for when I get back."

Chapter Three

I n the car, she queued up her lookin'-for-trouble playlist and turned up the heat. Winter was hanging around this year, and it was a clear, star-dusted night, the latest cold snap dappling everything with a sparkly coating of frost in the moonlight.

As she pulled out into the street, Melissa McClelland filled the Jeep with her moonshiney voice singing "Solitary Life":

> *Better keep the heat off 'till the snow falls,*
> *I'll fill up on whiskey, rye and reruns*

"Hmmph," Stella muttered to herself. A dire expedition, indeed. She turned down the volume and hit Chrissy's number on the speed dial. After a few rings, her assistant picked up and Stella could hear what sounded like a drunken fraternity party fast deteriorating into a riot in the background. In fact, it was a sort of family reunion, occasioned by a distant cousin's wedding. The ceremony itself had been a modest noontime affair, but it was the extended post-nuptials house party that prompted Chrissy's many siblings and aunts and uncles to make the trip to Prosper.

"It's me!" she hollered.

"Well, I can see that from the caller ID, Stella." Chrissy, too, was shouting to be heard. "Everything okay?"

"Not sure. Got a call from Priss Porter, of all people, wants me to come over to the farm, but she won't tell me what for."

"Did you say Priss Porter?" Stella could hear high-pitched screaming in the background and what sounded like dueling air-raid sirens. "I didn't know she was back. Man, I hate that stuck-up bitch."

"You know her?"

"Yeah, she babysat a few times until Mama found out she was going around calling us trash. Like the Porters was some sorta fuckin' royalty or something."

"What-all you got going on there?" Stella asked as a man's voice started barking orders.

"Oh, we're just cleaning up from dinner. My brother Mac's boys brought this toy car thing and they've run track all over Mom's sofas and I guess she's fit to be tied, and Dad wouldn't help so she threw a plate at him, and Tucker's got gum in his hair and Ginger's upstairs trying to get the boys to apologize only she's threatening to take a hairbrush to their butts and so things got a little out of control."

Stella never ceased to be amazed at the sheer velocity and volume of goings-on in the extended Lardner clan. Chrissy was one of six kids, most of whom had run through a spouse or two and produced a slew of towheaded cousins for Chrissy's two-year-old boy, Tucker. Chrissy herself was a widow; she'd started out as one of Stella's clients.

"I hope y'all are keeping the firearms locked up tonight."

"Stella!" Chrissy gasped. "Of *course* we are. There's *kids* here. We put everything away after the turkey shoot, and that was *hours* ago."

"Get anything?" Chrissy had told her all about one of the more colorful Lardner family traditions, which dictated that every male family member over the age of twelve sneak out to the state forest preserve early the morning of a wedding to shoot at wild turkeys. Lardners were generally crack hunters; the fact that they never managed to bag a bird was due to the other Lardner tradition of starting such mornings with ample amounts of schnapps in their coffee.

"Well, Pete and Mac got them a couple of squirrels. And then Dad almost took out a cow that wandered into the woods—that would of sucked. But Mom had a couple a store turkeys in the oven by the time they got home, so it all worked out. How'd your dinner go? Git you an extra large serving of sheriff?"

Stella ignored the teasing tone. At twenty-nine, Chrissy was about two decades more modern in her thinking than Stella was, and saw nothing wrong with a lady pursuing a gentleman full steam ahead. Stella herself was stuck in the wait-for-him-to-make-the-first-move habits of another generation, which might account for the fact that, despite the blistering kiss that had ratcheted up their relationship back at a party Stella threw to celebrate the wrap-up of her last big case a while back, things hadn't moved along perceptibly since.

That, and the man had been busy. A series of snafus at the county sheriff's office in Fayette, related to a recent murder case Stella had accidentally gotten involved in, had led to a flurry of butt-covering and reviewing of policies and reassessing of procedures by Goat's boss, Sheriff Dimmit Stanislas. Goat and his fellow deputy sheriffs, who hailed from Fairfax and Harrisonville and Quail Valley, had been spending a fair amount of time commuting to Fayette to be retrained and reoriented and re-dedicated and otherwise made to suffer for mistakes they hadn't personally made. The experience had left Goat both irritable and largely unavailable in the evenings and on the weekends, until now.

Tonight's make-out session in the kitchen could have been a breakthrough—at least, if Priss's call hadn't messed things up.

"I used the alpaca thing," Stella admitted grumpily.

"Aw, you did? That was one of the best ones!"

Stella had lined up a number of get-out-of-trouble contingency plans here and there all over the county. Most had been set up with the help of grateful ex-clients happy to do her a favor. Mindy, for instance, owed Stella for dealing with Rayburn Gish, a neighbor who made a habit of wandering over drunk and standing in the driveway howling up at her to come down and party with him, occasionally hauling out his man-parts and waving them around as an additional enticement.

Luckily, he hadn't been too tough to discourage, and in return, Mindy had promised to serve as an alibi the next time Stella needed one.

After making a quick call and apologizing for cutting Mindy's evening short, which Mindy reassured her was no big deal, since she'd only been watching the History Channel, Mindy rang off to let the alpacas out of their pens—to lend credibility to the story—and Stella drove the rest of the way to the Porter farm with nothing but Melissa McClelland's soulful tunes to distract her.

Lights were, if not blazing, at least switched on here and there around the Porter homestead. Set in a clump of dispirited-looking trees amid a patchy sprawl of alfalfa fields, the farming of which Liman Porter had contracted out to leave himself more time for lounging around the house in his undershorts after his mother's death, the house had seen better times. Paint blistered and peeled off the siding, the chimney leaned, and rails were missing from the front porch banister.

A car was parked at a haphazard angle in the roughly circular gravel drive that wound crookedly up to the house before quickly veering back to the main road as though it didn't want to get too close. The car didn't share the same hangdog air as the rest of the place: it was glossy and sleek and expensive looking.

Stella spotted a figure wrapped in blankets sitting in a weather-beaten wicker chair on the porch. She parked the Jeep behind the Mercedes and cut the ignition, then approached the porch cautiously, icy wind whipping her face.

"That you, Priss?" she called. Now that she was closer, she could see that there were towels layered with old quilts around the shivering figure, and that the person was huddled miserably against the wind. "What on earth are you sitting out here in the freezing cold for?"

"It's *Priscilla* now," the person said, standing and letting the blankets and towels fall to the porch. "I didn't realize you were going to take forever to get here. How far could it possibly be, Stella, not more than four or five miles—what took you so long?"

That gave Stella pause—here she'd left the comfort of her toasty warm home and that nice spiked coffee and the promise of more Goat than she anticipated being able to handle, to come out to what was left of the sorry Porter homestead to visit with a woman who was pretty much despised by everyone in town.

"I had to change. I wasn't about to come out here in my *nice* clothes."

Priss gave Stella's outfit a flick of examination and lifted her nose in the air—a nose that, Stella noticed in the dim light cast by a buggy porch lamp, had had the bump carved out of it. Porters all had ungainly noses; Priss was the first one who could afford to do anything about it, as far as Stella knew. She climbed the porch steps and took a better look, but in the poor light, she couldn't make out the rest of Priss's features to see if she'd bought herself any other alterations and enhancements.

"Is that your, ah, *professional* attire?"

Stella looked down at the hot pink fleece jacket she'd layered over a T-Bones sweatshirt and a pair of flannel-lined jeans and her fake-fur-topped snow boots. The jacket was sprinkled here and there with little sparkly crystals and featured a rhinestone-studded zipper. It had been a birthday gift from her friend Dotty Edwards, who had purchased it from QVC and owned one herself, in lime green. Dotty bought everything from drain uncloggers to fine faux jewelry to handcrafted teddy bears with little knitted sweaters from QVC, and she often got so swept up in the online-shopping rush that she couldn't stop herself from buying twos and threes of things—Stella was frequently the lucky recipient of the excess.

"This'll do, I guess," she said, narrowing her eyes at Priss's own cold-weather gear, which included a pair of shiny black boots with high pointy heels, and a shimmery black cape sort of affair that swung around dramatically but left long swatches of Priss's forearms exposed. "Depending on what you want to hire me for. Speaking of which, if you have in mind to get right down to business, which I guess you must, seein' as you've been waiting for me out in weather like this, how about if you show me a little good faith cash."

Up-front payment was something Stella rarely insisted on. In fact, finances were generally among the last things she and a client talked about, well after the litany of misdeeds and mishandling and mistreatment that brought them to Stella in the first place, and generally after a soothing cup of hot chocolate or a resolve-firming jolt of Johnnie Walker Black or a steadying can of ice-cold Fresca, whatever the client seemed to require. Sometimes it was several meetings before payment came up at all.

But Priss was pissing Stella off. Part of the reason was obvious—the woman had left town at the age when most other local gals were trying to decide whether to pop out their first baby before or after racking up a Prosper High School diploma. She'd headed for the city, where rumor was she'd earned not just an undergraduate degree but also a business school diploma, which showed the kind of gumption Stella could respect—but then she somehow landed a job that rained money down on her but didn't leave her time to come back and visit any of the local folks, even the few who'd managed to tolerate her when she still lived in Prosper. And that kind of thing—turning your back on the ones who brought you up—Stella didn't cotton to that one bit.

Still, an unpleasant thought lurked around the edges of Stella's mind, and she sighed and dragged it into focus: Priss's life path—all but the frosty, ungrateful bitch part—was uncomfortably close to the dream Stella had carried around for Noelle for many years until she finally got it through her head that her daughter had her own ideas about her future. Specifically, Noelle did not wish to be a doctor or a teacher or a scientist—she dreamed, since the age of five, about becoming a beautician, and now that she had become a darn good one, the girl had the sort of career satisfaction that Stella guessed everyone was entitled to.

Maybe, she admitted to herself, she ought not judge Priss quite so quickly for her own ambitions and decisions.

"Well, I guess you can describe the job first," she said, softening.

"I'll do better than that—I'll show you," Priss said, going down the steps in her high heels with surprising agility, leaving neat little footprints in the dusting of snow that had accumulated on the ground. She practically sprinted across the drive, the loose gravel not even slowing her down, and aimed a key ring at her car. It beeped and the trunk popped and Stella caught up just in time for the expensive German-engineered mechanism to glide soundlessly open, the tasteful interior lighting revealing one sorry-looking dead man who, judging by his color, had been departed from the living long enough to get used to the idea.

Chapter Four

There you have it," Priss said, hand on a hip in the manner of a game show hostess, gesturing at the unfortunate fellow with a flourish. "I think it's time we expedite his disposal, don't you agree?"

"Holy fuck," Stella breathed. "He's *dead.*"

Priss shot her a look of surprise. "Well, yes, obviously. That's why I called you." She gave the trunk lid a little shove, and it closed as easily as it opened, sealing its ghastly cargo inside. Stella couldn't say she wasn't grateful not to have to look at the dead guy—his lips had pulled back from his teeth in a sort of leer that, combined with his glassy open eyes, gave him the effect of an especially bold voyeur.

"Me? What do I want with *your* dead guy?"

Priss turned and started toward the house. "Stella, I realize that you usually like to do the job beginning to finish, but I just got it started for you. Don't worry, I'll pay your full rate, but all I really need from you is the, ah . . . cleanup."

"Hold on a minute," Stella said to Priss's retreating backside.

Her heart was going at a solid clip. She'd seen a variety of dead guys, starting with her own husband, four years ago. Ollie hadn't been very pretty with the side of his skull cracked open with his own wrench, but then again, he hadn't been a whole lot to look at on a good day, and the expression he gave her before slumping to the floor was one of mildly disappointed surprise, as though Stella had served him tuna mac twice in one week.

Besides Ollie, there had been that crew of Kansas City mobsters down at the lake last summer. They were a lot more pissed-off looking about being killed—and considerably bloodier—than Ollie. And then there were the mummified remains of Brenda Cassell that she'd accidentally gotten wrapped up with—not literally, of course—but Stella had never really got a clear view of that body before getting hired to figure out who did it.

The man in Priss's trunk was different from the rest of the bodies on Stella's list in one key way: He was decidedly not fresh. His odor confirmed it, if his unflattering coloring left any doubt. And to Stella's surprise, that made a considerable difference. She felt her tummy gurgle and surge in horror and realized she was close to losing the pleasantly digesting remains of the corned beef and Irish soda bread.

Priss turned just in time to see Stella lurch across the gravel drive to a row of winter-deadened lilacs that were in need of a good pruning. "Oh, for heaven's sake, Stella, how are you going to dispose of him if you can't even stand to look at him?"

Stella's yakking did have one happy side effect, which was to get her invited inside the house, out of the cold.

"But you *must* be quiet," Priss cautioned, holding a manicured finger to her lips as she opened the front door. "Liman is asleep—and he is ignorant of what has transpired."

Liman's ignorance was legendary, but Stella didn't bother to point that out. There was no way she was going to take the job Priss was offering her, but she also was well aware of why the gal had come to her rather than seeking out some other thuggery expert, and the situation called for a little finesse.

Stella didn't *kill* husbands or boyfriends for her clients. The only deaths she was responsible for were of the self-defense variety—and Stella had no problem including Ollie's demise in that category, since thirty years of getting smacked around surely justified some defensive maneuvers on her part, and Stella had long ago forgiven herself for unleashing them all in one three-second torrent.

She wasn't a killer for hire, but—understandably, since rumors of mayhem and mercilessness were part of her stock-in-trade—she didn't dispel that perception either. There had been half a dozen occasions when her case strategy had included intimidating and threatening a wrong-doing man right out of town—even out of state—with a clear understanding that return visits and, in fact, any sort of contact at all were actively discouraged. These men were missing, though they weren't missed enough for anyone to go filing reports or hire detectives to find out what parts they'd lit out for, and if folks presumed them dead, why, who was Stella to argue?

But that didn't mean that Stella had any intention of getting started in the murder business. Not even in the abetting of it, which getting rid of Priss's dead body would surely be.

"I'll come in and get warm," she said, "and then I'm going to turn around and head for home. You can count on me to keep my mouth shut, but that problem you got there, you started it and I'm afraid you're going to have to be the one to finish it."

"Oh, why don't you wait until we've had a chance to discuss things further, before you make a final decision on that," Priss murmured in a low voice. She tiptoed down the hall and peered into a darkened room, listened for a moment, then gently closed the door. When she came back, she pointed to a chair in front of the fireplace, which looked as though it hadn't been used in a long while, if the *Hustler* and *Off-Road* magazines stacked in sloppy piles on the hearth were any indication. "I'd offer you a drink, but my brother isn't exactly a connoisseur of spirits. I believe all he has is Budweiser. In *cans*."

Stella considered telling Priss that she'd downed plenty of Bud in her day and never found it particularly lacking, but then she figured that a bolt of Johnnie Walker Black in her own nice clean kitchen, even if the chances were remote that any of her guests would still be up and ready to party with her, was worth holding out for.

The room, even without a fire, was warm as toast, and Stella figured Priss had dialed up the heat when she arrived at her brother's place. She peeled off her mittens and the fuzzy pink and silver scarf her sister Gracellen had sent for Christmas and unzipped the sparkly zipper of her jacket with care. She took the seat she was offered, a squishy-cushioned old upholstered job that smelled faintly of mold. Dust puffed out when she sat, making her frown in distaste.

"Really, I'm warmer than I thought I was," she said. "Why don't I just give you a couple of pointers for that little cleanup job and I'll be on my way. Professional courtesy, the least I can do."

"Oh, Stella," Priss said, shaking her head in disappointment. "I'm so sorry to have to do this. Really, I hadn't wanted things to go in this direction. But you don't leave me any choice."

She reached for a manila envelope that Stella hadn't noticed sitting on the dusty coffee table. She reached inside and drew out a thin stack of photographs and considered them briefly, her lips pursed in disapproval, before shaking her head and handing them over.

They were black-and-white photographs, a bit grainy and blurry. Stella stared at the first one for a few moments before she realized that the looming figure in the picture, standing over a kneeling young man cowering on what appeared to be a dirt floor, was none other than herself—and that the object she was brandishing in what could only be called a threatening manner was a twenty-four-inch Stock Shock cattle prod—and that the young man in question was Ferg Rohossen, with his wrists trussed expertly and tied off with a series of neat bowline knots that Stella had perfected during a slow day in the shop last spring, practicing with a package of Wrights Hem Tape and a 1970s-era Boy Scout knot-tying pamphlet she'd bought for a nickel at a garage sale.

She flipped through the stack of photos. There were three pictures in all, taken moments apart, the final one clearly the pièce de résistance, showing a tearful, terrified, pleading Ferg on his knees wearing an expression of powerful entreaty as Stella hefted a sixteen-ounce claw hammer in the air.

Ferg hadn't been much of a fighter, Stella recalled as the rest of her brain scrambled to figure the angle of the photographer and remembered that, yes, there *was* in fact a dusty little casement window in that canning shed on the old Haversham Ranch. But no one had followed her that day—Stella made sure of it. She *always* made sure. And when she departed the shed, leaving a chastened and tearstained and changed young man behind to reflect on the many promises he'd made, there was no sign that anyone had been peeping.

But she had obviously been wrong.

"Who took these?" she demanded.

"Well, now, in Complex Litigation class at business school, I learned all about a concept called trade secrets," Priss said acidly. "This would be one of those situations where trade secrets apply."

Stella nodded slowly, her perception of Priss undergoing a real-time revision. It appeared that Priss had found and hired the kind of manpower whose stalking skills rivaled Stella's own. Which implied that Priss had contacts in some seriously unlawful circles. Which furthermore suggested that her own dealings skirted the aboveboard variety.

The way Stella understood things from the very cursory attention she paid to the business news, there were ample opportunities for crooks in corporate America—and if Priss had taken her career in that direction, it would certainly explain the Mercedes and the fancy clothes and all that gold on her wrists and the olive-sized diamonds in her ears.

None of this, however, explained what Priss was doing hiring people to build up a collection of incriminating evidence on *her*.

And Stella didn't like to be threatened. While being in the presence of a sharp and calculating criminal mind such as Priss's might once have shaken her to the very core, now that she herself was a deliberate flouter of the law, Priss Porter didn't scare her so much as make her very, very irritated.

"Tell me, Priss," she said calmly, handing the photos back. "Do you think my butt looks big in them pictures?"

Priss made a funny sound, a sharp sucking-in of breath that Stella supposed meant she was reaching the end of her tight-assed fancy-talking rope. Oh, well. Not her problem.

"These are the only printed copies," Priss said, tucking the photos back in the envelope. "But if you are considering some sort of retribution, I'll have you know that there is a digital copy on a flash drive in a secure location which, I assure you, you will not find. If any misfortune befalls me tonight, a series of events will be put into play that you will very much regret. Authorities will be notified. Justice will be served. Perpetrators will be punished."

"Oh, cut the drama, Priss," Stella snapped. "You think I'm going to kill you over a few amateur photos? I told you I'm not in the murder business."

"And I told *you* my name is *Priscilla*," she retorted, her voice going a little shrill. "Nobody calls me Priss anymore."

"Now, that's where you're wrong," Stella said, standing and slipping her fuzzy sparkly jacket back on. "Just about everybody still calls you Priss around here. That is, whenever anybody remembers to talk about you at all, which isn't very often because, to tell you the truth, under all that expensive makeup and clothes and shit, you just really aren't all that memorable."

"I can make serious trouble for you," Priss said, standing up herself and glaring at Stella. With her high-heeled boots on, she was a good three inches taller, and Stella had to tip her head back to return the poisonous gaze, but she took her time zipping up her jacket and slipping on her mittens.

"And I guess *I* could make trouble for *you*," she said. "Tell you what, though, why don't we just put this whole evening behind us. You drive on back up to Kansas City and find you some other sucker to clean up after your mess, and we'll just pretend we've been sitting here exchanging casserole recipes."

"I'm giving you one last chance, Stella Hardesty," Priss hissed as Stella walked toward the door.

"Give Liman my regards."

Only when the door slammed behind her did her heart start pounding like it wanted to bust right out of her chest. She sprinted for the Jeep and peeled out, wondering if she'd finally made the mistake that would land her in jail.

Chapter Five

By the time she pulled up Mindy's sloping drive, Stella's panic had simmered down to nail-spitting irritation. How the hell had Priss come across those photos? There were a fair number of people who could tick off a list of illegal things that Stella had done, but they were all clients, with ample reason for keeping the information to themselves.

Priss's threats of exposure hit closer to home than she could possibly know, since the front line in dealing with a situation like the one the photos seemed to reveal would be the sheriff, and he had let her slide several times when suspicions had pointed her way. Goat knew more than Stella wished he did, since he had on more than one occasion stumbled into the aftermath of a case that didn't wrap itself up neatly, though he had yet to put the pieces together and come up with a picture of Stella that he couldn't live with. That was a delicate balance right there, Stella knew, and she was well aware that she was playing with fire, and that one unfortunate coincidence or not-easily-dismissed lead too many might push the sheriff too far, and he would have no choice but to end their budding romance and turn her over to the justice machine, presumably to fry.

A smart woman would probably do everything in her power to keep away from the sheriff. She certainly wouldn't spend her days trying to figure out how to get in his pants. She wouldn't invite him for dinner or drive past his office on her way home from the sewing shop just for a chance of a glimpse of his fine lanky form striding across the parking lot.

But ever since Stella had got her first gander of Goat's glinting blue eyes and his smooth bald head and his work-rough hands, she'd been a goner. Reasonable wasn't a consideration when you had it this bad, and the fire between them didn't show any signs of settling down. So Stella had to find a way to make sure the sheriff never saw the pictures. Which meant she had to figure out how to get the flash drive from Priss.

Okay. She'd already ruled out option number one, which was to hire on as Priss's body-disposal service.

Option two: Find something to hold over her. Something threatening enough that Priss would be willing to trade to make it go away.

Well, that body in the trunk might make a fine start. If Stella could connect it definitively with Priss, she'd have the kind of threat that might get things moving in the right direction.

Only, something told her it might not be as simple as it appeared on first blush.

Stella thought back to the Porter siblings' school days and remembered Priss winning every spelling bee, every geography challenge, every speech contest the Prosper school system put on. Her methods had been simple: a ruthless evaluation of the competition followed by its decimation based on whatever weaknesses Priss could discover. Stella had been a young mother at the time, and she read about Priss's accomplishments in the *Prosper Standard* and heard about them in the grocery line and, at first, felt a sort of regional pride that one of their own had made good, and even hoped that Noelle might someday look at Priss as a sort of role model—until she began to hear the *other* rumors.

When Priss was competing for a space on the Mathletes team, Minnie Seevers mysteriously fell in a ditch the afternoon of tryouts and missed a chance to vie for the spot that went to Priss.

When the master list of final-round words went missing before the school spelling bee, no one believed the innocent expression on Priss's face. And when the Kiwanis offered a scholarship to the student voted most civic minded, Priss forced her way onto every highway cleanup, nursing home visit, hospital caroling, and food drive until even the Kiwanis ceded defeat and handed over the scholarship check.

So was it really such a surprise that Priss had found a way to set herself up with a backup plan that featured Prosper's one and only career criminal?

And, Stella had to ask herself as she walked through the light snow that had begun to fall, up the drive to Mindy's front door, was it really so different from the contingency plans that she herself had set up for circumstances such as these?

Before she had a chance to give herself an answer, Mindy came walking around the side of the house in rubber boots and insulated overalls, a hand raised in greeting. She was a sturdy, no-nonsense woman in her thirties, and she made a nice living for herself raising and selling alpacas to clients all over the Midwest as well as hiring herself out for shearing and grooming. Mindy's alpacas routinely won all manner of competitions, their bloodline having been proudly overseen by Mindy's mother and grandmother before their retirement. Alpaca tending, it seemed, ran only in the matriarchal line of the family; Mindy's younger brothers were pursuing more conventional careers in the construction and hell-raising businesses.

"Howdy, Stella. Your evening go all right?"

Mindy knew better than to pry into the particulars of Stella's business, but she was a well-raised kind of girl and couldn't help making a polite inquiry.

"Not sure yet," Stella said, following Mindy back toward the pens, where the bleating sounds of excited alpacas let her know their unexpected outing had come to an orderly end. "This one might have to simmer for a while. Tell you what, you mind if I get in there with them and work on my alibi?"

"Not a bit," Mindy said, and then she sat on the fence and chatted with Stella about her worthless brothers and the latest scrapes they'd managed to get into while Stella smeared alpaca shit on her clothes and endured the friendly scrutiny of a dozen gentle, curious creatures, one of which managed to eat a couple of bites of her jacket before Mindy intervened.

Stella was back in her driveway twenty minutes later. Her damn garage door was seriously in need of a service call. It wouldn't go up and down at all. For a few seconds, Stella chided herself for letting Priss's big payoff slip through her fingers. *It was tainted money,* she tried reminding herself, but she couldn't avoid the feeling that tainted money would spend just as well as any other sort.

As she got out of the Jeep, however, she noticed something she had missed in the swirling drifts of crystalline snow—the sheriff's truck was still parked under the sugar maple at the edge of her front yard.

Her heart sped up in her chest as she let herself in the front door. In the kitchen, the dishes were lined up tidily in the drying rack, and dish towels were draped over the oven handles to dry. Sitting at the head of her kitchen table, flipping through an old issue of *Quiltmaker,* was Goat.

"Hey, Dusty, 'bout time you got those alpacas put up. How far did they get this time, anyway?"

Was she imagining things or was there a devilish glint in Goat's eye?

"Most of 'em just wandered into the back pasture, but a couple got through the fence and ended up over across the road on Monroe's land," she said carefully. "We had a heck of a time with those two. Took me and Mindy nearly an hour to wrangle them back in the pen."

Stella lifted her leg to point out the streaks of mud and alpaca excrement on her jeans. She felt a little silly about planting that particular evidence—it wasn't exactly mood-setting—but careful planning like this was what separated amateurs from professionals.

Goat started to get up out of his chair, but then his nose twitched like a rabbit's and he glanced up and down Stella's clothes. "That's not just mud on your duds, is it."

"'Fraid not. We had to get in the pens with them. You know how it is, get an alpaca riled up, and it takes a while to settle them again."

"I didn't realize that. It, uh, does seem kind of funny that Mindy called on you in particular. You know what I mean? She could have called the Monroes—"

"They're over to Sikeston visiting Cressa's folks."

"Or the Spitzers, they're alpaca people. Seems like they might be a little better at the wranglin', no offense. I'm just surprised

Mindy would ask such a favor, seeing as you had company and all."

Stella examined Goat carefully for subtext. Was he suspicious? Was he accusing her of making up a bogus outing, perhaps?

"It's just that . . . well, I showed alpaca, in Four-H." Blatant lie. "Got ribbons, did okay in the pee-wee division. I know how they handle, you know? It takes a special touch."

"Yeah?" Goat advanced slowly, causing a shiver to launch itself right around the base of Stella's spine and slither and quiver its way upward. "What kind of special touch?"

He came to a halt when he was mere inches away, tilting his head down so he could regard her closely with those inky blue eyes. Stella sighed in anticipation and considered not answering at all, but Goat's mouth tipped up at the corners and his hands came to rest on the small of her back, drawing her almost imperceptibly closer.

"They, uh, require . . . reassurance," she whispered.

"Mmm?"

"They are a little bit insecure." Stella swallowed hard. "They need a firm hand. Someone to take ch-charge . . ."

Damn, her teeth were actually chattering in her head. Like she was planted over a hole cut in a frozen pond and ice fishing, instead of standing in her own kitchen, hoping this breathtaking man would kiss her.

You could kiss him first, an eager little voice suggested from somewhere deep in her mind. *Ain't any kind of law against that.*

But there was something extra-delicious about having the man you've dreamed of and lusted after for years hovering centimeters away, so that you could practically count his long fringy eyelashes, could feel the warmth of his skin through the charged air against yours. Something exquisitely delightful about the waiting. Stella wondered if she could be happy if time stopped right now, if she spent all of eternity suspended in the magical span of seconds before Goat's wide sexy mouth descended on hers and stirred up her insides with one of his soul-searing kisses.

She decided it wasn't a bad idea.

Except for the alpaca odor.

"If . . . if you'll excuse me," she said breathily, "I think I'll take a very very fast little shower. I need to, um, freshen up."

"I'll be waiting," Goat rumbled in reply before reluctantly releasing her.

Stella hightailed it to her bathroom and turned the shower on full blast. She dialed it extra hot, then changed her mind when she realized her body was already blazing, having got itself convinced it was headed for eight kinds of paradise. She stripped off her dirty clothes and got in, lowering the temperature to lukewarm and directing the spray carefully away from her hair—no time for a blow-dry now—and lathered up with her favorite Avon Naturals Cucumber Melon shower gel.

When she was finished with her shower, Stella patted herself all over with a clean towel and smoothed on body lotion. She paused, wondering if she should slip into her one slinky nightgown, a gift she bought herself on her birthday this year when she decided to try to get laid before she turned fifty-one. Instead she slipped on a clean pair of pajama pants—pale green, with a coordinated floral-print T-shirt. After a few seconds of deliberation, she skipped the matching slippers.

Going barefoot might send a message.

The sort of message she very much wanted to send.

Stella waited for a moment so her recklessness could sink all the way in, and then she padded out to the kitchen, putting a little shimmy in her step.

The kitchen was empty.

Goat was not in any of the chairs. Goat was not leaning rakishly up against the counter, arms crossed, eyebrow lifted. Goat was not getting a beer from the fridge and giving her a devilish grin over his shoulder.

Goat, Stella discovered after a few moments of searching, was stretched out on the sofa, long legs crossed at the ankles, eyes closed, chest rising and falling gently with the rhythm of deep sleep.

For a moment, Stella just watched him, reflecting that a man who could fall asleep in your living room after a long evening of socializing and pie eating and kitchen cleaning was a man who was plenty comfortable with you.

Which was good. Oh, it was very good. Even when you might have been hoping for a different sort of conclusion to the evening.

Goat stirred in his sleep, and Stella had the fleeting suspicion that he could sense her hungry gaze on him, and she blinked rapidly a few times to make sure that it didn't look like she'd been letting herself check out every lanky, muscular inch of him, maybe letting her tired eyes rest a little extra long around his midsection, where crisp cotton khaki covered up features that had been the subject of her frequent daydreaming.

Goat opened his eyes and yawned, a long luxurious yawn accompanied by a bit of stretching and the pop of a shoulder. As he sat up, he rubbed his eyes and gave her a sideways grin. "My, my, Stella Hardesty," he said. "You look like a little springtime blossom there."

Stella glanced down at the front of her lounge top, which

had fanciful flowers embroidered in a loopy scroll. "Is that a good thing?"

"Oh, heck yeah," Goat said. "All fresh-like. And I bet you smell good, too. Whyn'cha come on over here and let me get to findin' out."

So Stella went. It turned out that the space under Goat's long arm, well-muscled from his hobby of rowing himself around in a kayak on the sparkling waters of the Lake of the Ozarks, a habit that certainly gave him a fine hard sinewy wingspan, was a perfect fit for her. As she leaned against his chest and he tugged her in so she was snuggled up close, she almost felt . . . little, like he'd said. *Petite.*

"Oh," she murmured happily into the Tide-detergent-and-man scent of his pressed cotton shirt. It felt delightful. She peeked down at his broad hand resting lightly on her knee and just for kicks laid her own hand on top of it. Yup. It looked positively dainty there. She couldn't help a satisfied little giggle.

"What's so funny, Dusty?" Goat growled into her hair.

"Nothing, just, you're so—I mean, you're a big man, Goat, and next to you I feel . . ."

Safe. Protected. Cherished.

"Defenseless?" Goat suggested, and the growl got even lower and turned into a sort of purr, the kind of purr the most badass lion in the jungle would make before gobbling up the rabbit trembling in his paws, and it gave Stella a series of goose-bumpy shivers that turned into zingers when Goat shifted her onto his lap like she weighed no more than a sack of feathers. "Like you couldn't stop me from having my way with you if I felt like it?"

Stella giggled again as he turned her so that she was looking down at him over a space of a few inches. "Um. Maybe. A little."

And then she was kissing the man. She was kissing Goat Jones in her living room, sitting on his lap like a schoolgirl at a football game, and he was sliding his hands down her back, over her hips, drawing her closer against him, and when she was pretty sure she'd run entirely out of breath but didn't much care, when she thought she might go ahead and asphyxiate happily and expire right there, his hands found the hem of her T-shirt and slipped up under the hem and they were warm and rough against her back and she felt the trace of every callus, every work-roughened fingertip, and she kissed him harder and made a little sound that was kind of the girl version of his low-down hungry growl and then the phone rang.

Not her phone. Goat's phone, which she felt in his pocket, pressed in the nether region between his hips and hers, and which he reached for by sliding his hand in between them and sending one last emergency flare up along the nerve endings of her skin, rang the old-fashioned way, in a businesslike series of rings.

"This is Goat," he said gruffly, flipping the thing open, and though he made no move to remove Stella from his lap, she slid regretfully off him and rearranged herself awkwardly by tugging her various hems and waistbands back into place and patting at her hair.

She was pretty sure she was blushing.

"Uh-huh," he muttered. "Where? You don't say! And he was sober? . . . How bad, would you say? Okay . . . okay."

The conversation went on a bit, Goat asking questions and muttering terse answers, before he finally snapped his phone shut and regarded her with a mixture of regret and exasperation.

"This was really fun," he said, and Stella sighed. She wanted to tell him not to worry about it, not to apologize, because she of all people knew what it was like to get a middle-of-the-night summons. When you were in the justice business, there were plenty of nights when one's own needs, even a need as pressing as finding out what Goat Jones might be like between the sheets, came second.

"I had fun, too," she finally settled on. She stood up briskly and dusted off the front of her pants with short little pats, and put a smile on her face. "You want me to fix you coffee for the road?"

"No, I'm afraid this is more of an urgent-type situation," Goat said, shoving the tails of his shirt, which had somehow managed to come loose in all that furious making out, back in place.

He swung in for a peck, somewhere north of just-friends but way south of the fiery kisses of moments earlier, and made for the door. "Thanks for everything. Whyn't you see if you can save me any of that delicious pie, and I'll come back for it tomorrow if I can."

Of course, he didn't say where he was going—much as Stella wouldn't dream of telling him the addresses or particulars of any of *her* clients. She understood.

But there, Stella reflected ten minutes later as she pulled up her fluffy down comforter and snuggled deep down into her flannel sheets, was the problem.

They were on opposite sides, her and Goat Jones. Doing her job right required a certain amount of fast-talking and double-dealing and sneaking around and rule bending and exception making and creative interpretations of the *spirit* of the law while occasionally avoiding the *letter* of the law. For Goat Jones, the boundaries were far more precise. He was a man who believed in duty and order, a man who made pledges and oaths and kept them.

He was a bad choice, a truly terrible choice, for a vigilante such as herself. And she really had to stop. That was the thought she took to sleep with her, so why did her dreams feature Goat striding around in those just-tight-enough department-issue trousers with that service belt slung low and a look of fierce determination on his face?

Chapter Six

The lovely dreams were interrupted by the ringing of Stella's own phone, which she'd left on the bedside table. The fright she felt upon waking splintered into stomach-souring anxiety when she saw that the clock read two fifteen, an hour when the only news was likely to be bad. She pressed the phone against her ear, and in the split second it took her to choke out a hello, managed to cycle through her most fearsome worries:

Please-Please-Big-Guy-Don't-Let-Anything-Happen-to-Noelle-Chrissy-Tucker-Todd—

"Hello?"

"I don't guess you managed to get the sheriff in the sack when you got back from Mindy's, did you?"

"Holy shit, Chrissy, this had better be good. I think I'm having a damn heart attack."

"Well, hold off on that, Stella. You're gonna need your strength when I tell you where the sheriff is now."

"Where . . . what?"

"Just tell me, what-all'd you get up to with him last night? And I really hope you got you some in advance, considering what I got to tell you. Like I hope you laid in a good supply of nookie, you know what I'm saying?"

Stella tried to process the note of trepidation lacing Chrissy's forced cheer. "Everybody kept their clothes on. That's all I'm gonna share. Not that it's any of your damn business."

"Well, that's too bad, Stella, 'cause the sheriff got called out to Porters' a while back."

"*Liman* Porter's?"

"Yup. My sister Lorrie's youngest started cryin' and carrying on in the next room just now and woke me up, so I got up and fixed me some leftovers, and Dad left the scanner on, so I heard it. I guess he got called out to Porters' for a domestic, but now they're callin' for extra officers."

The patriarch of Chrissy's large extended family—Ralph Lardner, her father—had a long-standing practice of listening to the scanner the way some folks liked to keep easy listening tunes going in the background. It was a habit born during the days when his large brood of sons were making frequent bad decisions and misjudgments of the sort that resulted in law enforcement attention, and eventually Ralph figured he'd skip the step of getting called down to the station to pick up one or another of his boys for shooting out mailboxes or drag racing by hearing about it firsthand, which gave him a certain respected status with Goat's predecessor, Sheriff Burt Knoll. The pair spent many a long evening sharing nips from Sheriff Knoll's desk-drawer flask as the two of them let whatever young Lardner had most recently tested his hoodlum wings cool his heels in the holding cell before Ralph took him home. All that effort had more or less paid off, and Chrissy's brothers rarely got hauled in anymore, but Ralph had become accustomed to the soothing scratch and static of the scanner.

"Oh, hell!" Stella exclaimed. "Porters'? You sure?"

"Yeah. I'd call down there and see what I could find out, but it's Darja and Dorota on nights. . . ."

"Yeah," said Stella, thinking hard. The regular day-shift desk person, Irene Dorsey, was something of an ally and could often be counted on for a little information on the sly, but the Dzurinda twins—spinster ladies who lived in a tidy rancher next to the Saint Cyril's and cooked for Father Theodore "Tubby" Green as well as sharing receptionist duties at the sheriff's department—were sticklers for procedure. Even worse, they'd report straight back to Goat—and probably enjoy ratting her out.

"So what happened over there, anyway, Stella? You didn't do anything to Priss that's gonna leave marks, did you?"

It wasn't a serious accusation—Chrissy knew well that Stella never left evidence of her handiwork.

"No, but maybe I should have." She explained the evening's events, from her arrival at the farm through the incriminating pictures and Priss's threat. "I guess I need to see if I can do some damage control."

"You better haul ass," Chrissy said. "Mike and Ian are on their way."

Mike Kuzler and Ian Sloat were the Prosper sheriff's deputies, and what they lacked in brains and ambition they made up for in a sort of stolid, slow-moving dependability.

"I can't go over there. I mean, how would I explain that? Middle of a Saturday night . . ."

"I'm sure you're right," Chrissy said crisply. "Wouldn't do to just show up there and get creative, I guess. No sense trying when you can just lie down and let this thing drive over you."

"Hey, I didn't say—"

"Got to go, Tucker's climbed up into the dog food bin."

Stella thought it over for only a few seconds before dialing

Goat's personal number, one he gave out to very few people. She'd come to have it when a case went wrong several years ago, but she made a point of never using it unless absolutely necessary, like when she was bleeding out in a mobster's lake house and needed rescuing a few months back.

It had definitely made their relationship a little one-sided, since she was always waiting for him to call her. But that was a less immediate problem than finding out what had happened to the body in Priss's trunk and if she'd done anything foolish with it and most especially if she'd said anything at all to Goat about Stella's earlier visit.

This was not a call she was going to enjoy.

He picked up on the first ring. "Dusty?"

His tone wasn't exactly welcoming, and Stella found herself struggling to get a greeting out. "Hello, Goat, I was just—"

But Goat cut her off before she had a chance to finish her thought. "What the hell is your scarf doing in Liman Porter's living room?"

It took a few seconds for Stella to catch up with this new turn of events.

She'd been wearing the fuzzy pink and silver scarf Gracellen had given her, and she remembered taking it off along with her mittens when she unzipped her coat.

Because the Porter place had been stifling . . .

Because Priss Porter had turned the heat up . . .

And the scarf must have gotten wedged into the chair cushions somehow, and when Stella got up to leave, she must have accidentally forgotten it, which wasn't surprising, considering how eager she'd been to escape the collapse of her criminal career at Priss's hands.

"I don't know what you're talking about," she said, but it came out like a question.

"I know it's your scarf—you had it on when you went out to help Mindy with them sheep of hers."

"Alpacas."

"What the fuck ever. You had this thing wrapped around your neck when you left. So where'd you really go, Stella? What were you doing over here? And you better answer me quick, 'cause I got the boys on the way, they'll be here any minute."

"I—you saw me when I got home, Goat. I was at Mindy's. You can ask her. How am I going to get alpaca dung on my clothes at Liman's?"

"How do I know that was *alpaca* dung?" Goat said, his voice in the threatening register of irritated.

"How about if you send it up to Fayette so your girlfriend can run a whole passel of tests on it?"

As soon as the words were out of Stella's mouth, she wished she could take them back. Detective Daphne Simmons, head of the Fayette Crime Scene Unit and presumed future head sheriff of Sawyer County, had a crush on Goat that over the course of a recent case had taken a run-up from simmering interest to full-on sexual bartering. Which, Stella was confident, Goat had refused. But she still couldn't think of Daphne without an unpleasant rush of jealousy seizing her lizard brain.

And it certainly hadn't helped that when Sheriff Stanislas started assigning blame for the recent fuckups, he singled out the Prosper department to receive nearly all of it. Even if Stella didn't have a thing for Goat, she had as much civic pride as the next person, and it was very difficult indeed to stand by and watch their law enforcement team being forced to eat a giant serving of crow that they hadn't earned.

But Goat refused to take the bait. "Good idea. Best put

44

them jeans in a bag just in case I need 'em," he said. "Leave it on the porch, if you can't abide the smell."

Now he was just being testy. Well, maybe she deserved it: She'd lied to him, and they both knew it. But that didn't mean she was going to back down.

"Bet there's lots of scarves like that. And I hear Priss is back in town. It's probably hers. What does it matter, anyway?" she asked in a conciliatory tone. "Something gone wrong over there?"

"Like I'd tell *you* anything. Stella Hardesty, I trust you about as far as I can throw you, and that ain't any kind of far distance."

As Stella lowered her cell phone back onto the bedside table, she tried to convince herself that she hadn't just been hung up on, that Goat had just rung off in a hurry.

But as she tried to get back to sleep, she couldn't decide if she was more upset about getting involved in some new and unknown criminal dealings or about the complete absence of warmth in the sheriff's voice.

Chapter Seven

'm out on work release," Chrissy announced, holding up a pa-per bag as she let herself into Stella's kitchen a few hours later. Stella had managed to fall back into a troubled sleep before getting up with the dawn. "Mom says she'll watch Tucker for me today if I'll help her later."

"What-all does she need you for?"

"I need to help her clean up the rec room. Everybody got to dancing, and a couple of the ceiling tiles got knocked out, plus there's guacamole in the carpet. Least, I think that's what it is. And Mom wants to put up her crosses before everyone leaves."

"Wow. You're going to be busy." Chrissy had described her mother's habit of observing the Lenten season by decorating each of the house's street-facing windows with a four-foot cross made from scrap lumber rigged with bathroom lightbulbs; at night, the effect would be not unlike a high-wattage Mount Calvary.

Chrissy sighed. "I don't mind, only I can't help but feel like it's just a little bit tacky. But the little kids like it, so what can you do? Only Stella, promise me you'll do up your yard like you used to. I can't wait for Tucker to see it."

"Well . . . maybe."

When Noelle was little, Stella had decorated the front yard for Easter. It had begun with a few plastic eggs hung from the sugar maple, which had been a lot smaller in those days. Every year, she added something new: a family of ducks cut from plywood, painted and mounted on stakes; big plastic pots shaped like baskets, planted every fall with tulip bulbs; strings of pink and lavender lights strung along the eaves.

Easter had been her mother's favorite holiday. Pat Collier had loved everything about Easter, from sewing fancy dresses for herself and little Stella, to the corsage her husband always bought for her to wear to church, to hiding dozens of eggs around the yard, to baking a cake shaped like a lamb and frosted with fluffy coconut icing. Pat had been gone for six years, and even after Stella quit observing the holiday with more than a ham sandwich, it always brought back memories of happy times in the warm, safe bosom of her parents' home.

The boxes of decorations hadn't come down from the attic since Noelle had grown up and moved away, but folks in Prosper still talked about the Hardesty Easter display. Maybe it was time to stage a return. Stella hid a smile. She was liking the sounds of the upcoming holiday more and more. Waking up with a little one in the house again, experiencing the magic through his eyes—it had been a long time since Easter morning had been anything special. The last few years had been just plain lonely. "Now can I have my doughnut?"

"Yes'm, I got you them ones with the crunchy shit on top like you like. Only hurry up, 'cause Irene says the sheriff told her he'll be in by ten. I got her a couple a jelly and a couple a crème-filled 'cause I didn't know what she liked."

On the way to the sheriff's office, Stella got Chrissy caught up on the latest developments, including the reaction she got when she called Goat. When they pulled into the parking lot of the old Hardee's restaurant that had been converted into the Prosper Municipal Annex, Stella was relieved to see no sign of Goat's cruiser. Only Irene's old boat of a Chevy Caprice station wagon was parked in what used to be the drive-through lane. Much of the parking lot had been given over to a prefab equipment shed, so staff and visitor parking was somewhat limited.

Behind the glass double doors, Irene was squinting into a purse mirror and plucking her eyebrows. "Oh, goody," she said when Stella and Chrissy came in. "Chrissy, darlin', come on over here a sec. I know I got one a them strays down here somewhere, but I cain't see it with my old eyes."

Chrissy winked in Stella's direction. "Gimmee them tweezers and let me have a look," she said. "You picked the right girl for the job—my mom's always havin' me go hunting."

"Oh sugar, what would us old birds do without you young ones," Irene sighed contentedly as Chrissy located the offending stray chin hair and gave it a firm yank.

Stella fetched paper plates and napkins from the break room and sliced the doughnuts into quarters and arranged them in an attractive circle on the department's single chipped serving platter. She poured three cups of lukewarm coffee, and the ladies sat down at the Formica-topped conference table.

"He's in a foul mood today," Irene confided. Stella was always a little nervous around Irene, whose loyalty belonged unquestionably to Goat, but Irene had warmed to Stella and in recent weeks had asked for her help with a little situation of her own.

Stella gladly complied. The job involved corralling Irene's favorite great-nephew, who'd left his freshman year at SMSU to go on an extended bender with a few fraternity brothers.

Stella found the little band of good-timers drinking off a long weekend in an Arkansas State cheerleader's parents' rec room, and explained the costs and benefits of higher education to the entire group. Each and every one of them was now sending her a weekly update on their grades, and Irene was satisfied that her nephew was no longer failing all his classes.

Now it was time to test the goodwill Stella had built up.

"So, Irene," she began as casually as she could, once Irene had polished off several doughnut sections and had a fetching little smear of strawberry jam at the corner of her mouth, "what did Goat and them find out at Porters'?"

Irene fixed Stella with a stern gaze and tsked. "Is that why you two are over here bribin' me with sweets? To git me talkin'?"

"Of course not—it's just, well, I'm *concerned* about Priss. You know, coming back to town after all these years—why, it's just terrible that the welcome she's getting is in the form of a heapin' pile of trouble."

"How'd you even know the fellas got called out?" Irene demanded skeptically.

"I was listening to the scanner," Chrissy said. "I was stayin' out at my folks' place over the weekend and I couldn't sleep."

"Oh, your dad surely is one for the scanner. We used to have us a time, your dad and me and Sheriff Knoll and those brothers of yours." Irene's expression softened. "Your brothers were a hoot, Chrissy girl, even if they were a bunch of untamed hell-raisers. Well, listen, I suppose it won't hurt to tell you, since it'll be all over town soon anyway, once folks see Ian and Mike's car up there. What happened was, Liman called in a intruder."

"Liman?" So much for him being asleep, as Priss had suggested.

"Yup, he called Emergency, but he was so drunk, he couldn't

hardly get a word out. He kept sayin' there was people in the house, and they was comin' for him. He wouldn't leave his room. He locked himself in there while he was talkin' to Darja and told her if we didn't get somebody out quick, he was gonna jump out the window. And you know maybe that's what he done, 'cause when Goat got out there, wasn't a soul on the property."

"Wait a minute," Stella said, lowering her uneaten doughnut to the plate. "The house was *empty* when Goat got there?"

"Yes'm. Lights all blazing and Priss's car right out in front and nobody there, not Priss or Liman either."

"Then why'd they call out Mike and Ian?" Chrissy asked. "They figure to go lookin' for 'em in the dark?"

"Yes, they searched all the way back through the acreage and over to Monroe's land. They're back on it now it's daylight, got some a the boys from over to Quail Valley in to help out."

She gave them a conspiratorial gaze, her drawn-on black eyebrows lifting into impressive arches.

Stella took a deep and steadying breath. She was at a delicate juncture, and she had to proceed with great caution. There were things missing from Irene's recounting, things that could make the difference between a smattering and a mountain of trouble. Like, for instance, if Priss had disposed of the dead body before disappearing. Or, for that matter, if her little envelope of pictures had turned up in all that searching.

"What-all do you want to know?" Irene demanded, frowning.

"Nothing much," Stella assured her. "Just . . . what the sheriff found out there and maybe what else he's looking for. And, uh, how *hard* they're looking for whatever they're looking for."

Irene sat back and gazed at Stella thoughtfully. "That's kind of a lot of questions. Okay, but for that, I'm gonna want you to keep on Ricky all through the spring semester."

Stella thought about it for a moment. Being Ricky's academic guardian wasn't really taking up all that much time, especially since the boys had started sending their updates on a Twitter feed, which Chrissy had finally explained to her how to use.

"I suppose I can do that."

"And anything dips below a C, you go and visit him."

"But—"

"I will *not* have the first Dorsey to go to college flunk out on his first try!" Irene exclaimed. "You *got* to do this."

"All right," Stella sighed. "It's on my list."

"Well, all righty, then." Irene took a sip of nearly cold coffee and swirled it around in her mouth before swallowing. "What the sheriff found was, there was a mess in that house. Above and beyond the normal-type mess Liman's let build up over there. There was a lamp busted, a chair was turned over—and there was this big china beer mug or something broke on the floor, but it had blood on it and little hairs they think might be Liman's, seein' as it was short and brown, so they're gonna have the folks up in Fayette take a look at it."

"They think someone used it to hit someone else?"

"Well, you're the smart one, what do you think?"

"What about the door?" Stella asked, ignoring Irene's comment. This was a startling development, indeed, if things were being busted on people's heads—that kind of violence was generally a sign of reckless desperation. "Did someone break into Liman's room?"

"Sheriff didn't say nothing about that."

So the door probably hadn't been broken down, meaning Liman unlocked it on his own. Or maybe someone—Priss?—had a key. Only doors on the inside of houses rarely had keys anymore, did they?

Stella exchanged a glance with Chrissy, who was polishing off the last of the powdered sugar doughnuts and licking frosting off her fingers. Chrissy gave her a faint shrug.

"Did they search Priss's car?" Stella asked.

"Not yet, I don't think. I believe they're having it towed up to impound in Fayette. They'll probably take a look at it there."

There was simply no way to ask if they'd taken a gander in the trunk, not without raising Irene's suspicions even further.

"Well, I surely do appreciate it," Stella said, producing a warm smile. She'd have to remember to swing by with a Big Pig sandwich from the Pokey Pot restaurant—Irene's favorite—in the next few days to ceremonially mark the transfer of favors.

"Whyever are you so curious about this particular case, anyway?" Irene demanded. "Somebody beatin' on Priss? Wouldn't surprise me, that gal been stuck up since she got born onto God's earth. Why, I'd take her down a few notches myself, if I had the chance—though violence ain't ever the answer to anything."

Stella noted Irene's pious tone, and wondered if working in such close proximity to the official nerve center of the law made a person cleave more closely to the party line. "Not that I know of."

"What about Liman? Is he knocking some gal around? Though I don't believe that man's had a date in years," Irene interrupted herself. "Least not one that don't take place at the Honey Club."

"No, Liman hasn't done anything I know of," Stella said. She knew the "club" Irene was referring to—it was a flat-roofed cinder block rectangle where a fellow could buy a young lady a drink for eight times what it ought to cost, as an entrée into an evening of delectable pleasures, or at least a quick hand job in a thin-walled cubicle.

Not a very romantic setting, but Stella figured she didn't have any business judging other folks' pleasure seeking. As long as no one was hurting anyone else, and everyone was doing what they agreed to do for the price they agreed to do it for, and not being forced to do anything that wasn't in the plan, she guessed she could respect folks' rights to party as they saw fit.

"Did they find anything else? Maybe something come through evidence?"

An image of the offending scarf—one that Stella now realized she'd never much liked anyway, since it tended to pill and the little metallic bits scratched against her neck—came into her mind and complicated her efforts to look innocent.

Irene narrowed her eyes and considered Stella craftily. She was no slouch; Goat had inherited her from Sheriff Knoll, who'd hired her as a fresh and dewy fifty-something divorcée a couple of decades back. Now she was plowing through her seventies with all her important faculties intact, and every apparent intention of turning back the hands of time with vigorous attention to her beauty regimen, failing sight be damned. As a result, her makeup often looked slightly askew and her jet-black hair sported a solid anchoring of silvery roots, but she hadn't lost a bit of her hawkish attention to the details of running the sheriff's office exactly as she pleased.

Luckily, Goat had enough sense to back off and let the woman mind the shop.

"Nothing I know of," Irene said serenely, reaching into the top drawer of the desk. She took out a little plastic tote containing nail files and polish in several shades of hot pink. "But I'll keep you posted, hear?"

When Stella and Chrissy took their leave, after rinsing out

the mugs and serving dish in the old industrial sink from the building's fast-food days, Irene was well into giving herself an eye-popping fuchsia manicure. She wiggled her freshly painted nails in a good-bye wave.

Chapter Eight

Their second stop was a visit to the old Prosper library, which had been turned into a shop called the Den of Spirits a few years back. The Den of Spirits sold all manner of New Agey crystals and dream catchers and tarot cards and did, as far as Stella could tell, hardly a lick of business. It was a sturdy building constructed of massive blocks of limestone that had been brought in all the way from Cape Girardeau on the Missouri Pacific railroad a century ago. There was a handsome, broad set of stone steps leading up to the imposing entrance—which was now hung with feathery wind spinners and tinkling chimes—and it was up and down these steps that the Green Hat Ladies currently trudged.

"Well, hi there, Stella! And Chrissy, where's that little Tucker of yours?" Gracie Lewis practically bounded down the steps at a pace that was impressive for a gal in her late seventies. She was wearing a lime green track suit, and her matching sneakers were topped with hot pink laces. Her three elderly companions followed at a less enthusiastic pace.

"My mama's taking care of Tucker today, Mrs. Lewis," Chrissy said politely. "Are you all having a nice weekend?"

Shirlette Castro grimaced and clutched her stomach. "Yes, I suppose so, except we played cards last night, and Novella's onion dip gave me gas," she said. "That or them beets she puts in the Jell-O salad."

Novella Glazer glared at her friend as though she was considering shoving her down the rest of the steps. "I don't guess anybody *made* you eat two helpings."

"I didn't say it wasn't good," Shirlette said primly. "Only, I don't suppose you need to be putting beets in everything when ain't none of us can digest them anymore."

"Gerald likes the beets," Novella said. "He'd just be devastated if I left them out. I've been making that recipe since 1956."

The Green Hat Ladies had been meeting for lunch most days for years, over at the Popeyes restaurant. Recently, though, Gracie Lewis's doctor had warned her that if she didn't trim down a bit, her chicken-and-biscuit days were over, and she'd convinced the rest of the gals to join her in a pre-lunch walk through town, starting with a few trips up and down the library stairs to get the blood flowing.

"My heavens, Gracie, you've taken to this walking program like a duck to water," Stella said warmly. It never hurt to butter up the ladies when she needed information. "Soon you'll be running circles around me."

Stella herself got a great deal of exercise, owing to the demands of her profession. Daily workouts on her basement Bow-flex combined with runs through town several days a week had helped her shed a fair amount of weight and given her a firm layer of muscle underneath her curves; after her recent hospitalization, she added some tai chi and yoga moves that the physical therapist had introduced. She'd never felt better, physically speaking, and she was glad to see the old gals taking care of themselves, too. Stella had a sneaking suspicion that if women kept themselves in fighting form, they'd be far less likely to let folks mistreat them.

Gracie beamed. She loved being the center of attention. It was her husband who'd contributed the John Deere caps back when the friends had decided to form their own club, a considerable savings over the purple and red hats they were considering, since the Deere rep gave them away for free when he came to call on Ed Lewis's feed store.

"I've been thinking I ought to call them *Biggest Loser* folks," Gracie confided. "Give Novella and Linda here a little bit of extra motivation, line 'em up on the scale in nothing but their underthings, on national television. Bet they'd take off all that lard then."

Novella's jaw dropped and she raised a finger to point at Gracie. "I don't know who appointed *you* May Queen," she sputtered. "I'm large boned, is all. Always have been. Least I've still got a *figure*."

"I know you ladies are anxious to get back to your exercising," Stella cut in hastily. "Chrissy and I just had a quick question for you."

"Oooh, a *business* visit," Shirlette said, clapping her hands to her cheeks. "Why, you should of *said* so, Stella."

The rest of the ladies crowded closer. Above them, the wind chimes clanked mournfully in the paltry wind. Thick gray clouds obscured the sun, giving the day a downcast, pessimistic feel. On the streets below, few shoppers hurried by. They were all over in Fairfax, Stella would wager, where they'd built a mall a while back. Her own shop was closed on Sundays and Tuesdays. Occasionally Stella considered staying open an extra day, but she doubted it would bring in any more customers.

Which was unfortunate, given the state of her finances, and now that Priss's money didn't look like it would be coming through, she needed to be on the lookout for some other source of income.

Meanwhile, she had some proactive ass-covering to get to. "I hear there was a little trouble out at the Porters' place last night."

"Oh my yes," Novella said. "Claire Binham saw all them cruisers over there this morning. She thought maybe Liman'd drunk himself into some sort of tragedy, like what Reverend Spokes done."

All the ladies bowed their heads at the mention of the reverend, letting a respectful moment of reflection pass. The reverend, whose cheerful if largely inebriated presence was a staple at all manner of community events, had been trying to park his enormous church-issued sedan at an unaccustomed angle at the far end of the Bethel Baptist parking lot late one summer evening when the Ladies' Altar Society had called a meeting and taken up all the parking spaces. He'd run the sedan into the culvert directly behind the church and, tragically reckless about seat belt law, managed to get himself thrown out of the car and crushed beneath all those tons of Detroit steel, where he died a slow but, they all hoped, pleasantly inebriated death before he was discovered the following morning.

"Well, I don't think Liman got in any wrecks," Stella allowed. Experience with the Green Hat Ladies had taught her that parceling out a bit of not-commonly-known facts generally stirred up plenty of enthusiasm for helping. Which was often fruitful, given that between them, the Ladies had about three hundred years of residence in Sawyer County, along with it knowledge of the undersides and underbellies of most of the local families.

Stella had often reflected that if the nation's top law enforcement agencies would each get themselves a flock of old biddies, they'd be able to crack every stubborn gang stronghold and drug epidemic and crime wave in the country. But it had been her experience that the wisdom of mature ladies was often tragically undervalued.

Not by her, though, and she knew how to work them to get the most out of their collective wisdom.

"What do you mean?" Linda wheezed, eyes widening.

"Well . . . I probably shouldn't say anything, but when the boys got over there, there wasn't hide nor hair of Liman *or* Priss on the property," she confided, making sure to imbue her revelation with as much breathless gravitas as possible.

"*No,*" Gracie whispered.

"I'm afraid so." Stella caught Chrissy's eye; the girl was standing back a bit from the rest of them. Her assistant always had a hard time hanging on to a straight face whenever they dealt with the Green Hat Ladies. Learning to maintain a sense of calm decorum was part of her ongoing training.

"But how can we help?" Lola asked, rising to her full five feet three inches and putting her fists to her hips.

Stella assumed a serious expression and let a few dramatic seconds tick by. The ladies drew even closer, resembling a scrum of fashion-challenged female senior citizen rugby players.

"It's like this," she said conspiratorially, keeping her volume just high enough for their challenged hearing. "I need to know who-all Liman's been, you know, *consorting* with. Who his known accomplices are, and all."

There was a collective murmur. The ladies loved jargon, so Stella laid it on thick.

"If he's been in any illicit relationships . . . any deals gone bad . . ."

"Well, now, he is a *homely* one," Shirlette cut in. "Weren't any good looks wasted on him."

"He ain't getting any action," Lola said decisively, "'cept the kind that costs twenty dollars over at the Trucker World."

"*Lola!*" Gracie gasped.

"I *think* I would know what I'm *talking* about," Lola said, folding her arms over her chest and lifting her chin. "Pete can't hardly help but hear the other fellows talk."

Lola's husband, Pete Brennan, had been a long-haul trucker for over four decades. Stella doubted he was much of a familiar of the sorts of commerce that went on in the Trucker World parking lot on the far side of the truck showers. He was a nice old guy.

"What did, ah, Pete say?" she asked gently. "If it doesn't *pain* you too much to talk about it."

"Oh, Liman was a regular over there. Pete said he'd sober up once or twice a month, long enough to get his chain yanked."

"*Lola!*" Gracie repeated, her face turning a florid red that signaled cardiac distress.

"What? I'm just telling Stella what Pete said. It's *important*."

Chrissy rushed forward and took Lola's arm. "Are you all right, Mrs. Brennan?" she murmured. "Can I get you something?"

"No . . . no, dear. I'm just saying what needs said. I suppose we can't keep the evil out of the world, now, can we?"

"No, ma'am." Chrissy flashed Stella a fleeting *you owe me* glance as she worked up a wistful expression. "The devil does come calling every time we turn our backs, don't he?"

"He surely, surely does," Lola murmured, taking advantage of Chrissy's strong grip to do a modified swoon, though Stella noticed she positioned her ample backside against the iron railing for support.

"So Liman . . . uh, indulged in the comforts over at Trucker

World," Stella summarized. "But no other known vices or regular habits. No gambling, no drugs."

"None of that," Linda agreed. "He's just drunk, and kind of nasty, nothing else. But what about Priss? She always did seem to think she was a cut above other folks."

There was a round of vigorous nodding and harrumphing around the circle. Stella seized the opportunity; there was rarely a better time to get to the heart of a matter than when the ladies were in high dudgeon. "Can you think of anything, anything at all, that would help me gain a . . . a better understanding of Priss? And her possible whereabouts?"

There was a moment of silent concentration, and then Shirlette piped up. "Well, you know, she had a reputation for leadin' the fellas on in high school. Remember that? She could be quite a teasing bit of tail."

Stella reeled in her own startled expression. "You mean, ah . . ."

"Well, I'm just repeating what they always said about her," Shirlette said, coloring. "What, did I say something?"

"Pete said she was coldhearted," Lola said generously. "I think you're right."

Stella fought to control her facial muscles, which were dangerously close to betraying her. "So you are saying that Priss was, um, unfriendly to her suitors."

"Well, except for Salty," Linda exclaimed. "Remember?"

Nods all around. Even Stella vaguely remembered: Dalton "Salty" Mingus, captain of the marginal Prosper High golf team back in the early nineties. He had squired Priss around for most of their senior year before she left for greener and more prosperous pastures. He'd moped for quite some time, drifting from one job to another, even—if Stella remembered right—moving up to the city for a while, but nothing seemed to stick until a few years back when he finally got married and went to work in his father-in-law's restaurant supply business. Since then, he'd done well enough to buy a four-bedroom trilevel and lose any lingering traces of his once-athletic build.

"You don't think he was still in touch with Priss," she ventured. Her impression of the grown-up Salty was a wide-bodied guy in an assortment of colorful double-knit golf shirts, his ample gut gamely restrained with pleated shorts for his post-church nine holes, while his wife and couple of young Minguses repaired to the homestead to put on a buttery spread.

Bland. If she had to come up with a word for Salty, it would be *bland*.

"Well, love does demand its due," Shirlette said mysteriously, turning her lined face into the biting November winds that whipped down the street.

"What do you mean, doll?" Stella asked cautiously.

"Only, sometimes them things ain't over when they're over," Shirlette allowed, though she kept her face averted from the group. Stella wondered if she'd experienced her own tragic love and made a mental note to explore the subject at a later date.

She made a few more stabs at stirring up the ladies, but they didn't have anything more to contribute, and when she and Chrissy left them a little later, they had resumed their brave campaign up and down the steps, Linda checking her watch and demanding they get over to the Popeyes before it filled up with lunchtime customers.

On the ride home, Chrissy chattered about her cousin's wedding, and Stella tried to keep track of the story's extensive cast of characters, the members of the vast Lardner extended family, but her thoughts kept going back to Priss. Priss with her ridiculous boots and coat, her fancy car, her condescending airs.

Priss with her—on reflection, desperate—bid for help with the body in the trunk. A body that Stella knew as little about now as she did when she first laid eyes on him. Maybe things were not as they seemed. Maybe Priss was in over her head. Maybe she was being stalked or framed or threatened—all kinds of terrible scenarios flashed through Stella's mind, and she began to feel a wee bit remorseful.

Until she remembered the pictures of her beating the crap out of Ferg Rohossen.

Then the remorse evaporated in a hurry. If those pictures fell into the wrong hands—say those of Detective Daphne Simmons, who had made it clear that she didn't care a whit for Stella—there was going to be all kinds of hell to pay. At the very least, if the pictures got out, it would make it nearly impossible for Stella to continue her covert benevolent aid society for the abused.

But it would probably also mean that a lot of sketchy episodes from the last few years would be dug up and reviewed by Sheriff Dimmit Stanislas as he sat on his wide and lazy ass up in the county seat, and Stanislas had shown how eager he was to find scapegoats for any blight on the department. He'd be pleased as punch to go after Stella—especially if a conviction could boost his dismal reputation.

And even if Goat wanted to help her then—which was very doubtful, since he'd probably be fit to be tied when he realized the extent of Stella's lawbreaking—he'd be forced to join the efforts against her if he wanted to hold on to his job. Stella figured it was only the crazy red-hot pheromone-drenched electricity between them that had allowed him to overlook her escapades this long. But all the sexual chemistry in the world couldn't help her if he ever found out just how far she'd gone to deliver her brand of renegade justice, a brand that flew in the face of everything Goat stood for.

At least the envelope of pictures and the flash drive seemed to be blessedly missing, along with Priss and Liman.

But Stella had a sinking feeling that she wouldn't be able to track down the former without getting tangled up further with the latter.

Chapter Nine

"That's quite a striking outfit you got on," Stella observed that night as she and Chrissy hiked through a frost-dead field toward the Porter place, eyeing her assistant's stretch fleece yoga pants tucked into a pair of pink fake-suede Ugg knockoffs, and the camo-print sherpa-lined flak jacket she'd borrowed from one of her brothers, the hood cinched tight around her pretty face. "You could take that anywhere from a dinner cruise in the Arctic sea, to a hoedown in a hunting camp."

"Well, you might as well get your mileage out of me now, seeing as I got to mind the shop tomorrow," Chrissy said, ignoring Stella's teasing.

Since the farm was a suspected crime scene and all, they were taking the precaution of approaching it overland in the dark. Stella's Jeep was parked off-road on Monroe land, hidden by a grove of scrubby staghorn sumacs.

"I don't know about these here flashlights you got," Chrissy added dubiously. The Blue Dot police models had been a splurge that, on reflection, didn't merit the price; the white light could blind a person but didn't do the best job of illuminating the path in front of them.

Stella sighed. "Yeah, sometimes you don't get what you pay for."

She gave her backpack a reassuring heft. It was a BlackHawk R.A.P.T.O.R., designed for special ops use, which she bought herself for Christmas after an earlier model was lost in the summer's deadly outing to the lake. She might never use all the features—she doubted that the built-in jump harness would come in handy any time soon, for instance—but she loved how slick and lightweight and intimidating looking it was.

Inside the pack was her Tupperware spaghetti box full of lock tools. Some were professional models Chrissy had helped her find in dark and illicit corners of the Internet, but her favorites were the homemade jobs she'd crafted out of beer cans. That, and a vibrating Oral-B flossing wand that had its uses in certain situations.

The Porter house was dark. The winds from earlier in the day had died down and now another storm threatened, illuminated by a silver moon that drifted in and out of the clouds. Their footsteps on the porch sounded much too loud, and an answering skittering sound from the bushes gave Stella a momentary start, but the inky form that went flying across the scrubby yard was nothing but a large rat or a small raccoon.

Stella unzipped her pack and got out two pairs of latex gloves that she'd rubber-banded together. She handed one pair to Chrissy and slipped on the other.

"Going uptown, I see," Chrissy said, tugging the gloves over her hands. For everyday breaking and entering, Stella economized by using Ziploc sandwich bags, which were just fine when a person didn't need a whole lot of manual dexterity, and cost a fraction what the gloves did.

"Nothing's too good for Priss," Stella said sarcastically. "Why, she probably wipes her ass with silk scarves."

She jiggled the door handle, finding it locked but cheap. "Here, hold the flashlight for me, this won't take but a minute. I swear, you can't find a challenge anywhere around here these days."

"Whyn't you let me try," Chrissy said. "Might as well learn something, seein' as I'm missing family poker night at my folks'."

Stella selected a narrow tension wrench and handed it to the girl. "What happened to your principles? How you were just going to focus on the shop and the computer stuff and stay out of all the hands-on lawbreaking?"

Chrissy snorted, an unladylike sound that contrasted with the sweet frown of concentration on her full cherubic lips as she held the tool up and examined it in the powerful white light of the flashlight.

"Well, now, I guess I just ain't got enough starch to resist the lure of the dark side no more, Stella, not when I'm exposed to *you* every durn day. Which end of this am I supposed to use, anyway?"

Stella tapped it delicately with a fingernail. "That there— see where it's bent? Jimmy that into the keyhole."

Chrissy got it started, and Stella showed her how to finesse the pins with a narrow hooked pick, and soon the door opened up with a little rattle. "Why, it's just like Liman's *begging* to get robbed," Chrissy marveled.

"Don't go getting any ideas. We don't run that kind of out-fit." Stella slipped the tools back in the Tupperware container and snapped it shut with a satisfying little burp. Chrissy pushed open the door and entered the house, snapping on a light switch, which lit up a '70s-era bean-shaped lamp with a macramé shade. The single bulb made little effort to illuminate the room, casting yellowish shadows over the huddled low-slung furniture, the piles of newspapers and magazines on the coffee table, the collection of dusty beer steins lining the shelves of a laminate entertainment center. "You start on the bedrooms. I'll take the main rooms. And remember, this flash drive we're looking for is just a little thing, a—"

Chrissy stopped cold, so that Stella walked right into her, nearly falling on Liman's musty brown carpet. When Chrissy put her hands to her hips and planted her feet wide and gave her a withering glare, like Clint Eastwood in *The Good, the Bad and the Ugly*, Stella knew she'd messed up.

"What I meant was—"

"You were *not* about to tell me what a fuckin' flash drive looks like, Stella Hardesty," the girl fumed.

"I only meant that it's not very big, that we need to be looking in—"

"Whyn't *you* tell *me* what one looks like. Since you know so much."

"Now, Chrissy, don't be like that. You know I respect your skills. You know I consider—"

"You best be considering telling me exactly what I'm *lookin'* for. Take your time, Stella, and tell me all about it. Since you're the *expert* and all."

Most gals, Stella reflected, tended to the hysteria end of the spectrum when they got flustered. She'd seen it over and over among her customers: The female brain seemed to require a lot of extra oxygen and bosom heaving when it was processing trouble and disharmony.

Not Chrissy, though. Ever since the girl had faced down a pack of angry professional killers during Tucker's rescue over the summer, she'd developed a repertoire of reactions more suited to, say, a ninja warrior. Her eyes narrowed and her breathing slowed down to what a person might experience if they were laid out on an iceberg and chilled like a shrimp cocktail, and she managed to radiate pure focused menace, as if she could kill with her mind alone.

And that was with people she *loved*. Because, as Stella reminded herself now, Chrissy did indeed love her very much.

Only Stella had done it again, had crossed that one line that provoked Chrissy like nothing else.

She'd questioned the girl's competence. Unwittingly, perhaps; without judgment, perhaps; but she'd done it, and now there was a whole field of hot coals sizzling between them. Chrissy had taken up computer hacking a few months earlier while she was recovering from being shot up like a prize buck, and she'd spent enough of her growing-up years being told she was just a shade smarter than a stump, that she'd need to trade on her voluptuous good looks to get anywhere, that discovering her own innate technical aptitude was like a junkie discovering the powerful allure of crack.

Chrissy wasn't just *good* with computers; she was a tech goddess, a byte-whisperer, a cracker of codes, a bloodhound of networks. But on the inside, she was still dragging around the outdated self-image of a girl who barely graduated from Prosper High, who was more likely to be propositioned by her science teacher than expected to complete a lab report, whose own mother hoped only to marry her off to a boy who would support her while she started popping out babies.

"A flash drive," Stella said carefully, "is, like, a little old thing you stick into your computer that holds a bunch of documents on it. Or, you know, pictures." *Pictures of me beating the shit out of a scumbag in a barn,* she didn't add.

"Uh-huh. Right. You still ain't told me what it looks like. Bigger than a lipstick? Round? Square?"

Stella knew she was being baited, but there was no graceful exit. She sighed heavily. "I don't know. Um, like a, you know, plug or something?"

"A . . . *plug*? Stella, do you even know how to turn on your Mac?"

"I. Uh. Well, see the thing is, you always have it on already when I come in and—"

"Forget it," Chrissy snapped, and started down the hall. "Once I look around in here, I'll come back out and help you out, since you obviously don't know your butt from your elbow."

Stella went to work with a smile on her face.

They kept at it for nearly an hour. Stella worked the living room and kitchen and tiny foyer with the gloomy attention of someone who knows she is going through a pointless exercise. She didn't want to admit it, but she *felt* in her bones that the drive wasn't here. That nothing helpful, in fact, was here—no lingering trace of Priss's presence at all.

The beer stein that had been used to pummel someone in the head—that's what Stella was assuming, given the hair and skin; knock someone over the head and you were going to get that particular kind of detritus—was sitting safe and secure up in Fayette, under the watchful eye of Detective Simmons's crime scene staff.

Otherwise, there wasn't a whole lot to go on. Blooming smudges of black fingerprint powder surrounded the doorframes leading in and out of rooms, the light switches, objects on tables. A pair of chairs that looked as though they belonged on either side of the fireplace had been stacked next to the scratched old walnut hutch in the dining room. In lieu of the usual personal tchotchkes—framed snapshots, ashtrays, figurines—the tabletop surfaces featured wooden bowls of pretzel crumbs and empty beer cans and expired issues of *TV Guide*. Stella checked in drawers and behind the sofas and under the rugs, but the most unexpected thing she came up with was a ticket stub from a matinee showing of *Lethal Weapon 2*. Which suggested nothing other than the possibility that Liman hadn't cleaned under the rugs in two decades.

She was about to declare the search a bust when she heard the crunch of tires on the drive outside. Chrissy must have heard it, too, because she came hurtling down the hall and grabbed Stella's arm and yanked.

"Tub," she snapped, and dragged Stella into the hall bath. She tugged the door nearly closed behind them and led the way into the tub, which smelled of mildew. They stood close together behind the stiff plastic shower curtain.

There was a soft tapping at the front door. Stella could feel her heart pounding hard under her sweat-dampened T-shirt. She touched her pocket for reassurance, wishing she'd brought something a little more muscular than the little Bersa .380 she'd picked up on a whim in the back of an old bait shop in Sikeston. The lightweight little gun fit into a pocket but was probably better for settling arguments at a garden show than for dealing with any kind of real danger.

"You packing?" she whispered.

"You out of your mind?" Chrissy whispered back. "This was supposed to be a simple little treasure hunt. Besides, what makes you think whoever that is needs shot? Prob'ly kids, you know, figuring they can come around and get high and make out, seein' as the house is empty."

"I don't know. . . ."

"Stella, every last person in Prosper knows Liman's gone missing. There's folks that likes crime scenes, too, you know, like a little hobby or something? There's this bunch on the Internet, calls themselves the CSI-dols, get it, like *idols*—"

She broke off as there was a tinkling of glass—someone had knocked out a pane from the front door. Stella swallowed hard.

"Well, fuck me," Chrissy whispered softly. "I guess life's about to get interesting."

Chapter Ten

don't think this is any kind of innocent little social call."

"Maybe not," Chrissy conceded as Stella got the Bersa settled in her hand.

"Anyone here?" a voice boomed. Fast-thudding steps came in and split off into at least two directions, maybe three, from the sound of it.

Another voice, with a thick Chicago accent, chimed in. "Take the hall. I'll check the kitchen."

"Not kids," Stella whispered, stating the obvious.

Chrissy snorted softly. "Bunch a morons, is what that is. Just announced where they was going—what kind of way is that to search a house?"

"You an expert suddenly?" Stella whispered back, then clamped her mouth shut as steps surged past the bathroom and they heard someone open the door to the bedroom across the hall. Stella shut her eyes and pictured the way she'd do it if it were her—go in fast, left nearside corner, since the bad guy was likely to be right-handed. Aim down—those scenes in the movie where they draw next to their faces were the worst kind of bullshit. A bad guy could grab your arm, and all you could do was shoot holes in the ceiling—aim down, and you'd be shooting holes in their ankles.

There was a sound at the bathroom door and the door swung and bumped against the wall and a man entered the little room.

Stella yanked the curtain back and stuck her hand out at lighting speed, getting a handful of shirt, and yanked as hard as she could as Chrissy ducked neatly out of the way.

There was a satisfying thunk of skull hitting tile. In the light from the hall, Stella saw that she'd bagged a short round sort of a thug—he'd stumbled on the edge of the tub when Stella grabbed him. That the move had actually worked was a cause for surprise as much as delight, and Stella savored the feeling for a half a second while she grabbed an arm and twisted it up behind the guy while Chrissy did something to him that elicited a girlish shriek of pain. An object clattered to the tub floor, and Stella jammed her gun in the soft spot behind the man's ear and put her lips millimeters from his cheek.

"Make a sound and I'll blow a hole in you that you'd be able to put a fist through."

The man nodded very carefully. A familiar if unpleasant stench rose to her nostrils.

"Eww," Chrissy whispered. "You done pissed yourself, ain't you? You some sort a beginner or what?"

Their captive was evidently taking to heart Stella's command to keep quiet because he merely shrugged—a very small and cautious shrug.

"Take your foot," Stella said, "and move that gun you dropped as far as you can to the right."

"And hope you don't drip on it or I'm a knock you in the nuts again," Chrissy snarled.

The man complied slowly, toeing the gun gently like he was a ballet-shoe-wearing member of the corps.

"You know what to do, I guess," Stella told Chrissy.

Chrissy snatched up the gun and stepped out of the tub with the graceful agility of a cat. Her form as she slunk around the corner into the hall was flawless, leading with the guy's gun— she'd been shooting a variety of firearms practically since she was a toddler. The Lardners were a well-armed clan, with diverse interests—they'd laid in everything from game-hunting pieces to varmint-scaring to siege-threatening to apocalypse-surviving weapons, and Chrissy and her brothers and sisters were as conversant in their use and care as, say, a family of professional musicians might be with metronomes and batons and tuners.

"Lay down on your stomach," Stella suggested, "and leave your hands up on the edge of the tub. Facedown, now."

She almost had time to feel sorry for the guy, since from the smell and visible ring in the tub, Liman hadn't cleaned it yet in his natural life, but as she stepped gingerly out of the tub, the Bersa trained on him the entire time, she heard Chrissy barking commands in the living room.

"Drop that now!" she hollered. "Kick it out of the way and hit the floor or I'll blow a crater where your dick used to be!"

There was a clatter, followed by a clumping on the floor and a volley of colorful curses.

"Oh, dear," Stella said to the trembling form below her. "My friend does *not* care to be yelled at."

Sure enough, the next sound from the living room was a sort of pronounced "oof" followed by a low moan.

"There any more of you?" Stella demanded. For extra emphasis, she leaned over far enough to tickle the back of her gentleman's short haircut with the muzzle end of the barrel. He shook his head, face grinding into the cold porcelain.

"Just you two today? You sure?"

He nodded harder.

"Okay, here's what we're gonna do—we're gonna go join those guys. Make it like more of a party, see? What's your name, by the way?"

It was Jake, though it took a couple of tries for him to get it out. When he stepped out of the tub he stumbled, and Stella sighed as she gave him a little shove in the right direction, tapping gently at the small of his back with the Bersa.

In the main room, Chrissy was sitting daintily on the edge of a faded, sagging sofa. The man lying on the floor with his hands extended out to the sides looked—at least from what Stella could make out, since his face was pressed to the floor, too—like he might be the larger, leaner brother of Jake.

"What's his name?" she asked.

"Lawrence, is what he says, anyway."

"Okay. Well, Lawrence, I want you to kind of snake-crawl over there, and then you can sit with your back up against the wall. Keep your hands to the sides. And Jake, you go sit next to him, but leave a little room. Like in kindergarten, you know? Pretend you're lining up for recess."

She sat next to Chrissy on the couch and watched the two men carry out their instructions.

"This couch smells," Chrissy said conversationally.

"Jake smells worse."

"Well, I'm not sure about that. Might be a close contest. Hey, they're not much to look at, are they?"

Stella thought that assessment was a bit harsh; their two captives were merely scared witless, which gave them unattractive slack-mouthed expressions. "They probably fix up nice enough," she said kindly.

"So what-all are you up to, coming out here in the middle of the night?" Chrissy demanded.

No answer. Jake cast a nervous glance at his partner, then stared miserably at the incriminating stain on the crotch of his pants.

"Looking for something, maybe?" Stella suggested. "Come out here to, what—you couldn't have been planning to *rob* the place, could you? Maybe y'all are beer stein collectors?"

"There's some vintage vinyl in the back bedroom," Chrissy said. "That might be worth something on eBay."

"Is that it? Y'all lookin' to start a collection?"

"Don't think it would be worth a whole lot," Chrissy said dubiously. "I didn't recognize hardly any of it. There was some Queen. Couple a ABBA."

"Hmm," Stella said.

"Flash drive," Lawrence muttered, giving her a murderous look. "We're looking for a flash drive. That's all."

Stella's eyes widened. What a coincidence. "That so. What, uh, was on this drive?"

"I don't know. The client didn't say. She just said find it and bring it back."

She. Huh. Someone else was looking for the drive with the images of Stella and Ferg. Or a different drive entirely. If Priss was keeping backup scenarios queued up that featured Stella, it made sense she'd have dirt on other people, too—just like Stella had escape hatches stashed all over the county.

This other person wanted the drive bad enough to send these two armed clowns after it. Stella wasn't quite that desperate yet. Did that mean that this other gal's dirt was worse than her own?

"Who's your client?"

"Ain't sayin'," Lawrence said quickly.

"The hell you ain't," Chrissy said, and lifted the gun she'd taken off him and fired a neat shot that hit the wall an inch away from Lawrence's right ear before Stella had time to open her mouth. Lawrence jerked like a puppet who'd received a good hard yank on his strings, and Jake looked like he was about to throw up. "You might like to know that you ain't the first jackass to draw on me. Difference is, last time I moved a little too slow. Not gonna make that mistake again."

"Ah, maybe don't kill 'em quite yet," Stella said hastily. Chrissy's rage was a beautiful thing to behold, but like a wild horse or a summer lightning storm, it seemed like it might be difficult to contain. "Why don't we try asking once more, real nice?"

Chrissy nodded reluctantly. "Okay," she sighed as she lined up another shot. Stella guessed this time she was aiming for the vicinity around Lawrence's other ear. She could see why that would make a person nervous, and decided not to share that Chrissy was a crack shot and would no sooner hit him than shoot her own foot. "I guess we can try your way first. Who. The. Fuck. Hired. You."

"Marilu Carstairs," Jake said quickly. Lawrence shot him a dirty look, but Jake focused intently on his lap. "She's a judge up in Johnson County."

Johnson County was where the fancy-schmancy Kansas City folks tended to live. Stella had once tracked a textile executive who liked to drive all the way to Casey to beat up his mistress back to his seven-thousand-square-foot house in Johnson County.

"A *judge*?" she demanded, wondering what kind of dirt Priss had managed to collect on such a lofty member of the legal system. Her own experience with the judiciary was limited to

Judge Torrance Ligett, who had ordered her released after Ollie's death when dozens of friends and neighbors lined up outside the courthouse to lobby in her behalf, sharing the universally held opinion that she was married to nothing short of a dangerous lunatic.

Judge Ligett was nice. Stella sent him a Christmas card every year. But she guessed not every judge was such a sterling sort of person.

"What did she want the drive for, anyway?"

Jake shrugged. "I don't know. It's a job—we don't ask her business."

"She crooked? Take bribes?" Chrissy asked.

"Don't know."

"That's prob'ly it. How much was she gonna pay you for it?"

The men glanced at each other. Neither said anything.

Stella had an idea.

"Here's what's going to happen," she said. "I figure you got some cash on you. Bet she gave you some up front, and I bet you got it with you. Now, you'll probably tell me otherwise, and then it's just gonna get real uncomfortable for you. It'll be a shame if you're telling the truth, see, because by the time you strip down naked and go out and empty out every inch of your car onto the driveway, you're gonna be real cold. I figure y'all thought you could drive right up to the house like that 'cause you can't really make out anything from the road, right? Up here behind all those elms? But see, that's also gonna make it real convenient for me and my pal here to get cozy while you clean out the trunk and the glove box and dig around under them seats and all that, while we're turning your pockets inside out and goin' through your wallets—"

"I ain't goin' through *his* pants," Chrissy said darkly, pointing to the damp-crotched Jake.

79

"You can damn well—," Lawrence started, his face going a purplish red, before Jake cut him off with a sputtering exclamation.

"She gave us fifteen hundred up front!" he blurted. "Each. Then there was gonna be fifteen hundred more when we gave it to the judge. She said that Porter lady always carried it around with her, is how we knew to come down here."

"Shut your fucking mouth," Lawrence barked. "For fuck's sake."

"I just." Jake swallowed, looking wounded.

"No, no, you're doing real good, sweetie," Stella said, giving him an encouraging smile. There was always a weak link, and they'd found theirs. "Tell you what—tell me the rest, we'll let you keep half your cash."

"We're takin' *all* a yours," Chrissy added, glaring at Lawrence.

Jake nodded enthusiastically, while Lawrence rolled his eyes and muttered "idiot" under his breath.

Stella didn't blame him. He was clearly the more experienced criminal between the two, and as such, he would be very much aware that the odds were that she and Chrissy wouldn't let either of them keep any cash. But that's where he would be wrong. Because the two of them had *principles*. They had *standards*. Their business was committed to helping those in need, and—

—and, really, maybe she didn't have any business taking *any* of their cash at all, come to think of it. It kind of muddied the waters. Confused things. A conflict of interest, if you will.

On the other hand, she was broke. Dead broke. And with all those pressing household needs.

"Reach into your pockets, nice and slow, and take out your wallets," she said decisively. "We're aiming right at you, and your pockets are kinda close to your peckers, so you might not want to do anything to make us suspicious. Right?"

More vigorous nodding from Jake. An aggrieved sigh from Lawrence.

The wallets were removed and tossed over. Luckily, neither had been doused with urine. Chrissy counted out the money, and gave half of Jake's back, after only a little hesitation. Jake grinned wide, like he'd just received a new bike for his birthday, and answered the rest of their questions.

"Judge Carstairs found us 'cause we've done a little work for this one con she sent up a while back. Name of Titan Small. Nice guy, bad checks, gambling, like that—he hired us a few times—"

"He hired *me*," Lawrence said. "Because I'm a professional. Least I was until the day I took *you* on."

"Don't mind him," Jake said, warming to his account. "He's like this sometimes. Anyway, Titan had us doing some collections for him—you know, tracking folks down to get them to pay up—and the judge thought we could help her find Priss. Which was easy, we just drove over to her place last night. Only, come to find out, it wasn't her we were watching, it was her cat-sitter."

"You were *so sure* it was her," Lawrence muttered. "Swear on a stack of Bibles, you said. Bet your life on it, you said."

Jake frowned. "It was through *miniblinds*. And that chick did have the same basic shape, you got to admit."

"What I get," Lawrence said, addressing the opposite wall, "trusting an idiot."

"The cat girl told us everything," Jake said, ignoring his partner. "Didn't take much to convince her."

He had some of his swagger back. Stella was familiar with

this effect—let a man talk, and the fish he pulled out of the lake got bigger and the woman he took home from the bar got prettier—but she let Jake ramble, figuring it was the most direct path to the answers she needed. Besides, they'd nearly wrung the man dry, which was something of a disappointment—evidently he truly *didn't* know much.

"You threatened her," Stella prompted in a pleasant voice, as though it were the best idea she'd heard all day.

"No, no, get this—I threatened the *cat,* see? I mean, she's got to love cats, right, it's her job. So I picked up this big old gray one like this—" He reached around and got hold of his own nape for illustration, causing Chrissy to roll off the couch into a shooter's stance in a split second.

"Go easy," she said, her voice full of menace.

"Sorry, sorry." Jake pulled his hands away and left them out to his side in midair. The effect was of a man trying to levitate. "Anyway, it worked like a charm. She said Priss was visiting her brother for the weekend, a last-minute thing, and she knew the name of the town 'cause I guess her and Priss were friendly that way. All's we had to do was call directory assistance and turn on the GPS, and here we are."

"And you were, what, going to just wait around until they showed up? If you couldn't find the drive on your own?"

"Uh—I mean . . ."

"Would you be interested in knowing that she and her brother both have disappeared?"

It was almost too easy. Stella watched Jake's eyes flicker with the effort of trying to process what she was saying.

"Disappeared . . . like what *kind* of disappeared?"

"Like the kind where somebody called in a disturbance last night."

"Like the kind where there was all kinds of uniforms here last night and you are *so* fucked if they find you here," Chrissy added. "Didn't you notice the damn fingerprint powder everywhere? Whadda ya think, Stella, suppose we ought to tie 'em up and call it in? Let these guys tell their story all over again for Sheriff Jones?"

Stella pretended to consider it.

Pretended for several moments, long enough for Jake to look like he was about to cry and Lawrence to go through an entirely new string of curses.

Then she left Chrissy in charge while she went out to the Jeep to get a few supplies from the Rubbermaid totes she had loaded in the back.

When Stella was working on one of her bread-and-butter clients, the men whose wives and girlfriends had finally gotten tired enough of being smacked around that they were willing to hire Stella to convince them they were on a wrong road, she employed an extensive set of bondage and S&M equipment she had acquired over the years. She owned a range of padded restraints and cuffs and spreader bars and collars and irons for keeping them in one place. Crops and paddles and floggers and canes and whips for turning them around to her way of thinking. And, when necessary, a few really esoteric items that she found on a fascinating Web site—these she saved for tough cases, for giving the worst offenders something new and unforgettable to think about the next time the urge came over them.

But these guys presented a whole other challenge. They were a different sort of scum, the sort that had already demonstrated they didn't mind taking chances with the law. Abusive men generally managed to convince themselves—as astonishing as it was to Stella—that they were in the right, that the hurt they doled out had been earned by their defenseless and terrified women.

Thugs were different. They *knew* they were in the wrong—and they didn't care. While she was pretty sure she could scare them—particularly Jake—she doubted they'd stay scared longer than it took for them to hightail it back out of town.

So in the end, Stella picked out her camera and a few Rem Oil Wipes. She and Chrissy emptied and wiped the men's guns, just to be safe, since they hadn't taken off their latex gloves since they got to the house. They pressed the men's unwilling fingers all over the guns and packed them into a couple of Ziplocs. Then they had their new acquaintances pose for photos around the house, making sure the background was easily identifiable as being Liman's cozy abode.

As Stella was tucking away her insurance policy, Chrissy convinced Lawrence to hand over the keys to his car—convinced him by threatening to employ the same instep-stomping technique she'd used on Jake in the bathtub.

"Okeydoke," she said, twirling the key ring on her finger. "I'll drive on down to Grover's Shell and leave your car in the lot. It's about two, two and a half miles from here heading west. Stella here's gonna take her car. Both of us can drive and aim at the same time, so I'm thinking you don't want to come out that front door until we're good and gone. Then you can start walking. I'll leave your keys under the mat. Sound good?"

"Oh, but you're going to be kind of cold," Stella added, trying to keep from looking amused. "Y'all might want to root around in Liman's stuff, see if you can come up with something warm to wear."

"He's probably got him a extra flannel shirt or two in there. Maybe one a them *I'm with Stupid* T-shirts." Chrissy grinned broadly. "Bye now, boys."

"Why, you're just a *sadist*," Stella said as they backed out the front door, her gun trained on their new friends.

As they headed for the cars, she reflected that she admired her protégée more every day.

Chapter Eleven

Morning dawned with the lovely aroma of strong coffee. Stella stretched luxuriously. A while back, once she had become thoroughly accustomed to sleeping alone, without the snoring malodorous hulk of Ollie taking up more than his share of the bed, she'd bought herself a set of flannel sheets at the Linens 'n Things up in Fayette. Ollie never let her buy flannel—he said it made him too hot, and it was true, he sweated like a pig even on the coldest day of winter.

Being new to the whole independent-thinking thing at the time, Stella had been overwhelmed by all the choices and confined her search for new linens to the clearance table. There, she'd found a set of premium German-made brushed flannel sheets in a very odd print. It was floral—sort of. If the multihued blobs that looked like they were trying to mate with a background pattern of pretzelly curlicues were regarded through squinted eyes, the effect might be vaguely flowerlike.

But Stella didn't care. They washed up fluffy and unbelievably soft to the touch. And that was when she unleashed phase two of her new winter bedtime plan—she started wearing nothing but her panties and an old stretched-out camisole to bed, all the better to feel that wonderful warm flannel next to her skin.

Some nights, some decadent devil-may-care nights, she skipped the camisole.

Oh, but it felt delicious to slide under those velvety sheets in next to nothing at the end of the day, the weight of her fluffy comforter like a cloud that had settled down to gently embrace her. She went to sleep with a smile on her face. And she had wonderful, bad-girl dreams, often featuring the hands-off man in her life.

But Goat hadn't visited last night. Stella kept her eyes shut for an extra five minutes, shuffling through her dream memories, just to make sure, but she came up blank.

Then she started wondering who the hell had made coffee in her house.

By the time she came into the kitchen, wearing an old pair of pajama pants printed with lollipops and a Chicks-A-Plenty sweatshirt she'd gotten for free at the chicken processing plant's spirit day, she was brandishing a large-barrel curling iron, ready for trouble.

"Hey, Mama, I ate all your Pop-Tarts."

Stella's heart leapt to a crescendo—mother love on overdrive. There, tucked into a kitchen chair and stuffing cotton balls between her toes, was Noelle. She was wearing an emerald green slinky, sparkly sweater that looked about four sizes too large, and a lacy black bra and tight black knit pedal pushers. Her trumpet vine tattoo curled prettily across her collarbones and disappeared under the off-the-shoulder sweater to twine, as Stella well knew, down her back.

"Oh, sugar, thank heavens I didn't shoot you."

"Well, I love you, too, Mama. And—and—I think I might need a hug."

At that, Noelle burst into tears and Stella, fueled by an imperative as old as time itself, or at least as old as the first amphibian mothers to walk on land, all the while fretting that their children were keeping up on their little webbed feet—or perhaps as old as the cavewomen, who surely sat up at the cave mouth many a sleepless night waiting for their daughters to return from raids on neighboring tribes—Stella gathered her little girl in her arms and rocked her back and forth and let her baby's hot tears fall on her neck and made shushing sounds and hummed in the back of her throat. She kissed the top of Noelle's head, not even minding the gel in her spiky fuchsia hair, and then she kissed her right above her eyebrows, where the skin was warm and soft. And then she kissed her baby's soft-as-petals cheek.

"What's wrong?" Stella finally asked, knowing she'd let everything else fall to the wayside if it meant she could provide Noelle a moment's comfort. Let the bad guys surge forth over the land. Let civilization fall; let evil gain a toehold. Nothing in the world would keep Stella from this moment.

"Mama," Noelle finally managed to snuffle after burrowing her sweet face into the crook of Stella's neck and hanging on for dear life, "I took a leave of absence at the salon."

Stella kept rocking. She snuggled tight and weighed her words and considered her five decades of experience and her daughter's nearly three, and she bit down hard on her tongue to keep from saying anything until she got it planned out right:

"Is that right?"

"Yes, Mama," Noelle continued, oblivious of her mother's considerable psychic torment. "It was the best thing to do. I mean, I'm almost thirty years old. It's high time I figure out who I am. Who I *really* am. You know what I'm sayin'?"

Stella didn't know, not entirely, but she nodded encouragingly. "Does this have anything to do with your charming new friend?"

"Joy? Yes!" Noelle drew back to smile at Stella, her tear-sparkled eyes lit up with delight. "So you *sensed* it, Mama. The chemistry between us. Right? It was the kind of thing you just couldn't *help* but notice, wasn't it?"

Stella did a complicated end run around her sensibilities and forced a smile on her face. She didn't have any desire to know what her baby girl was getting up to—*that* way—or with whom. It wasn't that she had anything against Joy, or any other suitor, for that matter. It was just that thinking of one's child as being with—with—well, with anyone at all—thinking of one's child as possessing a robust sex life was a trifle awkward.

"Oh, Mama, I think Joy might be the *one*."

"Now, when you say 'the one' . . . do you mean like the person who, um, makes you feel like you've never felt before? Or do you mean more like the one who you intend to grow old with, the person who's going to change your Depends after you have a stroke?"

Noelle frowned, pursing her lips. "Mama. Do you have to take the romance out of everything? Come on, I'm young. You just don't remember how *intense* it can be."

Stella didn't much care for that, but she also wasn't about to tell her daughter that middle-aged motors could hum along just like fresher-minted ones, albeit with a few more kinks in the works occasionally. She was pretty sure her daughter knew about her ongoing flirtation with the sheriff, but if Noelle wanted or needed to consider her mother post-sexual, Stella guessed that was all right.

"So . . . you've pretty much decided you're a lesbian, then," she said.

"Oh, yes. I mean think about it, Mama. Why else would I have hooked up with all those losers for so long? I mean, unless I was secretly trying to, you know, *sabotage* myself so it never worked out?"

"My, that's—well, that's some complex thinking," Stella said carefully. She eased out of the hug with an affectionate little pat on Noelle's cheek and went to pour herself a big mug of coffee. This might be the sort of conversation that required artificial stimulants.

"No, really. I mean, every guy I've dated since Schooner's been mean as a snake. I think what I was doing was, I was punishing myself for ignoring my true authentic real self, see?"

Stella regarded Noelle carefully. "You been watching a little extra of those talk shows lately?"

"No, Mama." Noelle rolled her eyes, but her enthusiasm was sufficient to keep her from getting annoyed—yet. Stella remembered well from Noelle's teen years that one always had to be on high alert with one's daughter—they had a preternatural ability to get ticked off at conversational subtleties one wasn't even aware of exhibiting. "It's, like, *proved* and all. It's all about self-contempt. Denying your true nature can just cripple you. I went to this seminar when we were up at the regionals."

Ah.

Ahhhh. Now Stella was getting it. Noelle was a talented stylist, and in the last year, she'd been exhibiting and winning awards at several regional hair shows, where she met all kinds of wonderful and interesting people—and a few flakes. The beauty business did seem to attract a bit more of its share of odd ducks, judging from Noelle's stories. No doubt she'd run into some self-proclaimed New Age truth-spouter with an agenda.

Though, in fact, the basics that Noelle was spouting were sound. Who knew it better than Stella? She hadn't unleashed her own inner self until Ollie was gone, and though she didn't do regrets, a lot of years had gone by while that self, buried deep under a blanket of denial and victimhood and misery, paced unhappily like a caged panther.

Stella didn't want that for Noelle, that was for sure. She just wasn't convinced the girl was barking up the correct new and authentic tree.

Stella didn't have anything against gay folks. She'd had a few gay clients, in fact, and among other things, that had taught her that right and wrong weren't concepts that the straight community had any kind of patent on. Mean came in every stripe—and so did good. Sure, she'd like grandchildren, but there were all kinds of ways to come across those these days—hell, Tucker was kind of like a little grandbaby to her. Not to mention Todd and his sisters.

"Sooo. Let's say you *are* gay. Are you sure you ought to be putting all your chips on the first girl to catch your eye? Shouldn't you, you know, play the field a little?"

"Oh, but Mama, that's what *I* thought. I made a list of every gay person I knew, and at first I thought I'd just go right down the list, you know? Keep going until something clicked?"

Stella didn't really want to know what going down the list entailed, but she nodded brightly anyway.

"But then I saw Joy at a party over New Year's and there was this, like . . . magic. I don't even know what else to call it."

More nodding. Stella kept a smile fixed on her face. But inside, she was remembering Schooner, the first boy to ever ask Noelle on a date, when she was fourteen. Noelle ended up dating him until he enlisted two and a half years later. From the first time Noelle wrote her phone number on his Converse sneakers in the Prosper High School cafeteria, she couldn't think of anyone else. Stella suspected there might be some sort of

91

attachment disorder going on there or something—that Noelle got herself stuck on people the second she decided she might be interested in them. It would certainly go partway to explaining why, after hooking up with the hateful losers who littered her past, she stuck with them for so long.

With Schooner, there was never any overburdening reason to unstick the two of them. He was a nice boy, if a little gangly and awkward, and he treated Stella with shy respect and never failed to bring Noelle home on time. And maybe Joy would be an equally considerate and harmless romantic interest. But Stella hated to see her daughter shut down the field of possibilities so early in the game.

"Now, would you say that Joy is just as convinced of the, uh, magic between you, as you are?" she asked, switching tactics.

Noelle pursed her lips. "Well, now, see, she wants to take things slow, but that's because she's just naturally become *cautious*. She's been hurt before. It's sad, really."

Oh—the *I've been hurt before* line. It was like chick crack. If Stella had a nickel for every woman who'd gone chasing after some loser who made that claim—oftentimes a loser who was himself far more likely to be in the hurting business than any woman he'd ever dated—she could retire to a big old mansion. Still, that was the kind of truth that folks were just completely resistant to. Pointing it out would only make Noelle dig in her heels more.

"Oh," she said. "That *is* sad."

"I know, right? So I'm trying to let things develop naturally over time. I mean, I'm just plain sensual to the core, but I'm making a conscious effort to keep that part of myself under control and focus on getting to know each other and all."

"Are you two seeing a lot of each other?"

"Oh, yes! I mean, I hope we will be, anyway. That's why I thought of this leave of absence. It's only a few weeks."

"Your boss was all right with that?"

Noelle frowned. "Well, she wasn't, like, thrilled or anything. I mean, I *am* their top-booked stylist. But what can she do? I'm paying my rent on my chair and all."

"Can you afford that, sweetie?"

"Yes, Mama. I've been saving ever since I went out on my own, and since I don't have a car payment anymore, I've been able to put a lot away. I was saving up for a house, but this won't set me back much."

A few months ago, some of Stella's clients had given Noelle a nice bonus for ending up unexpectedly in a dangerous situation in their behalf, when she inadvertently got herself taken hostage, and she'd bought herself a pretty little blue Prius with it. Stella was relieved to know she didn't need to be concerned about her daughter's finances, but there was always something to worry about with kids.

"So . . . does Joy know that you've decided to devote all your time to—" Stella was about to say *chasing her around* but switched gears just in time. "—strengthening your relationship?"

"Um, well, I didn't exactly put it like that. I don't want to, you know, *crowd* her or anything. I told her I had some things to catch up on. Which I do. I mean, like being here with you and helping with the shop and Tucker and Todd and the twins and them-all. I mean, they're like family, right? Plus I know how you get about Easter." She hesitated, and added shyly, "How you *used* to get, anyway. I thought it might be nice to make a fuss again for a change."

She flashed another of her beautiful megawatt smiles, and Stella melted further and considered that only moments earlier her daughter had been near tears and hanging on for dear life. She was certainly riding an emotional roller coaster—well, maybe it really *was* love.

"And I love having you here." Stella had a thought. "Listen, sugar, any chance you might want to watch the shop for a few hours today? I've got a little job I need Chrissy for."

For a long time, Stella had been unsure if Noelle knew what her side business entailed, but getting driven around at gunpoint on that recent case had pretty much blown the lid right off the situation. Luckily, Noelle was as proud of her mother as if Stella had accepted the secretary of state job. But she had no desire to join in the business, which frankly made Stella happy. Unlike Chrissy, her daughter had no natural gift for vengeance or violence. What she did have was a cheerful friendly way with the customers, when she occasionally helped out in the shop, and she could get them to spend more than they planned on supplies and notions simply because they were busy chatting.

"Sure, I guess," Noelle said, yawning. "Joy don't get off work over at the laundry until three anyway, so what else have I got to do?"

Chapter Twelve

By eleven o'clock, Stella and Chrissy were sitting in the Jeep outside a nice-looking trilevel home set off by precisely trimmed hedges and shrubbery that looked like it had been made to behave. A big red GMC pickup shared the driveway with a dusty green minivan. After a moment or two, the garage door went up, revealing an interior crammed with workshop tools and stacked lumber and supplies, and a man came out dragging a trash can.

"He's trimmed up some," Stella observed. Salty had, indeed, lost much of the spare tire he'd been growing around his middle. He was dressed in a fleece jacket and nylon workout pants that didn't show him to best advantage, but Stella judged him a nice-enough looking man—you could still see the shadow of his former athletic self, and he still had a full head of dishwater blond hair.

Salty noticed the Jeep pulled up in front of the house and hesitated. "Let's get him now, before he decides he's not feeling friendly," Stella suggested.

They got out of the car as Salty gave them a tentative little wave. Stella wasn't surprised by the lukewarm nature of the greeting—everyone in Prosper knew she was an unconvicted murderer, and plenty of them had heard rumors about her more recent endeavors. It tended to make even innocent men uncomfortable.

"Mrs. Hardesty, is that you? I haven't seen you in an age."

"Well, hello, Salty," Stella said, edging cautiously up the icy drive. "It *has* been a while. This is my friend Chrissy Shaw."

Salty gave Chrissy a carefully appraising look. "I think I remember you. You were in middle school when I was in high school, isn't that right?"

"Yeah," Chrissy said, taking hold of her jacket zipper and tugging it down far enough that the top of her low-cut sweater was visible. Salty watched, his mouth gaping open. Stella hated to admit it, but Chrissy's extraordinary cleavage had helped them out in more situations than she could count. She always felt a little uncomfortable using her assistant's considerable natural appeal on the job, but it was just so darn effective. Men couldn't seem to keep their minds on concealing the truth when they were faced with her impressive curves and sexy pout and wide, pale blue eyes.

Chrissy jutted one hip out provocatively and narrowed her eyes. "You were on the golf team or some shit like that."

She said it in the same tone that she might have used if she'd said he'd been on the stable-mucking crew, but Salty stood straighter and sucked in his gut. "I was the captain, actually," he said modestly, pushing the trash can over the curb into the street and wiping his hands on his pants.

"You building something in there?" Stella asked, pointing to the project laid out in the garage.

"Oh, that. We're putting in a shed out back. Doraleigh—my

wife—she wants to park in the garage, so I needed a place to move all my crap into. Oh well, it keeps me out of trouble, ha ha."

"I was wondering if we could ask you a few questions," Stella suggested. "We have a friend in common . . . and we're a little worried about her. You know Priss Porter?"

Salty's pale eyebrows shot up, and he pursed his mouth. "Priss? Why sure, I know her, but I ain't heard from her in quite some time. What, has she—"

Just then the door leading into the house opened and a woman came striding out, holding a baby and poking at a cell phone with her free hand and talking away, in the middle of a sentence. "—get that mess swept up, because I need to—

"Oh," she said when she finally noticed that they had company. She slipped the phone in her pocket and hitched the baby up higher on her shoulder. He was a handsome little baby, with her dark sturdy looks rather than Salty's rather bland and featureless ones. She ran a hand through a cascade of badly dyed curly hair and produced a harried, insincere smile. "Hello."

"Doraleigh, you remember Mrs. Hardesty," Salty said. "And Chrissy Shaw, well you probably don't remember her. She was a few years behind me. Doraleigh's two years older than me," he added, giving Chrissy a little smile.

Doraleigh shot him a look that contained about as much warmth as an iceberg. Then she turned to Chrissy and gave her a cool once-over. "I've met some of your kin, I believe. Seems like there's a lot of Lardners around these parts."

"We're good at that," Chrissy agreed. "Reproducin'."

"And of course I remember you, Mrs. Hardesty," Doraleigh added with only slightly more warmth. "Would you care to come in? I could put some coffee on. I'm sorry the house is in such a state—I'm trying to get Salty to clean up the mess he's made out back, since we're having company tonight."

She couldn't have made it more clear that the timing of the visit was inconvenient. The little boy in her arms started making a huffing sound as if he was winding up into a wail. Which was good, because Stella had hoped to talk to Salty by himself.

"Oh no, I wouldn't dream of it," she said. "I'm sorry to intrude on your afternoon, I was just—"

"They're here on account of the blanket drive that the highway patrol's putting on," Salty said quickly, and gave Stella a look that could only be described as pleading.

"Huh," said Chrissy.

"Oh yes!" Stella exclaimed, blinking with surprise. "My dad was a patrolman. I just like to give back a little. In his memory. What a successful campaign we're having this year, too." She gave Doraleigh Mingus an expression that was as beatific as she could come up with on short notice, and gestured at the Jeep. "Just loading up with blankets and quilts, gonna drive them on over to the station. . . ."

Doraleigh considered them dubiously. "Is this like Toys for Tots? 'Cause usually I put the toys in the bins they got at church."

"Yes, yes," Stella agreed. "We do that, too. I, um, forgot that you and Salty had kids already. Seems like you two just tied the knot yesterday."

"Hmm," Doraleigh said as her son wiped a fist under his own runny nose and hiccupped in agitation. "I got to get in, I left Emma in the baby swing."

"I'll just be a minute, hon," Salty said, visibly relieved. "I'll get the back straightened out and then I can give you a hand with the kids."

"Hmph," Doraleigh said in a tone that implied she'd believe her husband was going to give her a hand around the very same time that pigs started flying through the air. She shot Chrissy one more doubtful look and then gave them a brisk nod. "Take care."

"Oh, and you do the same," Stella said sweetly.

Nobody spoke until the door to the house shut behind Doraleigh.

"Sorry about that," Salty said in a low and agitated voice, as though he suspected his wife of having supersonic hearing. "Doraleigh's just . . . well, she's kinda jealous. She don't like hearing about any of my old girlfriends, you know?"

"Priss and you were *involved*," Stella said unnecessarily.

"Oh, I remember you guys in high school," Chrissy said with a note of scorn. She had clearly decided to take the "bad cop" job this time around. "She was so smart, I couldn't ever figure out why she was going out with you. No offense."

"So you haven't heard from her at all? Have you talked on the phone?"

Salty rubbed his chin with a big, meaty hand. "No, no, nothing like that. We just sort of fell out of touch."

"But I thought you were living up in Kansas City a while back," Chrissy said. "I heard you worked for Priss up there."

"Oh. Uh, yeah, that's true, I worked for her for a while, but it's been years."

"How many years?" Stella asked. "Just curious."

"Well . . . about three, I guess."

Not that many, Stella thought darkly. "And look at you now, married to a lovely woman and with a couple of beautiful children already. Isn't it wonderful how things work out, sometimes."

"Uh, yeah."

"What-all kind of business were you and she in?" Chrissy asked.

"It was, ah." Salty pursed his lips into an *o* and looked at the ground. "Well, it was . . . landscaping."

"Landscaping?" Stella exchanged a glance with Chrissy. The

Green Hat Ladies had said he hadn't stuck to a regular job, and she remembered him doing construction here and there, but it seemed unlikely that he and Priss, with all her business acumen, couldn't have come up with something a bit more ambitious. She was pretty sure Salty was lying.

"You ran a crew? Did design and installation? Bid on projects? That sort of thing?"

"Um, that was her end. I was, like, the guy who *did* the landscaping. You know, like a gardener."

"Uh-huh. Well, like I said, we're mostly just worried. Seein' as she's gone missing."

Salty blinked. "You're kidding," he said in a stilted voice.

Chrissy shot Stella a look of disgust, and Stella knew she wasn't buying it either. "I'm afraid so. There was some trouble out at Liman's the other night, apparently, while she was visiting, and now they've both disappeared."

"I didn't know she was in town," Salty said hurriedly.

"No, I didn't mean to imply that you did," Stella said. "I think this was a last-minute trip."

Salty swallowed. "Well, then, I bet she just turned around and went back home. You, uh, tried her there?"

"Oh, yes," Stella lied. "I tried all her numbers. That's what's got me so concerned. Seein' as you and she used to be close, we were wondering if you might be able to help us out with some ideas on where she might have gone. If, you know, she was in need of a little privacy, for instance."

Salty appeared to be holding his breath. A variety of emotions duked it out on his face: alarm, doubt, and uncertainty—and not a little bit of fear. "Like I said, it's been a while. Priss and me don't keep up much. Um, if you don't mind me asking, what are the two of you doing looking for her?"

Stella fixed him with an unblinking gaze. "I do a little . . .

investigative work, on the side. Looking for things that folks have lost. You may have heard."

Little beads of sweat appeared around Salty's hairline, despite the rapidly plummeting temperature. He'd evidently heard something closer to the truth.

"Who hired you? If you can say."

"Oh, I wish I could," Stella said regretfully. "Only they got all these client confidentiality rules."

"I ain't bound by them rules," Chrissy said. "I'm just the assistant. Only, I don't *feel* like telling you. I think you know more about Priss than you're saying."

"Oh, Chrissy, can it," Stella chided. She gave Salty an exasperated smile. "I apologize, Salty. Chrissy's new to the investigatin' business, and she hasn't learned the number one rule yet. She's just got all that youthful passion built up and sometimes she can't hardly control it."

Chrissy scowled and tugged her zipper down a little farther, and flicked her blond curls with her fingers. Then she heaved a huge sigh, throwing her shoulders back.

If Salty was put off by her irritability, he didn't show it. "I sure wish I could help you," he said, addressing her breasts.

"Just a couple more questions," Stella said, "and then we'll be on our way. Why did you leave Priss's employ?"

"Why did I what? Oh, you mean why did I quit?"

"Yes. Exactly."

"It was . . . I didn't . . ." A little twitch formed over Salty's left eye, and he put a thumb to his mouth and gnawed at his nail for a moment before he added, "Difference of opinion, is what it was."

"Opinion over what? Over your performance?"

Salty's gaze darted to the left and the right, before coming to rest on his shoes. He stared intently, as though seeing if he could untie his shoelaces with his mind. "S'pose you could say that," he finally muttered, and even Stella was surprised at the depth of the bitterness in his voice.

"What—you couldn't mow a straight line?" Chrissy prodded him disdainfully.

Salty glanced at her nervously. The tic near his eye danced and throbbed in a fascinating manner that made it difficult for Stella not to stare.

"Couldn't handle your trowel? The quality of your fertilizer didn't impress her?" Chrissy took a step forward and jabbed a finger at him. "Didn't do much for her blossoms? Couldn't much navigate her patch? Huh?"

After a moment, Salty seemed to wilt. His shoulders slumped, and his chin ducked down toward his chest. "We had professional differences, and that's all."

"Mmm-hmm," Stella said in a soothing tone. "You get much call to go up to Kansas City these days, Salty?"

"From time to time. I work for Doraleigh's dad. We work with a few vendors up there, so sometimes I'll have a meeting—you know, not real often."

"Just how often would you say that happens?"

Salty shrugged. "Dunno—maybe one or two times a month. But don't get any ideas. I don't visit Priss or nothin'. She's got her uptown life now, with her Mercedes and her country club membership and her fancy house. I mean, I got my pride."

"What's that mean?" Chrissy asked in a cruel, lilting tone. "What kind of pride we talkin' 'bout?"

"You know—*man* pride," Salty said, blushing.

On their way to the car a few minutes later, Stella shook her head in disgust.

Man pride. What a concept. As if that half of humankind needed any more reason to feel superior.

She started the engine and drove slowly down the street, watching Salty setting up his ladder in the rearview mirror.

"So what is it, anyway?" Chrissy asked.

"What's what?"

"The first rule of the detecting business."

"Oh, that." Stella smiled and turned up the heat. "Same as any other business, really. Something Ollie used to say: Screw them before they screw you first."

Chapter Thirteen

By early afternoon, they were seated behind a couple of pulled pork sandwiches at the Pokey Pot. Binny Planche, the restaurant's owner, had done a little unorthodox decorating for Easter; his oldest girl was studying art over in Rolla, and she'd got hold of the kind of paint that can be used on glass, but rather than the traditional rabbits and chicks and baskets of eggs, she'd gone for cavorting pigs with a nice assortment of holiday trimmings. Besides a little gal pig in what looked like a naughty bunny costume and high heels on her back hooves, there was a pair of porkers who looked like they were pelting each other with jelly beans and bellowing with rage; a large and dignified looking sow in regal pastoral vestments; and, most inexplicably, an almost photorealistic rendering of a Shelby Cobra that appeared to be roaring toward a trio of little piglets wearing crowns of thorns on their sweet little heads, possibly intending to flatten them into bacon.

"I don't believe I've ever seen Brittany do anything quite like this," Stella said, licking sauce off her fingers. She and Chrissy had each ordered the Pokey Pot Baby, the smallest sandwich on the menu, which had about twelve pounds of delicious pork falling out of the bun.

"But remember when we had lunch here back in July—"

"Oh, yeah, that naughty Uncle Sam . . . forgot about him. With them little trousers of his . . ."

For a few moments they reminisced about their favorite painted tableaus, a feature of the restaurant since little Brittany Planche had been old enough to hold a brush. Her parents were proud of both their offspring, though only her big brother, Jeremy, had decided to follow in the family footsteps, working back in the kitchen.

"Whyn't you fire up that laptop of yours," Stella said when they were finished and had washed up at the trough the Planches had installed in the front of the restaurant and fitted with faucets, and refilled their iced teas. "Seein' as it's going to be the ruin of me, might as well get some use out of it."

She was secretly pleased every time they had an opportunity to use the thing. It was a sporty little Mac model, the bottom of the line but no less impressive to Stella, who had taken to finding out where in town there was free Wi-Fi to be had since it still tickled her no end to watch Chrissy hack into the DMV or check out the sports scores from, say, the parking lot of the Calvary United Methodist Church.

"Don't give me that, Stella Hardesty, you cheapskate. I'm the laughingstock over at the U-Pub. They all got Airs. Wouldn't a cost you but a few hundred bucks more and it runs circles around this piece of junk."

"What you get for hanging out over there—you ought to be embarrassed," Stella teased. The University Pub, fifteen miles down the road in Harrisonville, was a hangout for grad students in the computer science program at the state college. After three decades of mostly dull-witted men, Chrissy had developed a fixation on geeks—particularly those who could teach her whole new ways to sneak around on the Internet.

By and large, they were—to a bespectacled and pocket-protected man—overjoyed to receive the attentions of a slightly older, far more worldly, and amply sexed lovely woman with curves and soft places to spare. After a couple of failed marriages, however, Chrissy was taking a break from the whole monogamy thing, and Stella feared the day would come when she'd made her way through the entire pack of young men who hung out at the U-Pub.

At least there was a fresh crop every semester.

"Don't see why I should be embarrassed," Chrissy said, staring intently at the screen, fingers flying, "when I can do this."

She spun the laptop around and Stella dug in her purse for a pair of reading specs and slid them on her nose.

"Well, what the heck am I looking at?" she demanded. It was a bird's-eye view of a cluster of tile-topped buildings surrounding a sparkling pool and a couple of angled tennis courts. "Time shares in Hawaii?"

"That ain't Hawaii, Stella," Chrissy exclaimed. "That's Kansas City. Judge Marilu Carstairs's condo, to be specific. Very swanky address."

"How'd you—?" Stella began, but Chrissy's fingers were flying over the keys again.

"She bought it in 2006 for two hundred thirty thousand," she said. "Oooh, put thirty percent down, let's see, looks like she probably still has a little bit of equity in it even after—oh, dang, tough luck, the rest of her investments ain't done a whole lot for her. What d'you suppose a judge makes, anyway?"

"I'm sure you'll tell me momentarily," Stella drawled, taking a healthy sip of her tea, "and her bra size and blood type, too."

Chrissy, in the next half hour as they sat drinking tea and enjoying the Pokey Pot's late afternoon lull, did not in fact find out Marilu Carstairs's measurements. But she did find out her address and phone number and the convenient fact that Marilu's condo featured a fenced side yard where a person, if she were to find herself wedged between the shrubs and a window, would have a nice view inside.

After all that, making reservations online at a Super 8 down the road from the condo seemed almost too easy.

They swung by Chrissy's parents' place long enough to kiss Tucker and his swarm of little cousins and pick up a few things for an overnight trip. A handful of Lardner relatives lay about the house in various stages of recovery from the weekend's strenuous schedule of celebrating. Chrissy's mom, Loreen Lardner—a couple of years younger than Stella but well on her way to a stroke with an out-of-control carb habit and no exercise to speak of besides hollering at her kids and grandkids—asked Stella to show her a few of the tai chi moves she'd added to her exercise routine in physical therapy. Stella showed her the Part the Wild Horse's Mane and White Crane Spreads Its Wings moves, and the two of them went through the motions a few times while Ralph Lardner looked on in astonishment.

"We're sure glad Chrissy's working for you," he said when they were finished, laying a heavy hand on Stella's shoulder and offering her a bracing nip from the flask he carried in his pants pocket as he and his wife walked them out to the Jeep. "Got to appreciate the good folks in your life. Why, you're practically an honorary Lardner."

There followed a confusing volley of boozy hugs from all the out-of-town Lardners.

On the drive to her own house, Stella told Chrissy how much she envied her that large extended family, since her only living blood relatives were Noelle and her sister, Gracellen, all the way in California.

"Hey, don't get to envying me that bunch," Chrissy said with more than a trace of disgust. "They're fun and all, and I love every last one of them, but it does get a little old. They just can't help butting into everyone's business all the time."

"Yeah, but . . ." Stella hesitated, then figured if she couldn't say it to Chrissy, who could she? "You know how we were talking about Easter at lunch . . . well, holidays are different. They're supposed to be about family."

She didn't add that the prior year, back when Noelle and she were still in their not-speaking-to-each other phase, she'd spent Easter Sunday with only Johnnie Walker Black for company, watching *Beaches* and sniffling and eating an entire package of Gardetto's Roasted Garlic Rye Chips, and while that still beat any holiday she'd spent with Ollie, it wasn't anything she cared to repeat.

"But, Stella," Chrissy said, sounding genuinely surprised, "you got tons of people. *We're* your family. We'll all be together for Easter—I don't think I got the starch to get through another big do with my folks so close to this one. I was kind of thinking I'd bring Tucker over and you and me and Noelle could go to church and then we could do, you know, the egg hunt and baskets and bake up a ham and all that at your house."

Stella felt her heart lift up considerably. "That would be great," she said, "especially since Noelle seems dead set on running off with that Joy gal—wouldn't surprise me if she'd rather spend the day on her doorstep like a stray cat than with me, she's so whipped."

Chrissy giggled. "She *does* seem taken with her, don't she?

And that Joy's not a *bad*-looking thing—bet she's got her a figure under all them mousy clothes. Only I didn't exactly think there was a whole ton of chemistry going on there the other night."

"Really? How can you tell?"

"Well, I don't know, it just seemed a little forced, but maybe it was just that Noelle was being so darn obvious about it. Might be better if she backed off a little. You know how it is, sometimes when a person plays hard to get, you just get more stuck on 'em. Kind of crazy, you ask me. Why, any fella I ever got sick of, those were the ones I couldn't get shut of."

"You and your suitors. It's like you're catnip to 'em. Why, if I had half of your natural appeal, I'd have my pick of the whole county."

"Wouldn't matter none," Chrissy said, grinning. "You still wouldn't have eyes for nobody but the sheriff."

Stella tried to come up with a retort, but as she pulled in the drive, she noticed a vaguely familiar Dodge Challenger pulled up to the curb behind Noelle's Prius.

"Hey," she exclaimed, "I believe that's Joy's car. What do you know—maybe things are going better than we thought."

"Is that a good thing?"

Stella paused, her hand on the handle of the car door. "You know," she said slowly, "there was probably a day I wouldn't have known how to answer that question. Back when I figured everything ought to work out the way I planned it—you know, my daughter growing up to be a princess or at least ladylike—I sure wasn't expecting those tattoos and I guess I figured on a bit more conservative hairdo . . . but nowadays I think plain old happy's a good goal. Happy, and not getting beat on by anyone."

Chrissy shot her a grin. "Some folks would say that's settin' the bar pretty low."

"Well, some folks ain't seen what I seen and done what I done. And don't forget, sugar—happy's more rare than folks like to think."

"Ain't that the truth," Chrissy agreed.

Stella gave the door a good hard knock just in case the girls were getting up to something amorous, and she was rewarded with a wet snuffling on the other side of the door, followed by a joyful bark.

Roxy nearly knocked her down when she opened the door. The black and white speckled mutt had come to live with her a couple of months earlier, a refugee from a series of tornadoes that had ripped a swath through central Missouri, and she had made herself at home and devoted herself to her new mistress with doggy abandon.

"Okay, okay," Stella said, putting her hand down so Roxy could shove her cold wet snout into it, a greeting ritual she never seemed to tire of. Chrissy followed suit with a little less enthusiasm.

"When you gonna teach this dog some manners?" she asked. "Oh, my gracious mercy me—what are you *doin'* to that girl, Noelle?"

Stella followed Chrissy's line of sight and found herself staring at Joy Benagle dressed in an iridescent plum-colored smock, her hair sticking out in every direction in clumps that appeared to be glued to shiny foil strips with frosting. Only then did she notice the acrid smell in the kitchen.

"Highlights," Noelle said cheerfully. "And lowlights, too. Oh, it's gonna be awesome."

"It better be," Joy grumbled, looking none too pleased as Noelle's quick, sure hands fussed in her hair. Considering the unflattering getup Joy was dressed in, Stella was able to focus on her face without any distractions, and she decided that it was

110

true: Joy *was* a pretty thing. "I don't know how I let you talk me into this."

"Oh, sure you do," Noelle said, giving her shoulder a playful poke. "When you lost at strip poker, remember?"

"Oh my," Stella said, wondering if she ought to go back outside.

"It wasn't *strip* poker," Joy said, "and you shouldn't oughtta talk that way in front of your mama anyhow. It was *regular* poker and you were cheating."

"She wouldn't strip." Noelle shrugged. "So she had to let me do this. Fair's fair."

"Yeah? Then how come you ain't messin' around in anyone else's hair that was playin'?"

"Who-all was playin' poker?" Chrissy asked. "Reason I ask is, my family was fixin' to play last night and they usually have the neighbors in."

"This was a different crowd, I'm pretty sure," Noelle said, "unless your folks like to play in *gay* establishments."

It seemed to Stella that her daughter put a little extra emphasis on the word, but she let it pass.

"Don't think so," Chrissy said. "Least, not last time I checked. Hey, thanks for covering the shop for me today. How was it?"

Noelle shrugged. "I printed off the register tapes for you. They're over on the counter. Had a carful of ladies from over in Quail Valley who were stocking up on fusible web and trim and metallic thread and all kinds of shit for some butt-ugly wall hangings they were gonna make. I tried to talk 'em out of it."

"Noelle, you were trying to talk people *out* of spending money at the shop?" Stella demanded, incredulous. "Are you gonna come visit me in the poorhouse? 'Cause that's where I'm headed if we don't make the numbers this month."

"So long as you pay me first, I'll visit you," Chrissy said, peeling foil off a platter on the counter. "Oooh, somebody made them little cookies with the chocolate kisses—I love those. Stella, run along and get your stuff, we have a date with a minibar."

"Where are you going?" Noelle demanded.

"Long story—I assume you don't want all the details?"

"Damn right, if there's bad guys involved. I'll just wait and hear about it when you're done and back safe."

It was their deal, and it was a good enough one.

Still, after Stella had packed a couple of outfits and her toiletries into a duffel, helped herself to a couple of the cookies that it turned out her good friend Dotty Edwards had dropped off, and given Joy a sympathetic smile as she sat perched on towels on the edge of the couch waiting for her color to set, Noelle followed her and Chrissy to the door.

"Be careful, Mama," she whispered as she hugged her close. "Don't let the bad guys win. I need you."

Stella let Chrissy drive, against her better judgment. Chrissy didn't lack confidence, but unfortunately she was indifferent to the conventions other drivers generally observed, like sticking to a consistent speed and reserving the left-hand lane for passing. By the time they found the Super 8, they'd incurred the wrath of half a dozen apoplectic drivers who employed a variety of gestures to illustrate their feelings about sharing the road with the two of them.

"Gosh, Stella, there is just so much *hate* in the world," Chrissy sighed as they got their bags and checked in.

She perked up in the room, though, sitting down on the bed closest to the bathroom and giving it an experimental bounce or two. "Do you know," she said, "I ain't stayed in a hotel but twice? Once was on my honeymoon up in Wisconsin Dells, and once was this time we were going to see Mama's people over in Bolivar and we had a blowout and we all stayed in one room at this little motel that looked like it came right out of an Elvis movie."

"That must have been crowded," Stella observed. There were six Lardner children in all, born over an impressively brief and amorous span of the Lardner parents' marriage.

"Oh, it was, and I had to sleep between Lorrie and Danyelle, and you just don't *ever* want to sleep with them two—Lorrie farts all the time and Danyelle snores."

Stella left her to check out the rest of the room while she slipped into her favorite sneaking-around outfit: an old pair of stretchy black yoga pants and a fleecy top that had once been solid purple but had had an unfortunate bleach accident on an especially inattentive laundry day and now had a pale Florida-shaped stain near the hem.

Her cell phone rang and she squinted at the display. GOAT. Her heart did a little shuffle.

"Hello," she answered in a voice that aimed for sexy indifference and came out a little like she was talking around a sizable ice cube.

"You want to tell me what your prints are doing at Liman's place?"

Stella gulped. She shut her eyes and replayed the conversation she and Priss had in the Porter living room. She hadn't touched anything, had she? She was sitting in the smelly chair, she hadn't accepted anything to drink . . . and on their return trip, she'd had gloves on the whole time.

"Um. It was . . . see . . ." She cast around frantically for an explanation, and came up empty. "I had a date. Um, a few days before all the, uh, trouble. With Liman."

There was a silence, a long one, and Stella could practically feel the thunderclouds building and blowing along the cell towers toward her. She resisted an urge to duck.

"You went on a *date* with Liman *Porter* just before his sister abandoned her *car* in his driveway and the two of them *disappeared* under suspicious circumstances," he said, coming down hard every few syllables with a force that made Stella flinch.

"Uh. Yeah."

"And rather than take you to a restaurant or a movie theater, he, what, invited you over and before you could touch any other surface in the house—because we checked, Stella, I know you think me and Mike and Ian are a bunch of backward yobs, but I assure you we turned over every stone—he got you in such a position that you had to hold on to the side table for balance?"

Oh. The *side* table.

The image in Stella's head backed up and replayed, and she remembered sinking into the musty old armchair much more quickly than she expected, its cushion's stuffing being considerably less ample than it appeared, and grabbing the table in surprise.

Damn.

In the years before Stella killed Ollie, she'd stuck to a single tactic in the face of his ranting and crazy accusations: She would deny timidly, protest softly, and generally just wait quietly until he wound himself up tight enough to blow spectacularly out of control.

Since then, however, she'd switched gears.

Stella didn't grovel for anyone. And she didn't much care to explain herself. Especially when she knew she hadn't done anything wrong. And while the law might frown on her reasons for being at Liman's that night, and while it might be very interested in the photographs with which Priss had lured her inside the house in the first place, Stella was still well within her own ethical comfort zone.

So she took a deep breath and tried not to think about what the pissed-off man on the phone was doing to her a mere forty-eight hours earlier, lest she lose her momentum, and she said, "I don't believe I need to describe exactly what position he had me in, Goat—that's private."

The silence that ensued was much shorter and accompanied by sputtering. "Stella, not only is Liman Porter at *least* a dozen years younger than you, he favors the kind of company a man pays for, which, as far as I know, is one branch of lawbreaking you ain't yet got around to, and—"

"Keep talkin' that way, and I'm hanging up," Stella warned. She didn't brook insulting, not even from Goat.

"Hang up, and I'll come over there and haul you in," Goat said. "I'm mostly doing you a courtesy by letting you know that you hadn't better leave town until we get this figured out. You hear?"

"I hear."

"So I can count on you being where I can find you on short notice if I need to?"

"Sure," Stella said breezily, closing her eyes and crossing her fingers so the lie wouldn't count.

"You made him mad," Chrissy guessed after Stella hung up.

"How do you know?"

"It's obvious. Honestly, Stella, how are you *ever* gonna get any if you keep pissing him off?"

Stella sighed and explained the sheriff's discovery.

"Oh. Well, he ain't hauled you in yet. That must mean he's, you know, *protecting* you. That's kind of romantic." Chrissy didn't sound terribly convinced.

Stella fretted for a few more moments, then gave herself a mental kick. She would *not* waste time regretting things she couldn't control.

"Let's go, girl. Time to get my pictures."

Chapter Fourteen

They called every number Chrissy had managed to find for Judge Carstairs—home, mobile, and office—and came up empty. Stella figured the judge would keep until morning, and they had a quick dinner at a Red Robin next to the Super 8 and headed over to Priss's address in the inky darkness. It was a fancy if smallish house in a neighborhood tucked behind tall stone walls. The homes were fairly new, but they'd had all manner of trim slapped on them to make them look like they'd been plucked from the Italian countryside and replanted in orderly rows.

Priss's place had a fancy drive-through overhang thing leading to the garage, which shielded the entry from anyone looking in from the street. After leaving the Jeep in a cul-de-sac in the next block, Stella and Chrissy darted through the darkness to the front door. This time, the lock was a bit more of a challenge, and after letting Chrissy try for a few minutes, Stella figured the cover provided by the overhang didn't really justify conducting a full-on breaking-and-entering lesson, and took over. Thirty seconds later, they were in.

Luckily Priss had lamps on timers in nearly every room, probably so that it would appear that someone was home if she had to work late. At her *landscaping business,* Stella thought darkly, shaking her head over Salty's inept lying.

She and Chrissy worked until well after midnight, taking a couple of breaks to drink Priss's fancy imported beer and eat the little individual fancy cheese balls that constituted half the food Priss kept in her fridge, passing up the moldy mass in a Chinese takeout container that had apparently taken up residence there some time ago. The cat that Jake and Lawrence had mentioned, a large and skittish gray one with yellow eyes, slunk back and forth and watched them malevolently.

They checked drawers and shelves and all the obvious places, then turned to less likely spots under pictures and along baseboards and behind electric sockets and in the lining under the upholstered chairs—anywhere a flash drive could be hidden.

It wasn't particularly satisfying work. "It's like she ain't ever been introduced to a stray thought," Chrissy said after they'd finished up in the living room.

"At least she's got good taste," Stella said, gloved hands on hips, surveying the expensive interior. The furniture was all fine woods and expensive fabrics and free of even a speck of dust. There were few mementos or pictures, just a couple of silk floral arrangements here and there.

"Yeah, 'cept for that little display there," Chrissy said, jerking a thumb at the shelves of a mahogany glass-fronted bookcase that looked like it might be at home in a lawyer's office. Inside appeared to be every textbook Priss had ever owned, from a series of algebra and history and science books stamped PROSPER HIGH SCHOOL through a dizzying array of economics and finance books. There were also several years' worth of a magazine called *Financial Times,* whose editors appeared to have worked hard to present the driest information they could find in as lusterless a fashion as possible while making sure not to waste any extra paper on illustrations or pictures. "That's just pathetic."

"Yeah, well, that's kind of funny coming from you," Stella retorted, "seeing as you've gone and turned your living room into a geek lab." Last time Stella visited the little apartment that Chrissy and Tucker shared, around in the back of the China Paradise restaurant, a row of books with titles like *Nmap Network Scanning Basics* and *ASA/PIX/FWSM Firewall Strategies* were neatly lined up on top of the pass-through from the miniature kitchen to the tiny living room.

"Hey, that stuff's *useful*," Chrissy said hotly. "You think Priss really needed to read *Finance Econometrics Models* to run her little garden business?"

Her bedroom revealed no clues. Expensive but plain tailored jackets and pants were lined up with military precision in the closet, along with a dozen white blouses. The dresser drawers contained lingerie that had to cost plenty, despite its matronly style. "I wouldn't wear this to clean house in," Chrissy exclaimed, holding up a pair of silk hipster briefs between her thumb and forefinger as though they were toxic. "It's a wonder she got close enough to a man to kill him in these—they're like man repellent."

"First of all," Stella huffed, noting that the panties didn't look all that different from some in her own drawers, other than the fact that hers came three to a pack, "not every man wants a woman to be tricked out like a tramp when she takes off her dress. And second, we don't know if she *killed* anyone."

"Oh. Right. 'Cause it's just real, *real* common to pop your trunk to get at your jumper cables and find out, oh *damn,* somebody stashed a fuckin' *body* in there when I wasn't lookin'."

"We don't presume," Stella said stiffly. She agreed with Chrissy, but she still had to set an example. Even when the would-be client in question—innocent or otherwise—had complicated her life plenty and pointed her down a path that might well lead to jail. Even then, she had to assume Priss was innocent and act accordingly.

The thought caused her legs to go a little wobbly, and she sank down on Priss's expensive custom duvet with its silk cord edging. *Dang,* she asked herself silently, *do I really mean that?*

When she first got into the vengeance business, she didn't have a clear set of guiding principles. Women arrived on her doorstep with tales of woe and hurt, some of them far worse than anything she'd experienced at Ollie's hands, and she simply reacted. Partly as a way to continue her own healing, she now understood, she'd seized upon every case with a furious zeal and given everything she had until she was certain the abuser would never hurt anyone again. And though the danger to herself was real, especially in those early days when the layers of fat had yet to be hardened into taut muscle, when she couldn't tie a restraining knot and didn't know a slide lock safety from a recoil spring plug, she never hesitated, because going down in flames was a better alternative to living one more day in the victim place where she'd spent most of the last three decades.

Now, though, she had something to protect. Noelle. Friends she loved. A shot at a future. And *still* she wasn't ready to abandon the client who looked as guilty as any she'd had yet, who had already threatened her with ruin and shown every indication she'd follow through.

Stella had got herself some *integrity,* it appeared.

She wasn't sure she liked it.

After a moment, she shook off the jelly legs and rejoined Chrissy in the search. The office was more interesting; Chrissy disconnected the laptop and slipped it into Stella's backpack for further study after determining that the documents folder was locked. Besides the laptop, there were a few Post-its with cryptic notes in Priss's precise, cramped hand.

The rest of the apartment didn't yield much. Chrissy pocketed a tub of face cream—"This is the shit that costs three hundred bucks, I read that in *US*, Angelina Jolie uses it"—and when they were finished with everything, Stella found herself in the kitchen staring at the pink KitchenAid mixer, which looked like it had never even been turned on, though it coordinated nicely with the traces of salmon in the granite counters.

"You know," she said slowly, "Sherilee sure does like to cook."

Chrissy glanced at her curiously, then smiled. "Yeah, she does. And I got to say, when you're fixing French toast for three hungry little kids, that's a lot a eggs."

"Don't you hate when the recipe says to cream the sugar and butter?" Stella continued, caressing the machine's shiny, spotless base. "I mean, that takes like ten minutes, just standing there with the bowl."

"Tough on the wrists, too," Chrissy said. "Me, I'd be worried about carpal tunnel."

"Well, I guess that decides it, then."

While Stella packed up the mixer and hunted down its attachments, still wrapped in plastic in a drawer, Chrissy wiped down a coffee bean grinder and slipped it into her backpack.

Before they left, Stella took a final tour through the apartment. She felt discouraged. "It's like there wasn't a whole person living here," she explained to Chrissy.

"Well, you can't take on that burden," Chrissy said kindly. "Folks want to live a life of quiet desperation, why, who're we to stop 'em?"

"Wow—that's, um, profound," Stella said. "You make that up yourself?"

"Nah. Something I remember from senior year English class. That was Henry David Thoreau, I b'lieve."

"No shit. You know, Chrissy, sometimes I think you're a hell of a lot deeper'n anyone ever gave you credit for."

As they slipped out of the house into the eye-stinging cold night, Stella felt a little better.

She had interesting work. A loyal partner. So she wasn't getting laid. . . . Two out of three wasn't bad.

Chapter Fifteen

Oh, I do love me a sausage biscuit," Chrissy sighed happily as they enjoyed a Burger King breakfast the next morning.

"Look at you, with that metabolism of yours," Stella sighed enviously. "I used to be able to eat like that. Now I got to watch it every single day."

Her own breakfast, which consisted of orange juice and black coffee and only half a serving of Cheesy Tots, was a concession to vanity. A combination of the hospital stay earlier in the fall, along with a stepped-up exercise routine since she'd picked up some new moves in physical therapy, had helped her drop twenty pounds, and she was now as slender as the day she married Ollie, which was to say, pleasantly rounded. So some of the rounding had shifted a little—so what. That's what they made all those high-tech supportive garments for.

"Why, Stella, you're slim as a whip," Chrissy said, setting down her biscuit and licking her fingers. "Get any skinnier, and we won't be able to see you when you turn sideways."

"I don't care how thin I am, I just want to be healthy," Stella lied modestly.

"And you're looking mighty fine, now you finally got Noelle on you to take care of your upkeep. It's *refreshing,* is what it is, seeing you take a little trouble in the morning."

Stella snorted, but she was secretly pleased. It was true—she'd let Noelle teach her a few makeup tricks; they had all these new products that really went a long way toward covering up what wanted covered, and highlighting her assets. Noelle had brought her a soft pink eye shadow that made her green eyes sparkle brightly, and taught her how to apply eyeliner so it looked almost natural and stayed mostly where it was supposed to. She'd introduced Stella to a variety of concealers—creamy ones for the dark spots under her eyes, mineral powders that covered up redness. And there was this new plumping lip gloss that was practically magic, giving her a va-voom bedroom pout with just a few swipes.

She'd been noticing a general uptick in the sidelong glances and outright admiring stares she received from gentlemen in recent months, and while part of her figured it owed to her new pantherlike figure and updated makeup, another part of her suspected it was simply a matter of the energy she was putting out into the universe.

That bit of wisdom came courtesy of an article in *Cosmo* that she read while she was waiting to get a filling replaced at the dentist a few weeks ago. In the article, a relationship expert laid it all out like this: When you put out confidence, a kind of a couldn't-care-less-what-anyone-thinks vibe, it messed with men's basic woman-noticing habits. Their fragile internal compasses, the same ones that generally pointed steadfastly toward anything with big bosoms and mile-long legs, got sent spinning when they suddenly confronted a woman who didn't have any plans to worship them just for giving her the time of day.

They'd done this study where they coached women to go into a party and repeat certain phrases in their heads. One bunch of gals was directed to repeat over and over in their minds *"I'm the smartest, most attractive woman here, and I don't need a man to be complete,"* while the other group was directed to compare themselves to every other woman in the room in terms of looks and cleverness and sex appeal. Well, it wasn't much of a surprise that the first group got themselves showered with fellows asking for dates and phone numbers, while the second group ended up standing around alone at the punch bowl.

It wasn't this article that got Stella to rethink her place in the world of singles. In fact, looking back, she wasn't quite sure she could pinpoint what it was. Part of it, to be sure, was her side business taking off and growing to the point where she often had more clients than she could manage: she simply didn't have time to worry about how other folks viewed her as she went through her day. And part of it was surviving a near-fatal encounter with a murderous branch of the Kansas City mob. That certainly taught her not to sweat the small stuff.

And a final part was, undoubtedly, the comfort of having Noelle back in her life, along with all the other people who constituted her extended family. For the first time in many years, Stella rarely felt lonely.

So, yes, Stella felt basically content with herself, with her body and her looks and her opportunities for professional fulfillment. She'd gotten almost Zen-like—she didn't actually know a whole lot about Zen or Buddha or anything like that, but from what she understood, they were the serenity experts—in her long view, and if life just rolled along the way it had been, with its challenges and rewards, she could be content for the rest of her days.

Except for one thing.

One heart-skipping, mind-messing, breath-catching thing.

Every time she saw Goat Jones, her little pillar of serenity crumbled like a house of cards, leaving her feeling as uncertain and vulnerable as a newborn baby fawn. And every time their relationship took even the tiniest step forward—when he brought her flowers in the hospital, when he took her for a trip out on Lake of the Ozarks in his canoe, when he kissed her at a barbecue a few months ago—she found that she was spending more and more of her waking hours mooning over him, and more of her nighttime hours dreaming blush-inducing scenarios in which he featured most prominently.

And since he'd kissed her the other night—the hottest kiss yet—she found that thoughts of Goat intruded on nearly every minute of the day.

And that was no good. Not when they had incriminating evidence to hunt down and possible killers to evade.

"Chrissy," Stella said briskly, crumpling up wrappers and paper cups and collecting them on the tray, "thanks for all the encouragement and kind words, but it won't much matter what I look like unless we get the job done. Unless I figure out where them pictures of me and Ferg went to, they're liable to end up in the wrong hands."

"You mean the sheriff's hands?"

Stella grimaced. "That'd look nice, wouldn't it—I guess then he'd have no choice but to haul me in as a suspect, seein' as I'd have a heck of a good reason to be out to get Priss, *and* my fingerprints over at the last known place she was visiting at. Motive and opportunity, I believe it's called."

"Yeah, I guess then you'd fry for sure," Chrissy said glumly, "seein' as they already run your prints and all a couple of times in the past. You'd be in a three-strikes situation."

There was that. Stella didn't remember being printed when they came for Ollie—didn't remember much about that day at all, other than staring down at his no-good carcass on her kitchen floor and wondering how he got there. But she did remember when Goat had covered for her after the altercation that nearly left her and Chrissy dead, when their prints had been identified on a number of weapons—luckily, they'd been ruled weapons of self-defense.

Of course, she hadn't been *convicted* in either of those situations. Still, there was only so far a person could hope to push the police, even in a sleepy town like Prosper, even in a mostly rural county like Sawyer.

"Well, dwelling on it ain't gonna help anything. Let's go figure out what the heck the judge was wanting so bad, she sent them guys after it."

Halfway over to Marilu Carstairs's place, Chrissy asked a question that had occurred to Stella, too. "Wonder what would of happened if them two clowns had found the drive first."

"Well, we don't know if it was the same drive," Stella said.

"Well, duh, I know that. They've got so cheap, if I was Priss, I would have had a separate one for all my, uh, subjects."

"If Priss is in the blackmail business, there's no telling how many of those she's got."

"That wouldn't be a bad business," Chrissy said. "You probably wouldn't need to have the dirt on all that many people to make the rent every month. Just sayin'."

"I'll keep that in mind," Stella sighed.

The looming front gates of the judge's development came into view. Stella thought it looked more like a Vegas good-times ranch than a condo complex, with its gold lettering on the signs and fancy fountains and columns everywhere, but she had to admit that the place was kept spruced up nice. Expensive cars sat in driveways, snow was shoveled with ruthless precision from the walks, and ice crystals sparkled on the spindly trees tied up to stakes lining the streets. Evidently the landscaping hadn't had time to get going yet.

The condos were grouped in twos and threes, the buildings separated from each other with tall fences, which did detract some from the cozy neighborly effect.

"There—there it is," Chrissy hissed as though someone might hear, pointing at a duplex at the far end of the first turn in the road. "Drive on past."

"Thank you, junior sleuth. I wouldn't of thought of that. Fact, I was gonna just pull right up in the drive and holler at her to come on out."

"No need to get nasty about it," Chrissy complained. " 'Sides, there wouldn't be room for you."

Sure enough, a car had pulled into the driveway ahead of them, a newish Camry. The driver didn't get out right away; it looked like a man, and he was doing something to his hair, looking at himself in the rearview mirror.

Stella cruised slowly to a cluster of mailboxes centered on three guest parking spots, and pulled in and cut the engine. They watched the man in the car, but he kept at his grooming or whatever it was he was doing. He was too far away to make out any features.

"How long you figure he's gonna keep us waiting?" Chrissy said. "Fuck this, let's go."

"Go where?" Stella demanded in alarm.

"Go do what we come for."

Stella had no choice but to follow Chrissy as she grabbed

the backpack from the backseat and got out of the car. At least the girl walked in the opposite direction from the condo in question, looking for all the world like she was out for a casual stroll.

"We can go around the back," she muttered when Stella caught up with her. They slipped around the next building, winding around past a little duck pond and a gazebo, and tracked back until they were looking at the fence at the back of the judge's unit.

"Now what, you gonna catapult me over that?" Stella demanded. She couldn't see a thing over the top except for the judge's second-floor windows, which were shaded by thick draperies.

"It's tempting," Chrissy said, and then she flattened herself against the fence and started inching along toward the front yard. "Cain't nobody see us from over there, though."

They crept to the front, where the fence took a sharp corner and ended in a gate leading around the side of the building. This was familiar from the aerial views they'd seen online. Bushy hedges on the other side of the fence shielded the path from the wall—if they could get there. For the moment, they ducked behind a tall shrub and peered out at the visitor's car.

The man was parked no more than ten feet away, but he appeared to be absorbed with looking at his lap.

"What *do* you think he's doing?" Stella demanded, mystified.

"Texting, no doubt."

"Oh. Right." Stella blushed. Texting was something she hadn't quite mastered yet; when Todd occasionally sent her a few misspelled lines, generally if he was too bored to think of anything else to do, she always just called him back rather than try to pick out those tiny little buttons with her thumb.

Judging from their subject's look of concentration, he didn't have the same problem.

"Now or never," Chrissy said, and went for the gate's latch.

Chapter Sixteen

Before Stella had a chance to hiss at Chrissy to get her ass back to the bush, she was in—and Stella gave the man in the car only a cursory glance before following.

Once through the gate, she closed it carefully and leaned against the building's stucco wall, heart pounding. "He could have seen us!"

Chrissy shrugged and unzipped the backpack. "Yeah, so, we'd figure something out. We always do."

Stella started to reply, and then gave up. So what if the gal was a little trigger happy, a little free and loose with their safety—that was part of the reason Stella kept Chrissy around: She didn't scare easy. In fact, she barely scared at all. The only time Stella had seen terror in her eyes was when Tucker was kidnapped; now, with her son safe and sound in a house full of drunken revelers, Chrissy was cool as a cucumber.

Stella watched as her assistant set up the Bionic Ear that she'd found online. The thing was supposed to amplify sounds forty times and block out background noise, and it had come with lots of boldfaced warnings about how it was illegal to use it to intercept oral communication.

"Ain't we lucky," Chrissy continued as she took out the parabolic dish component and set it up to point through the window. "No curtains, and I can see right into the living room. Our girl's doing something . . . with some sort a implement and a—a—could that be a onion? Oh, this must be that *cooking* everyone's always talking about. Quick, Stella, check it out, you might learn something."

"Ha, ha," Stella grumbled. "I wouldn't be bustin' on my cooking, considering I fed you a home-cooked meal just last week."

"You did no such thing. I happen to know you didn't make that chicken parmesan you tried to pass off as homemade—you drove your bad self over to Casey and picked it up at Handy Sam's restaurant and stuck it in your own pan so's everyone would think you made it yourself."

Stella's mouth fell open. She was so sure she'd gotten away with it. But before she could demand how Chrissy had figured it out, the girl held up her palm to shush her.

"Our man's in," she whispered excitedly. "Judge Marilu's meeting him at the door. Oh, and don't she look special."

Stella pushed through the scratchy shrubs, getting up on her toes to look through the window. The floor of the condo was raised above ground level, and she had to peer through the legs of a side table, but she could make out a brunette woman's petite, slender figure, dressed in a flowing sapphire blue pantsuit.

But what really caught her eye was the gentleman she was kissing on both cheeks. Oooh—sizzling.

He was at least a decade and a half younger than Marilu, who Stella guessed to be around her own age. Not that there was necessarily anything wrong with that, of course. It would take a heck of a lot of cradle robbing for women to catch up with all the May–Decembering that men had been practicing for centuries.

But this man was more than simply young. He was smooth and muscled and had a full head of thick inky hair and wore a black silk shirt that slid provocatively over his generous shoulders and tucked into his expensive-looking trousers. When he slid his hands down Marilu's back to cup her ass against him, and took the kiss past anything that might be mistaken for friendly straight into R-rated territory, Stella whistled softly.

"And at this hour of the morning, too," she said, impressed.

"You gonna get all pissed off at me if I wonder if he's after her money?" Chrissy asked.

Stella thought it over. "I don't know. I should. But I'm kinda thinking the same thing."

They were silent for a few more moments of the show, as Marilu got herself backed up against the pantry door and one of her high-heeled shoes ended up falling off her foot as the pair wrestled and writhed. To Stella's surprise, their breathing and exclamations of unbearable pleasure came through loud and clear on Chrissy's listening device.

"That's some sound quality," Stella finally said as Marilu's mewling little murmurs gave way to smacking wet suctiony hickey noises.

As though they'd heard, the judge and her boy toy finally pulled apart.

"You do have a talent, Beau," Marilu said with admiration as she went to the fridge and poured herself a glass of water from the tap in the door, without offering anything to her guest.

"Only because you inspire me," the young lothario said in a throaty voice, as though he were auditioning for *One Life to Live*. Stella was amused and a little disappointed to hear a flat Arkansas twang in his voice. She never could abide an Arkansas accent—especially since Beau, if that was really his name, looked like he ought to be named something exotic like Antonio or Stavros or Dmitri.

"Come now, dear boy, let's both just admit that what inspires you is all the zeroes on the checks I write. Yes?"

Beau ducked his head and fluttered his eyelids as coyly as any blushing young virgin maiden. *If you insist,* the gesture seemed to say, while keeping alive the fantasy that he had landed in her kitchen by the unknowable forces and tides of pure lust.

"Speaking of which, here's for today," she added, taking a white envelope off the kitchen countertop and handing it to him. He slid it into a pocket without giving it a second glance. "I trust that now we can focus on just having a nice time?"

"I'm always up for that kind of nice time," Beau murmured, aiming his full lips and sculpted nose and cheekbones in for a nuzzle to Marilu's neck, but she ducked neatly out of the way, laughing.

"Hey, precious, keep a little in reserve, there," she said, picking up a sheaf of papers that was lying under the envelope. "Besides, you need to study up while I finish getting ready."

"Oh, all right," Beau groaned as though he'd been barely able to contain his man-lust for her quivering body, but Stella couldn't help noticing that as soon as Marilu padded out of sight down the hallway, he quickly straightened up out of his sexy slouch and took a seat at the kitchenette table, and began going over the papers.

"What do you suppose—?" Chrissy murmured.

"Well, see, I think that boy is the type of date a lady *pays* for," Stella said carefully. "I mean, for special services that go above and beyond the keepin' company area of the date."

"I *know* that," Chrissy snapped. "You think I growed up

under a rock or somethin'? I was just wondering what-all it's costing her."

"You mean, per hour?"

Chrissy cut her off with a guffaw. "Stella, that ain't how it's done. There's like special charges for every little thing. You get pure and simple company included in the price, and plus they throw in a little messin' around no-charge. Like maybe he'll stick his tongue in your mouth and run his hand up your nylons, you know, like that. But it's mostly to get your motor running so you'll spring for the other stuff."

"Chrissy Shaw," Stella exclaimed, startled, "however do you know this?"

Chrissy shrugged. "One a my brothers? Mac, the one with the mustache? It was, like, his dream job in high school. Only he didn't pass the entrance exam."

"What—?"

"Too short," Chrissy said matter-of-factly. "Ain't no cure for it, lots of ladies want a tall fellow, and no amount of offering up creative business proposals was about to change their minds, unfortunately for Mac. Which is I think the cause of the start of his troubles, gettin' his feelings hurt that way."

Stella knew that Mac had done a stint up in Fayette at the county jail for robbery. Somehow she doubted that being turned down by an escort service ought to qualify for a personal devastation, but then again, she'd never entered what was clearly a competitive industry, if their current mark's Academy-worthy performance was any indication.

"So that thing he's reading, is that like a takeout menu for what-all she's plannin' on getting up to with him?" Stella asked. "Like in the hospital when you got to circle what you want off the menu they send around?"

Chrissy inclined her head thoughtfully. "Could be. You know, we ought to get one a them special scopes, I could read that thing from here."

Stella snorted. "Yeah, well, and I surely would like to go on a pleasure cruise to Aruba, but if you ain't heard, the economy's kinda in the toilet, so I don't suppose that's in the cards."

"Hey," Chrissy said, giving Stella a quick jab in the shoulder. "Don't be talkin' that way. It's practically spring already. Season of renewal and hope and all. Why, even that painted Jezebel in there's got more Suzy Sunshine goin' on than you."

Stella followed Chrissy's gaze to the other side of the room, where an enormous bowl painted to resemble a head of cabbage held a clutch of fake peonies from which a plastic bunny peeked coquettishly.

"Well hold your horses, I ain't even put away the shamrock salt and pepper shakers yet."

"If I don't git on you, it won't get done," Chrissy scolded. "Tell you what, I'm coming over there next weekend, whether you like it or not. I ain't lettin' Tucker wake up Easter morning without all the decorations and shit."

"Well, if you don't like the way I do things, you could just wake up at your own damn house," Stella said, secretly pleased.

"I'll bring Tucker's basket and some eggs, but you got to get all them boxes out of the attic," Chrissy continued, unruffled. "Whyn't you git the sheriff to help you?"

Stella grumbled, but the idea wasn't half bad. After all, wasn't that the kind of job men had programmed into their DNA? Fussing with ladders and toting heavy objects—and all the while she could be whipping up Irish coffee and wearing that cute little sweater with the fuzzy trim around the neckline, the one that dipped far enough down to show that she meant business. Maybe she ought to look into that bra her friend Dotty kept going on about—the one Oprah liked so well.

A low growl got her attention trained back inside the house. Young Beau had got himself out of the chair, and Marilu had changed into a neat little pink suit, the fabric of which must be awfully fascinating, since Beau was running his hands all over it.

"You sure we need to get to that brunch already?" he murmured, speaking directly to her collarbones, brushing them with his lips.

Marilu ran her manicured fingernails through his perfectly cut hair.

"I'm afraid so," she said. "My cousin Dorcas's bastard grand-baby's only getting christened once, and she'll never forgive me if I don't show up. Besides, that side of the family barely lets you get out of the room before they start talking about you behind your back."

"We can't have that," Beau murmured, nuzzling his way down. Either that, or he was being shoved—Stella couldn't help admire the take-charge attitude Marilu seemed to have adopted concerning getting her needs met.

"On the contrary, we most certainly *can* have that," she laughed. "That's what I'm paying you for, remember? To give them something to talk about, so I don't have to spend one more family gathering with every nosy maiden aunt asking me when I'm going to meet some *man*."

Marilu spat the word *man* as though it were a cat turd she'd accidentally discovered in her mouth, but Beau didn't appear to be the least bit offended on behalf of his gender. "I'll give 'em a show," he promised.

She disentangled herself gently from Beau's roving fingers and face, and he held her fingertips in a courtly gesture, as though he were about to take her for a waltz around the dining room. Damn, but the man was smooth. Stella had the unkindly thought that it wasn't only height holding back the Lardner

137

boys—that kind of suave probably had to get started in the home, when a boy was just a wee thing; once he got to the man stage, it was probably too late.

"I'll just get my things," Marilu murmured, crossing the floor on her high-heeled black alligator pumps and fetching a long black wool coat from the closet. Beau rushed to help her into it.

"She sure has got him trained," Chrissy marveled. "So you want to sneak in there and wait for her to come back?"

Stella considered. Breaking in and waiting was probably the most sensible course of action, especially since the judge was bound to have better snacks than Priss. But Stella didn't think she could stomach watching Marilu and her rent-boy groping each other in the foyer again. The way they carried on, he was likely to have her dress ripped off before Stella could properly intimidate them. "I think we better follow them and see where they go."

Inside, Marilu was buttoning her coat while her lover boy fussed with a silk scarf around her shoulders. "Now did you have a chance to go over everything?" she asked.

"Yes, ma'am. Cousin Dorcas Severance, fifty-nine. Her husband is Jim Senior, of Belk, Glazkov, and Severance. Two daughters, Minette and Ashleigh. Ashleigh's the homely one, and the mother of little Tremayne."

"What a *dreadful* name for a child," Marilu said, shuddering, as she buttoned her coat.

"It didn't say if Tremayne was a boy or a girl," Beau said, slipping his folded cheat sheet into the same pocket that held the check the judge had given him.

"The little bastard *better* be a boy," Marilu exclaimed. "I got the blue rattle from Tiffany's."

Beau chuckled as though she were a great wit. Well, money probably made anyone a little more amusing.

138

"Let's go, precious," Marilu said, picking up a pink calfskin handbag and a little beribboned box. "We can go over the rest of the names on the way. The sooner we get to that brunch, the earlier we can leave."

"And the sooner we can get back home and get busy," Beau purred, allowing himself to be led to the door like a prize pony.

Chapter Seventeen

t wasn't too much of a surprise that Beau drove, though it was Marilu's big, solid Acura RL they followed through the streets of Kansas City rather than his tidy little compact. Stella figured it wouldn't do to show up for a fancy party in a car like that.

"Too bad we cain't hear what-all they're saying," Chrissy observed as Stella dodged in and out of traffic, trying to stay with the Acura. She'd suggested she take the wheel, having spent some time a couple of years ago learning a variety of tricks for following folks who you'd just as soon didn't know you were doing it, but she'd never had a chance to try them out in heavy traffic. Traffic around Prosper generally kept to a leisurely pace.

She was finding that the additional lanes of traffic had advantages and disadvantages. On the one hand, all those cars made for excellent cover; her pretty little Jeep Liberty had a dusting of road grime that went back a couple of snowstorms, since Stella hadn't had time to run it through the car wash all month. On the other hand, her usual driving practices, while not exactly tame, lent themselves to the pedal-to-the-floor-on-a-straightaway-type thrills rather than the dodge-and-feint variety that city folk seemed to favor.

After nearly clipping a slow-moving minivan, and getting stuck in the blind spot of a flatbed truck stacked with crates, Stella almost lost their quarry several times in the fifteen-minute drive into Kansas City's downtown. It was with great relief that she spotted them in the right-hand lane in front of an imposing old redbrick high-rise hotel. She followed as they rolled into the circular drive and up under the fancy covered valet station, and then braked hard.

"What the hell're you doing?" Chrissy demanded, jolted forward against her seat belt.

"I don't want them to see us," Stella said, glancing in the rearview mirror for traffic as she tried to figure out what to do.

"Well, if you get folks honking behind you, they're gonna notice for sure," Chrissy said. "Keep driving. You know where they're at now."

Stella eased past, keeping to the outside of the overhang, as a uniformed valet leapt to attention and practically fell over himself helping Marilu out of the car. Thankfully, neither she nor Beau looked their way. Out the other side of the circular drive, she found herself back in traffic. "Now what?"

"Find a spot," Chrissy said, "and make it quick."

Dang the insanity of the city pace, Stella thought as she dodged a pedestrian darting across the street. Up ahead, she noted a spot opening up as an old Cadillac pulled out, and turned on her signal just as a sleek BMW shot past her and nearly caused a head-on collision when it stopped abruptly.

All set to steal her space.

Uh-uh. Not happening.

Stella's temper, on a hair trigger already due to the stressful traffic, ratcheted up toward the atmosphere. The Cadillac, which they now saw was being piloted by a tiny little man about 150 years old, was moving at a glacial pace, the driver backing up a matter of inches and turning the wheel with a mighty effort before reversing forward a paltry bit and repeating the process.

Stella jammed the Jeep into Park and got out. She stalked the ten feet to the would-be spot-stealer's driver's-side door and rapped on the darkened window, which glided soundlessly down. She found herself staring at a florid man in a starched shirt and tie, a little headset corkscrewed into his ear, talking a mile a minute.

"—have her shoot me those financials," he barked, holding up a finger and glaring at her.

"That's my spot," Stella said, raising her voice. "I had the blinkers on."

He raised one eyebrow, his expression of irritation taking on a quizzical cast.

"You might hear me better like this," Stella said, reaching out and giving the earpiece a yank. It came out of his ear with a jerk, and she tossed it over to the passenger seat.

"What the hell!" His cheeks flushed an even deeper shade of red.

"What I said was, don't even think about taking my fucking parking space. I'm not in the mood." Stella leaned down, forearm resting on his open window, until she was looking the man in the eye, their faces inches apart.

"Yeah? Well, I don't care what sort of menopausal hissy fit you got going on," he snapped, and in the fraction of a second when his gaze tracked from her to the space that was finally being vacated by the elderly gent, when his hands shifted on the wheel, when his foot began its journey to the pedal, Stella had a rush of the kind of killer instinct that she'd honed to a razor edge, which had served her well in so many of these good-versus-asshole moments.

She shot out her hand and grabbed a handful of crotch, dug in her fingers with the concentrated force of all her might, just like she'd learned to do during all those months of physical therapy, and gave a ferocious twist.

He screamed. Stella dug in and twisted some more.

"We clear?" she demanded, so close now, she could smell his aftershave, mixed with sweat and fear.

"Yeah-yeah-yeah-please-yeah-please," he blubbered, scrabbling with his damp and squishy hand, trying to dislodge her iron grip. But he was messing with an angry woman who'd cleared the midcentury mark with attitude to spare, and that put him at a distinct disadvantage.

"Drive forward very slowly," Stella suggested. "If you go too fast, I'm liable to keep your balls as a souvenir."

The car began to move, at about the pace an ocean liner would go if it had started at a standstill on calm waters. Stella strolled along until she was satisfied that her new friend had time to process the situation.

"Now, explain to me how you just had a moment of poor judgment, which has thankfully now passed," she said. "And how you feel about that little incident a few minutes ago."

"I'm so-so-so-sorry I tried to take your spot," he stammered. His face was now turning an interesting shade of green.

"And I won't do it again to some other lady in the future."

"And I wo-wo-won't . . . I won't . . ."

Well, that was good enough, she supposed. She released him and gave the windowsill a little pat. "Drive safe now," she said as she stepped back and the car shot forward.

Back in the Jeep, Chrissy was shaking her head. "You and your violent ways. Got to solve everything with pain, don't you."

"Don't sass me, little girl. I ain't in the mood."

She executed a perfect three-point parking job, which surprised even her—there wasn't much call to put those skills to the test in Prosper—and grabbed her purse and made a hasty exit.

"We cain't go in there like this," Chrissy said as Stella fed coins into the meter. "We ain't dressed for the occasion—we'll stand out. Come on." She grabbed Stella's arm and spun her down the street in the other direction from the hotel.

"Where we going?"

"To fancy up some." She led the way down the street at a good clip and force-marched Stella into a storefront whose sign had big sparkly red letters spelling WIG'N'MORE. In the windows, as the name suggested, a variety of hairdos were displayed on featureless foam heads, decked in piles of glittering costume jewelry, draped with scarves and boas and crystal-studded eyeglasses.

"That isn't gonna help us," Stella complained. "Besides, I bet they mark everything up to city prices."

"We ain't exactly bustin' out with options here," Chrissy insisted. "And we don't want to miss that party, do we? In case you haven't noticed, we are in the middle of a city we don't know nothing about, and far as I can tell, it's this joint or nothing. Besides, we got that hush money from Jake and Lawrence—it won't kill us to spend a little. So shut your damn trap and let's see what they got."

Stella's fears about blending into the party were set to rest the minute they entered the ballroom marked with a sign reading

SEVERANCE CHRISTENING. It was jammed with people—easily over a hundred guests milled about, helping themselves from the buffet line, lining up at the open bar, admiring the ice sculpture of a cherub riding a dolphin.

And it wasn't just the crowd that put her at ease, or the fact that it appeared to be open seating, with the guests milling about on a wave of boozy good cheer despite the fact that the usual cocktail hour was quite a ways off.

No, what really heartened Stella was that the bastard child—baby Tremayne—appeared to have sprung from a blended family. Blended in the sense that half the guests looked like they rode over on the *Mayflower*—the men dressed in navy blazers and striped ties and even the occasional ascot, the women in more conservative versions of the solid-colored suit that the judge wore. But the other half had taken a decidedly more lowbrow interpretation of the dress code. The women wore giant-print dresses and miniskirts and high-heeled sandals and ankle bracelets. The men sported a fair number of slicked-back mullet-esque haircuts, and shiny double-breasted jackets and silk shirts open at the throat, all the better to show off their gentlemen's jewelry.

"Why, some a these gals make me look downright sophisticated," Chrissy marveled, echoing Stella's own unspoken sentiment.

Not that Chrissy looked bad. In fact, she had a certain preening charm that was not lost on any of the men in the vicinity. Wig'n'More had yielded a lace-up bustier top, which, coupled with the black pants Chrissy had been wearing as well as a pair of lime green mules that had been tucked away in the sale shelf at the back of the shop, looked quite fetching. She had accessorized with a pair of dangly green crystal chandelier earrings and a chunky gold bracelet, but the most memorable accessory had to be her own cleavage, which had attained an astonishing new level of magnificence with all the extra support lent by the stiff leatherette material from which the bustier had been crafted.

Stella had to settle for something a bit more sedate. The proprietress of the shop—CALL ME MYSTI, her name tag had commanded—gave her only the briefest of once-overs before fetching a number of things from the "hold" rack, claiming that they were so much better with Stella's fair coloring and lovely eyes that it would be a crime for her to selfishly hold them back for another customer. All of which Stella saw right through, but when she slipped on the silver burn-out velvet jacket over the matching stretch-velvet tank top, and added some fake pearls that would have had to come out of twenty-pound oysters, she had to admit that she looked fine, fine, *fine*.

Now, scanning the room, she was aware of the smooth stretchy fabric keeping her midsection nicely restrained, of the jaunty stance forced on her by the new silver-strapped sandals of astonishing height. The shoes might be the death of her, seeing as they were barely walkable, but it would be a pretty death, at least—Stella would go out clutching the sparkly handbag that their new friend Mysti had talked her into.

The clothes were an unexpected expense, it was true, and something Stella hadn't budgeted for. But they were a *business* expense, and that ought to count for something. Plus, maybe she'd get herself invited somewhere special for dinner and dancing by a certain gentleman friend. The silver ensemble would come in plenty handy then, wouldn't it?

Stella had a firm rule: She refused to engage in any of the petty competition that seemed to come over so many women when it came to men. Stella rued the millennia it must have taken to lodge in the female mind that they had to brawl for limited resources, except nowadays instead of fighting over a berry bush or roasted brontosaurus leg, women seemed ready to throw down over any kind of man, including the good-for-nothing ones. Why, it was epidemic—as anyone who flipped on the *Maury* show could see.

Marilu, however, didn't appear to share that perspective. She was standing in a circle of ladies, all appearing to harken from the old-money clan, with Beau hovering behind her as though he were there to hold an invisible train. Stella couldn't make out her words, but it was clear she was the center of the conversation, talking and laughing and occasionally touching the arm of her handsome escort in a decidedly proprietary way.

"What we need to do," she said thoughtfully to Chrissy, "is we need to separate those two."

"You want to git the judge off by herself?" Chrissy asked, piling a plate high with mini quiches and darling little deep-fried puffs of something glistening and golden. "Can I just have me a snack first? I ain't really had a lot of sustenance yet today."

Stella helped herself to a puff: cheesy, and spiced up with little chive bits. "Put some in your purse for later," she advised. "I don't think we want to wait—you know how these things are, folks start drifting off when all the good stuff is gone, and nobody really wants to stick around to watch them open up their baby gifts."

"Oh, yeah, I hate that," Chrissy said. "Every fuckin' baby shower I go to? First they make you play all them stupid diaper-pin games and then you got to sit there and watch 'em and it's like, get over it, it's another damn bib and you know the kid's just going to puke all over it."

"That's a terrible attitude—and you a mother yourself," Stella clucked, shaking her head. "What do you want 'em to do, show porn movies? Set up a poker game?"

"Just sayin'."

"Okay, Little Miss Sunshine, I'll take lover boy. Give me ten minutes or so, and then get the judge off somewhere you two can talk."

"Whyn't *I* take him, and you deal with Marilu?"

Stella rolled her eyes. "Right. I know you can't leave a piece of man candy alone for thirty seconds without taking a bite. Besides, we got to give that gal a reason to crack."

"Oh, so you're fixing to beat him up?"

"Come on, now, you don't want me to take all the surprise out of it, do you?"

Stella popped one last cheese ball in her mouth and wiped her fingers on a paper cocktail napkin—light blue, so maybe the tyke truly was a boy after all. She made her way through the crowd of folks, scoring a glance at the guest of honor, a wrinkled, homely little thing being passed among a thicket of starchy older ladies with ponderous handbags who appeared to be examining him for defects. Stella couldn't help noticing that the old gals from the other side of the family seemed to be having a lot more fun; they'd set up camp in a cluster of upholstered chairs in a corner, a trio of champagne bottles in the center of the table, and several had taken their shoes off and a few had their wigs askew and their lipstick a little sloppy. One had brought, in lieu of a purse, a recycle bag from Green Foods, the kind you were supposed to carry around so they didn't waste a paper bag on you; on the side was emblazoned BECAUSE WE CARE, and its owner was tipping an entire tray of mini sandwiches into it.

My people, Stella thought warmly.

She circled Marilu's cluster of acquaintances, easing behind a balloon-festooned column and listening carefully.

". . . conversational Mandarin," Marilu was saying. "Isn't that right, Beau?"

"Um, yeah." Beau nodded and flashed his megawatt smile.

"I imagine that's very helpful in your business," one of the ladies said, appearing drawn toward him like a magnet.

Another gal, one who bore a striking resemblance to Marilu herself, but lacking the expensive polish, made a harrumphing sound. "And what exactly was your business?" she demanded. "I don't recall."

Marilu shot her a look that could freeze lava. "Beau works in futures," she said frostily. "Really, Dorcas, I doubt we want to bore anyone with the details."

Stella slipped from behind the column and tapped Beau on the arm. "Sir," she murmured, "you have a call from Tokyo. I'm sorry to bother you, but he insisted it was most urgent."

Beau's eyebrows shot up with surprise. "Me? I didn't—"

"The gentleman explained that you had given strict orders not to be disturbed," Stella said hastily, aware of the ladies' sudden and keen attention. She shifted slightly so her back was turned to Marilu. "He was terribly sorry, but said to mention there is a crisis in the, uh, London office that requires your immediate attention."

For a moment Beau glanced around, openmouthed, as though looking for guidance. Stella gave his sleeve a little tug, but he seemed rooted to the spot. Not an improviser, she observed, and perhaps not all that bright after all.

"Go, sweetie," Marilu said, the first to regain her composure. Stella chanced a quick look and found that the judge's eyes were narrowed with great interest as she examined her. "That sounds important."

"Oh. Okay. I. Um."

Stella tugged more firmly and led him away from the group. She dragged him down the hall and into an alcove, where a bank of pay phones lined up in lonesome neglect, keeping up a steady stream of chatter about the party and the hotel, and maneuvered him easily into a corner out of view from passersby.

Then she slipped her little handgun from her purse and pressed it to the front of his pants.

Chapter Eighteen

Hey!" he yelped. "What the fuck!"

Stella jabbed a little harder, getting a grunt in response. "Don't move, and keep your voice down. Put your hands together behind your back. Easy now."

He did as she asked, very slowly, while his face displayed three kinds of wonderment and confusion. "I think you might have me confused with someone else," he finally said.

"Don't think so. Beau your real name?"

He managed to look hurt. "Yes. I mean, I use a professional last name, Mandrake— Hey, did Priss sic you on me?"

Stella tried to keep the surprise out of her face. What a fascinating development. "We'll save that conversation for upstairs. How much cash you got?"

"How much . . . you want my *cash*?"

"*I* don't want it, no. But the nice lady at the front desk is going to want it when we march over there and get us a room."

"You want to get a room? Christ, lady, you could of just *said* so. I mean you didn't have to go threatenin' me this way. Only, it's not going to help my performance much if you plan to keep that gun on me the whole time."

"Hold on, bucko, that ain't what I got in mind. You're not my type."

He gave her a world-weary eye-roll. "Trust me, I'm your type. I'm *everyone's* type. I mean I don't mean to brag or anything, but there's a reason I'm the second-most-requested guy in the company."

"Yeah, well, not today." Stella explained what she had in mind and tucked the gun into her purse, and then they walked companionably to the lobby, avoiding the party, her arm looped through Beau's. He paid in cash and managed to stay remarkably calm. When the desk clerk insisted on seeing a credit card, Stella squinted at it and read BEAU FAHRQUARDT.

Mandrake, indeed.

"So, all you rental fellas use made-up names?" she asked as they rode the elevator to the fourth floor.

"I don't believe I like your tone," he said, blushing, and they stayed silent the rest of the way to the room, where Beau slipped the key card into the lock and held the door for her. She had to admit that his manners were very nice.

Inside, she motioned him to the bed farthest from the door, and sat on the other bed and kicked off her shoes, which were rubbing across her instep painfully.

"I *knew* it," he exclaimed, a look of resignation taking over his features. "So *now* we get down to it. You must a got something awful nasty in mind if you couldn't even find anyone to *pay* to do it."

"I told you I ain't interested in your professional skills," Stella snapped.

Beau's whispered "dyke" was quiet indeed, but not so quiet that Stella didn't catch it. *Figures,* she thought stonily, *tell a man you aren't interested and suddenly you're gay.* Maybe Noelle was on to something after all—at least if she hooked up with another gal, she wouldn't have to put up with this kind of nonsense.

"I got a few questions for you, and I ain't real interested in the long version, so you might as well get right to the point. First. Why'd you think Priss sent me? How do you know her?"

Beau's neatly groomed eyebrows took another trip north. "Huh?"

"I said—" Stella repeated herself, slowly and with great care.

"I. Work. For Her," Beau said, replying with an identical spacing and emphasis of words, looking at Stella as though she might be slow. "She. Is. My. Boss."

"I *get* that, fucktard, but what is it you do for her? You, um, service her or what?"

Beau's eyes narrowed and he looked at her with great suspicion. "She owns the business."

"What, the landscaping business?"

"What the—? No, she owns Elegant Company. You know, the whole thing. Eighteen employees. Well, seventeen, now she killed Keller."

"Now that she . . . slow down. What's Elegant Company?"

Beau gave her a look of incredulity. "The escort service! Are you sure you know what you're doing? 'Cause you sure don't seem to know much—"

Stella slapped him medium hard with the side of the gun barrel. "Shut up and let me think. Priss Porter runs an escort service. Not a landscape business, not a, a, *legitimate* business of any sort?"

"Yeah."

"And you think she *killed* one of her employees? Another escort?"

"Yes, Keller McManus. A couple days ago, she sent us all an

e-mail saying—well, it's not like she came out and admitted she killed him, 'cause you can't go writing that kind of stuff in an e-mail, but she said he'd been disposed of and shouldn't none of the rest of us be asking questions unless we wanted to worry about our own futures. Mighty threatening, you ask me. "

"What'd he look like, anyway?"

Beau touched his hands to his hair, which maintained its sassy razor-cut fullness despite the rigors of having been kidnapped at gunpoint. "Well, *good,* of course. Kind of a Matthew McConaughey build. Probably around a forty-two long. Circumcised—"

"Blond or brown? Facial hair?" Stella couldn't add much about the rest of his features, since they'd been, well, *dead,* and grayish and unfresh and quite possibly swollen. "Wearing a brown leather coat?

"Oh, yeah, he got that at Macy's—looks just like the Armani. Cost him three hundred bucks, forty percent off."

Stella thought for a moment. "What did she kill him for, anyway?"

Beau scowled fiercely. "As a warning."

"A warning about *what?* You boys not showing up for work on time? Coming to work soused? Raiding each others' clients?"

"Organizing. You know, labor. It's, like, union-busting. It's complicated."

"Now hold on a blessed minute," Stella said, growing more confused by the moment. "There ain't any kind of prostitution union in this state I'm aware of, and it would take a whole lot more than just a couple dozen of y'all to start one, so unless you're all in cahoots with the, ah, brotherhood, all your colleagues and shit, that doesn't make a lick of sense."

Beau shrugged, and Stella considered how often men tended to dig in harder the more their dumb-assed views were challenged. "You'd have to know the whole history, I guess. Like I said, it's *complicated*."

"Uh-huh. And your, um, *client* down there, the judge, she fits into this how?"

"She doesn't have anything to do with it," Beau said, shaking his head as though it was working on his patience to have to explain a simple concept to her. "She doesn't care about the details as long as I'm keeping her satisfied. See, it's all part of the arrangement. It's a whole experience we provide, a mystique. We shield the client from the business aspects, so she can focus on living the fantasy."

"That sounds like you memorized it off a brochure or something," Stella said, and by Beau's hurt expression, she could see that she'd made a lucky guess. "So you're sticking to your story, that Judge Carstairs down there is nothing but a satisfied customer who has no ax to grind with your boss."

"If that's how you want to put it."

"One last question for you—what do you know about a flash drive Priss might have had, that might have been worth something to someone?"

Beau's expression of vacant confusion was convincing. "Nothing."

Stella thought about the lack of records anywhere in the apartment, about the locked folder on the laptop. "Maybe she keeps a separate set of books? I mean, she must have a legitimate-looking set for reporting, and another for her own use. . . ." Stella thought it through as she talked.

Beau shrugged. "I don't know anything about that. Priss does it all. We give her the checks from our clients, but we keep our tips in cash. And then she cuts us checks every two weeks. And, you know, sometimes . . . well, depending on what the client wants, the tips are like way more than the paycheck, you know?"

"Wait, so a lady can hire one of you pretty boys for nothing but, what, a date to the movies? No hanky-panky?"

"Sure, I guess. Only that would be pretty steep. We start at eighty-five bucks an hour and that's with. You know. No extras."

Stella started to ask another question about the cash flow situation and realized she was getting way off track, as fascinating as it was. She was here to figure out why Judge Marilu Carstairs had hired a pair of thugs to go rooting around in Priss Porter's life, not to do a study of the male escort service business model.

"Okay, well, I'm gonna call your client now," Stella said. She flipped open her phone with her free hand. Before hitting Chrissy's speed dial, she had a thought. "Look here. I know you're close to the judge and all, but this can go a lot quicker and easier if you do things my way."

"What do you mean?"

"When I do this—" She jabbed the Bersa in his direction, toward the vicinity of his trim abs. "—you pick up that pillow and holler into it. Sound scared, not mad. No—sound like I'm hurtin' you real bad, 'cause that's what I'll do if you don't cooperate."

Beau nodded glumly.

Chrissy picked up after one ring. "Took you long enough," she complained. "Me and the judge don't exactly have a whole lot in common and we done run out of chitchat."

"Where are you?"

"We're sitting by the inside pool. Got the whole place to ourselves, but it's real steamy in here. Don't guess it's doing much for my hair."

"Good for your pores, though."

"If you say so."

"Did you have to draw on the judge?"

"Only a little," Chrissy said, sounding bored. "She didn't put up much of a fight."

Not a whole lot of brain power in either of their new friends, Stella reflected. After all, it wasn't like she or Chrissy was about to go shooting anyone in the middle of a crowded hotel. All they would have had to do was say "no thank you" when a gun was presented, and walk away, and Stella and Chrissy would have been left standing there feeling might stupid, and without a plan B.

But folks rarely thought things through when they were in a surprised state on the other end of a gun.

"Put me on speaker," Stella advised as she did the same, setting the phone down on the bedside table. She pointed at the pillow, and Beau immediately picked it up and started wailing into it.

Not yet! Stella mouthed, exasperated, drawing a forefinger across her neck for emphasis. Beau stopped midwail.

"What was that?" Marilu's voice, shrill and annoyed.

"That, sister, is just a little taste of the hurt I'm gonna put on your boy if you don't tell me what I want to know."

"I know you're working for Priss," Marilu said. "She wouldn't let you do anything to one of her boys. They're her bread and butter, she wouldn't risk damage to the goods."

"I didn't say I was gonna leave any *permanent* damage," Stella said. "I'm just going to make him hurt."

There was a fraught moment when Beau's expression went worried and Stella hoped some sinking-in was happening.

"So Marilu, why'd you send those clowns down to Priss's, anyway? What's on this flash drive you want so bad?"

This time Stella let less time go by. *"Make it real,"* she whispered to Beau, gesturing at the pillow he was clutching with the business end of the gun.

Beau set to howling then, and Stella raised her eyebrows, impressed. It was a good thing the pillow muffled most of it, because the carrying on was Oscar-worthy.

"Hey!" Marilu snapped, but Stella waved her gun to encourage Beau and he kept it up, adding a snuffling hiccup between wails.

"Stop it!"

Stella circled her finger as a cue for Beau to stop and he lowered the pillow, his face flushed with exertion. She gave him a curt little nod of approval.

"What are you doing to him, anyway?"

"Like I said, nothing that will leave permanent damage. I've got him tied up, and I've rigged up this little dick-squeezing mechanism. Clever, really, you know that phrase 'dick in a vise'? I mean I don't think a vise would really be such a good idea, but what I've got is this spring-loaded—"

"Take it off him," Marilu snarled.

"Thought you didn't care," Stella said. "Aw, that's sweet."

"Don't take it all the way off," Chrissy piped up. "Just loosen that one wing nut a little. It's a bitch to get that thing on proper in the first place."

Stella smiled; her assistant was developing a real talent for ad-libbing. "Now can we please get down to business? Why-all'd you send those boys down there?"

"In the first place, I didn't send them anywhere. I should have guessed that their incompetence would get in the way. I just asked them to retrieve, ah, something . . . from Priss's possession. I told them to follow her, but I had no idea she was going to head out of town. For the rates I'm paying, you'd think they might have checked with me before they headed down to the sticks."

Stella considered whether to let the "sticks" reference pass,

158

not liking the woman's tone. "Yeah, good help is so fuckin' hard to find, ain't it?"

"You might could a seen it like they was just usin' a little initiative," Chrissy suggested.

"Or that they were more incompetent than I guessed, considering they were stymied by the two of you. Ow!"

"Oh, sorry," Chrissy drawled. "These darn fake nails. They can be sharp, cain't they?"

Stella grinned. "What was it you sent your boys after, anyway?"

"I should think you already know," Marilu huffed. "I'm sure you didn't waste an opportunity to ask them."

"Yeah, well, I just want to hear you say it."

There was a silence that stretched longer than Stella cared for. "Did I mention these here nipple clamps I rigged up from the tongs that came with my old Fry Daddy?"

"Damn it, Stella, I don't really think it's material, what I needed to get from Priss. It doesn't have anything to do with you."

"That's for me to figure out, I think," Stella said.

"It's just a flash drive with some images on it that I'd like to keep . . . private."

Stella, who was watching Beau slowly recuperate from all that huffing and blowing, noticed his face screw up in surprise. "What, did the two of you take pictures of your little parties?" she asked, as much of him as of Marilu.

"No," he said quickly. "I'm not into that, and besides, it costs a *lot* extra."

"You rig something up on the sly, you bad girl?" Chrissy broke in.

"Of course not!"

"Well, then . . ."

"Now, look, Beau, honey, don't get offended—this is not a reflection on you or my, my satisfaction with you. . . ."

"What?" Stella demanded.

"You ought to see this," Chrissy interjected. "She's turnin' every shade of pink."

"I, um, had a date with Turk."

Chapter Nineteen

Turk!" Beau barked. "Turk? You went out with *him*? And just when were you going to get around to telling me *that*?"

"Hold on," Stella said. "Who's Turk? And, ah, what does it matter? I mean, it's not like y'all are going steady or anything."

"Turk's one of the other Elegant Company employees," Marilu hedged.

"Turk's a client-stealing, steroid-jacking, fake-tan pretty boy," Beau bellowed.

"He's, um, the highest-grossing escort," Marilu continued in a chastened tone. "The other men are, er, a little sensitive sometimes."

"He's got no principles!" Beau blurted. "He'll just do anything to anyone to make a buck."

Someone coughed delicately—either Chrissy or Marilu—and Stella figured they were all trying to let Beau's brain catch up to his last comment.

"So what happened, he take a compromising picture of you?" Stella asked. "Give it to Priss and now she's holding it over your head? Blackmail, maybe?"

"It was . . . ah." Marilu's discomfort was plenty clear even through the phone lines. "More of a . . . video clip, you might say. Actually, um, several."

Beau's eyes widened with fury. "Bastard," he whispered.

"I don't get it," Stella said. "What do you care? I mean, you're not her boyfriend. You've got lots of other clients. Face it, the woman pays for your time, not really a romantic relationship, you know what I mean?"

"Turk Hardpole crosses the *line,* that's why I care," Beau fumed. "Every quarter, Priss sends the top earner on a trip. All expenses paid. Turk's been to Reno and Myrtle Beach already last year."

"I could take you to Jamaica . . . ," Marilu said in a small voice.

"I don't think so." Beau was frosty. "Besides, I'm not *allowed* to take videos. Remember? It's in the contract."

"I didn't know he was doing it," Marilu protested. "I never would have allowed that. He must have had it rigged up somehow in secret, which certainly raises all kinds of ethical issues. Why, the reason I used Elegant Company was because they are very, very discreet."

"Right up until they start extortin' you, I guess," Chrissy said, not without sympathy. Stella knew that the girl had been burned in the past by naughty Polaroids.

"Turk and Priss evidently have a system," Marilu explained bitterly. "He turned over the videos to her—"

"Shit, just how many *were* there?" Beau demanded.

"Well . . . a few."

"Do you *know* what that does to my numbers?"

"It's just . . . he has this one special thing he does . . . it's kind of, you might say, an aberration. A, er, physical attribute of sorts that . . . well, I was curious, that's all, sweetheart," Marilu said in the most placating tone. "Look, Stella, could you put me on with Beau in private for a moment?"

"Hah," Stella said, at the same time Beau made a snort of contempt.

"I'd sure like to hear about that," Chrissy added quickly. "Was it, like, a birth defect?"

"Curious is *one time,*" Beau whined. "You kept going back for more. I don't know that I really feel that I can continue our relationship, knowing what I now know."

"Oh, for fuck's sake," Stella said, rolling her eyes. "This is ridiculous. You two are squabbling like a couple of chickens in the corn. Chrissy, this ain't getting us anywhere, so I guess you all might as well come on up."

While they waited, Beau closed his eyes and assumed an expression of great grievance. Marilu and Chrissy arrived within a few moments, and the judge looked them up and down with a frown.

"Where's all your interrogation equipment?" she asked suspiciously.

"Folds up tiny," Stella said. "Fits in my purse. Genius design, really."

Chrissy dragged over the desk chair and the upholstered ottoman and they sat. "This is cozy," she said. "Now all's we need is some pretzels and we can watch stomper pulls on pay-per-view."

"We're not staying," Stella said. "Things to do, people to see, you know how it is. So just to tie up any loose ends here, there's a tape out there of you doing nasty things that the Johnson County District Court probably wouldn't be too happy to have in circulation. That about the size of it?"

"It's—I'm—"

"Uh-huh," Stella said, getting up off the bed and gathering her purse and slipping on the uncomfortable shoes. "What I thought. Well, think on this. I'm on the lookout for something of my own, and it's entirely possible I might run across your tape while I'm looking for it. So, what I'm saying is, you might want to keep me in mind as a friend."

"I suppose you think *you* can squeeze me, too, if you find it," Marilu said darkly.

"No, no, that's not my style. It wouldn't be very sisterly, would it?" Chrissy and Stella walked to the door. "Just consider it a favor I might need to call in someday. Trust me, the day I or one of my clients need help from a judge, it ain't gonna be anything that's gonna tax your conscience too bad. Hear?"

Marilu nodded slowly, a calculating expression on her face. "I'll keep that in mind."

"What about me?" Beau demanded. "What am I supposed to do now?"

"Well, y'all got this nice room," Chrissy said. "Might as well someone have a little fun today. Whyn't you two kiss and make up."

In the elevator down, Stella couldn't help giggling. "Oh, the expression on his face."

"He just had his feelings hurt's all." Chrissy shrugged. "You know how delicate men can be."

"Men don't think there's anything wrong with payin' a hooker. And I doubt they spend a lot of energy worrying about her feelings. But if they're on the other end—well, hold the show—everybody's got to be all concerned about whether they're upset."

"Yeah, well, that's a man for you, I guess. Wants you to fuck him and tell him thank you and he's the best you ever had and buy him lunch."

They were silent for a moment, thinking it over.

"Gotta say, that wouldn't be the worst deal in the world," Stella finally remarked.

"So we got us one dead male prostitute," Stella said glumly half an hour later.

They were sitting in Arkansas Joe's, polishing off a couple of slabs of ribs. The joint had been recommended to Stella by a client, but she and Chrissy agreed that they preferred the Pokey Pot's sauce. Still, it was convenient, just a little ways off 435 near Raytown, a perfect place to stop before they headed for home.

"By the way, do you know, what's the word for that? I mean, is he like a man hooker?"

"*Hooker* don't sound right, I got to say," Chrissy said, licking sauce off her fingers.

"There's *gigolo,* I guess, except I can never say that word without conjuring up Richard Gere."

"Eew."

"*Eew,*" Stella repeated. "Eew what?"

"Richard Gere's disgusting."

"*What?* He's entirely fine, Chrissy. I'd do him in a second."

"Well, you just go on ahead, then, you got my blessin'. Only he'll probably have to have his private nurse there. Isn't he like ninety years old or something?"

"Christina Jaynelle Lardner Shaw," Stella gasped, "sometimes I forget what a child, truly what a *baby,* you really are. Richard Gere was . . . like . . . like a young *god* in *An Officer and a Gentleman.* Every woman in America wanted a piece of that action, I guarantee it."

"Whatever. Never heard of it."

Stella shook her head in wonderment and dismay and set down her unfinished rib, her mood sinking even lower. Nowadays, half the men on the *People* magazine covers barely looked old enough not to need a babysitter, while all the truly fine-looking men were sitting on the shelf. Where was Tommy Lee Jones? Where was Harrison Ford?

The media acted like middle age was a shameful secret, like folks over fifty might ought to just go find themselves an iceberg and float quietly out to sea. But what was so great about youth, anyway? Other than taut skin and twenty-twenty vision and remembering where she left her keys, Stella's youth had frankly sucked. In the brief span of time between leaving her parents' house and marrying Ollie, Stella had lived an anxious existence. While she certainly wished many times during her marriage that she'd cherished her brief independence and maybe held on to it, what she most remembered was the crushing weight of her own self-doubts. Was she pretty enough? Funny enough? Interesting enough? Smart enough?

She'd been all those things and more, Stella guessed, if only she'd been brave enough to let them out of the box. Maybe the younger gals got it right. Chrissy never seemed to waste time worrying what the rest of the world thought of her choices, of her looks, of her desires and ambitions. And Noelle—well, she'd found the fortitude to pursue at least one dream, and she had a great job to prove it. And now she had the courage to pursue another. However this whole new romance of hers worked out, Stella had to admire her for that.

"Hey, anyone home?" Chrissy prompted, waving a french fry in front of Stella. "You were saying, how we got one dead man hooker?"

"And a missing madam—"

"Maybe it ain't called a madam, with men," Chrissy pointed out. "Come to think of it, maybe she'd be the pimp, d'you think? A woman pimp? Kind of an equal rights thing."

"Okay, we got a missing pimp and her missing brother. Unfortunately, we now know Priss likes taking picture evidence of her employees and their clients so she can blackmail them."

"We ought to go see that Turk," Chrissy said.

"You mean to find out who else they were blackmailing?"

"Yeah, sure, that and . . . well."

"Well, what?"

"Well—just—what do you think it was that he could do, in the lovin' department, that was so special? I mean you got to figure if he was the only one out of all them guys who could do it—"

"Chrissy, we are *not* spending company time figuring out how to do some dirty porno act!"

Chrissy pouted. "You don't need to get all ugly about it. How's it dirty, if two folks are having a nice time? Or even if one person's having a nice time and the other person don't much mind, especially if they're getting paid decent?"

"It's—what it is—you can't—" Stella left off sputtering, and then realized she didn't have a leg to stand on. Chrissy was parroting her own philosophy, more or less.

In fact, Stella realized, the philosophy she'd actually evolved without giving it a whole lot of thought was that things she liked to do or hoped to do or was even a little curious about were, by definition, healthy and natural and normal. By comparison, if she were truly honest with herself, the things other people did, that didn't light a fire for her, that she *didn't* hope to do—those things she considered just plain *wrong*.

But that didn't seem terribly fair.

And then there was the complicated situation with Noelle. Plenty of folks in Prosper still felt that men getting it on with men, or women with women, was a sin on a par with all the deadly ones, that you had to turn in your Christian card and hang your head in shame and maybe rot in jail if you happened to want to spend your zestful lovin' hours with someone whose chromosomes lined up more or less with your own.

And that did not strike Stella as one bit right.

"I'm sorry," she said, chastened. "I don't mean to judge what folks are getting up to. Only if I do find the judge's tapes, I'm holding on to them."

"'Cause they're *useful*," Chrissy clarified. "Not because they're dirty."

"Yes. Okay. Agreed. Now can we get back to the crime solving?"

"Be my guest. I ain't stoppin' you."

A squawking issued from her purse, and Stella quickly wiped her fingers on a wad of paper towels and squinted at the display.

"Aw, shit. It's Goat."

"Well, answer it!"

"I can't. He told me to stay in town."

"So, he doesn't need to know where we are."

"But what if he, you know, wants me to come over right away or something—"

"Then you tell him you're giving your legs a hurry-up shave and you'll be there quick as you can. Damn it, Stella, if you don't answer that thing, I will!"

Before Stella could decide, Chrissy snatched the phone away from her and flipped it open.

"Stella Hardesty's phone," she chirped. "Chrissy speaking. May I help you?"

Stella could hear Goat's voice from three feet away, and he didn't sound happy. She strained to make out what he was saying, but Chrissy leaned away from her and batted at her with her free hand. "Mmmm," she said. "I see . . . uh-huh . . . oh my goodness, I'd surely love to, but the gal wouldn't let her take the phone in the fitting room. . . . Oh, down here at, uh, Sears, actually. We're over at the Casey one. And it's like a new security thing? . . . Yeah, cell phones and, um, cameras."

Stella rolled her eyes furiously and grabbed at the phone, but Chrissy fended her off. "I surely will, Sheriff. It'll probably only be forty-five minutes or so—"

Goat's voice rose in tone and Chrissy held the phone away from her ear, sighing. "Well, sure, but you shoulda seen the stack of garters and thongs and shit she took in there. It's gonna be a while, I'm telling you. Uh-huh. Uh-huh . . . sure."

She snapped the phone shut, shaking her head slowly.

"That was the stupidest lie I ever heard you tell," Stella said. "No *phones* in the *dressing room*? Couldn't you have said I was, I don't know, getting a massage or something?"

Chrissy jumped up impatiently. "Come on, you can yell at me on the way home. We need to haul ass if you're going to pull this off. Is it like a crime or something to leave town when you're a suspect?"

"Why, what did he say?"

"Only that you better be in his office in half an hour. Want me to drive?"

The phone rang again and Stella put it to her ear with an exaggerated sigh while she hustled out of the restaurant, practically jogging to keep up with Chrissy.

"Mama, you don't care if I have a dinner party here tonight, do you?" Noelle's breathless voice was full of excitement.

"You want to do *what*?"

"Because Joy turned out so cute, just wait until you see, Mama. She's like, maybe, Natalie Portman if she was blond. We're going to invite some of the girls from Sidewinders. And you can come, too. And you can bring the sheriff if you want to."

"Sugar, you know you can't cook!"

Noelle had actually been kicked out of home ec for setting fire to the test kitchen years earlier when she was trying to take a shortcut on a frittata. Stella didn't bother adding that the sheriff wasn't likely to feel festive after the day he'd had.

"I can make cookies," Noelle said defensively.

"That ain't makin' cookies, when you pry off a lump of that shrink-wrap dough and cook it," Stella said. "That's just fakin'."

"Well, I saw you got some frozen chili in the freezer. How about I thaw that out and maybe you can fix some corn bread?"

"You want me to—Noelle, honey, I am on my way to see the *sheriff,* who is likely to put my ass in a *jail* cell for leaving town when he's got all manner of unsolved criminal *behavior* on his hands."

"You'll sort that out. He's into you, Mama. Just flash him your tits or something. Oh, and can you do that thing with the cream cheese and the chili sauce, you know that you serve with the Ritz crackers? That would be great. Gotta go—we're doing green tea facials and I'm dripping all over the counter."

Stella slipped the phone in the pocket of her new silver jacket as they approached the car. The restaurant parking lot glinted with snow crystals in a sliver of afternoon sun.

"What'd you just agree to do?" Chrissy asked as Stella slammed her door a little harder than necessary.

"Looks like I'm fixing dinner for a bunch of Noelle's new friends. Want to come?"

"I'd love to, 'cept if I don't get home, Mama's likely to let

Tucker go sledding with the bigger boys and that's no kind of good idea. Did it occur to you to just tell her no?"

"It occurred to me," Stella said darkly, "but heaven forbid I should get in the way of true love."

Chapter Twenty

Goat slammed something down on the desk in front of Stella, making her jump. She was sitting in the uncomfortable molded plastic chair Goat had dragged in from what used to be the dining area of the Hardee's that now housed the Prosper sheriff's offices. The old dining room had been carpeted, the booths replaced with a reception desk that backed up to where the order counter used to be, and a few vinyl-upholstered chairs were arranged in a sort of waiting area. A handful of offices and a cramped conference room had been carved out of the remainder of the old restaurant. The deep fryers and refrigerators and the rest of the equipment had been sold off, the proceeds funding a new photocopier and phone system.

Goat kept his broad hand flat on whatever he'd thunked down, leaning across the desk and glowering. He covered the distance between them with no effort at all, his long arms stretching his polyester shirt tight against his broad shoulders.

"You left town," he growled, "after I ordered you not to."

Stella couldn't help a shivery zip skipping up her skin even as she bristled at his words. She didn't much figure any man had the right to order her to do anything—she'd had several lifetimes' worth of that nonsense during her marriage—but when Goat said things like that, they somehow took on a deliciously perverse challenge. Stella kept her chin up and stared Goat right in his baby blue eyes until he finally leaned back in his chair and folded his hands on the desk. She glanced down: in front of her was a lavender ceramic dish shaped like half an egg, and it was full of jelly beans.

"Oh, is this that tropical mix?" she said, stirring it with a finger, looking for the pineapple ones.

"I don't know what the hell it is. It's Irene's."

"Bet she don't know you're in here threatening me with it."

"I *confiscated* it because she was giving *candy* to the *Girl Scouts,* what come around selling cookies," Goat growled. "That just encourages them to come back."

"Wow, good thing you nipped *that* in the bud," Stella said. "I mean, coming around here in their little knee socks and sashes? The nerve!"

Goat's face, which even in the middle of one of the coldest Marches on record retained the ghost of a tan from his frequent trips to the lake, where he paddled around in his kayak or his canoe, depending on his mood, darkened a shade. "Let me tell you about my morning, Stella."

"Why don't you. Seein' as you interrupted my shopping and all."

"Oh, like I believed that whole yarn of Chrissy's. That gal of yours can't lie for shit."

"How was your morning, Sheriff?" Stella asked as sweetly as she could manage.

"Well, let's see. When I got here at seven, I had an e-mail from the crime scene folks up in Fayette. One of those fellas stayed up way past his bedtime last night working on Priss Porter's car. Care to guess what-all they found?"

"Open containers of beer? Stolen street signs?"

"*Blood,* Stella. I don't know why this is all so damn funny to you. There was a significant amount of blood trace all over the trunk. They're sending it off for DNA now."

"Isn't that, like, confidential information?" Stella said. "I'm pretty sure the handbook says you're not supposed to share that kind of stuff with regular citizens like me."

"Damn it, Stella!" Goat smacked his hand down on the edge of his desk, causing the ceramic dish to skitter close to the edge. Stella hastily pushed it back before it could tip to the floor. "Why do you think I have you in here? Don't you think I might be cutting a corner or two that I don't have any business cutting? You're here so you can tell me exactly what the fuck you were doing there the other night."

"I didn't—"

"There's enough blood in there that it's a distinct possibility whoever it belongs to's dead, especially as live folks don't generally make a habit of lying down in automobile trunks without puttin' up a fuss. I want you to tell me everything you know about Priss Porter and Liman Porter and whoever they stashed in that trunk, because I'll tell you right now that if I don't come up with something quick, Detective Simmons and her merry fucking band of chore boys are going to be camping out in my office while I fetch her coffee, and that is something I *know* neither one of us wants."

He was right about that, at least. One of the problems with being the smallest outpost of the county seat was that Goat was at the mercy of Sheriff Dimmit Stanislas and his staff. Stella was willing to bet that Detective Simmons had put a lot of effort into helping Sheriff Stanislas forget all about her recent blazing show of incompetence and that she'd relish an opportunity to come down and show off, even if she hadn't been sweet on Goat. All in all, Stella would be pleased as punch for her to stay up in her end of the county and leave Prosper alone.

"Do you want to come to dinner tonight?" she blurted. "It's, ah . . . a party. I guess. Kind of."

Goat stared. He looked like he was trying out half a dozen different responses before he sighed and shook his head slowly. "You are about half a fly dick away from me throwing you in the dumpster until you decide to play by the same rules as everyone else, Stella Hardesty."

The "dumpster" was Prosper's single holding cell, for anyone unfortunate enough to need to be locked up for any matter of time before being hauled up to Fayette to be processed at the county jail. It wasn't really a dumpster, but it was built on the site of the walled enclosure that held the trash containers during the Hardee's days. It had been finished off with a concrete floor and a fourth wall and a roof with a skylight, but the baseboard heaters didn't work very well, and it still smelled faintly of rotting garbage.

"You wouldn't," Stella guessed, crossing her fingers under the overhanging edge of the desk.

"Oh, I would. You might think, just because you've got me worked up a time or two, that you have some sort of special privileges around here. But you'd be wrong, Stella Hardesty. The law comes first. A crime's a crime, no matter how pretty a package you tie it up in, and way I see it, you refusing to cooperate on this thing is capital-O obstruction, and that puts you on the other side from me, any way you slice it."

Stella kept her features carefully fixed in a neutral expression even while, on the insides, her heart felt like it was melting into a runny mess.

It wasn't exactly a ringing declaration of undying love. Not that she expected one. Their relationship was, if not in its infancy, certainly in its awkward toddlerhood, stumbling around in circles, full of enthusiasm but lacking direction. At least, that's how she'd thought of it. But Goat dismissing it so easily—that stung.

"Let me tell *you* something, mister," she said, pushing back the chair and standing to her full five foot six so she could stare down at him. "I care about justice every bit as much as you do, maybe more, and I don't care for you implying otherwise. The minute I have anything to say to you that's gonna make any of this mess right, I'll be in here saying it. Meanwhile, if you want me back again, I guess you'll just have to arrest me, 'cause I got better things to do than sit here and let you scold me."

She grabbed her coat off the back of the chair and stomped to the door of the office. Before yanking it open, she spun around and added, "And that dinner invitation? Don't you worry yourself over it. I'm sure you got way more important law-type stuff to do than have dinner with a bunch a your lowly constituents."

She slammed the door behind her and stalked across the lobby, managing a little wave for Irene, who was kneeling on the floor in a pair of purple polyester slacks and a fuzzy yellow sweater, taping decorations to the front of the counter. EASTER, Stella couldn't help noticing, was at a decidedly crooked angle to HOPPY, and the paper daffodils were curling and drooping under their own weight.

Stella stopped by Walmart on her way home. Cream cheese, chili sauce, green onions, shredded cheese . . . heaven on a cracker. She tossed in a few bags of snack mix, the good kind with the crunchy Cheetos, and added a fresh soldier—a liter bottle of Johnnie Walker Black. Might as well be well prepared, and she did have a nice stack of cash in her wallet, what remained of her half of the money they took off Jake and Lawrence. A twelve-pack of Miller High Life—Stella paused and wondered if lesbians were more likely to prefer fancy beer or plain, before giving up on the question as beyond her experience—a few bottles of wine and eggs and butter for the corn bread, and then she headed toward the registers.

Through the men's section.

Past the stacks of nubby sweaters, the racks of flannel over-shirts with corduroy collars, which Stella paused to smooth with her fingers, imagining how they might look on Goat.

Then she remembered him chastising her like she was some vagrant Mike and Ian had dragged in, and felt the blood rush to her cheeks. She steered her cart back toward the front of the store.

Paused at the book aisle. Cast a sidelong glance down the neat rows of best sellers. She used to love to read, her bedside table stacked with thrillers and mysteries and historical romances from the library. Once Ollie was dead, she treated herself to an occasional hardcover—she loved the feel, the smell, the sensa-tion of letting the pages flutter against her fingertips. Only, ever since she'd taken up the banner in defense of the defenseless, it seemed like her days ended in the kind of exhaustion that didn't do well with reading a chapter or two.

But that didn't stop her from wondering what Goat might like. Was he a history buff? Maybe one of those types that liked biographies—Stella found them dry as dust, but her father al-ways had one on the little table next to his easy chair, his place marked by a crisp dollar bill.

She passed up the page-a-day calendars and a coffee table book featuring classic cars of the '70s without a second glance.

At the end of the aisle were the travel books and there, squeezed in between a bedraggled stack of atlases and a copy of *Midwest Capitals on Twenty Bucks a Day* was a slim volume titled *Wonders of the Yukon*.

Stella picked it up. On the front was a gorgeous photo of a crystal blue lake laid out in front of a range of pristine, snowy mountains. On a peak in the middle distance, a man in hiking gear raised a hand to shield his eyes, while a brilliant sun peeped out through a layer cake of yellow and pink and orange sky.

All that was missing from that picture, Stella thought, was this rugged yet sensitive man's woman, dressed in a slimming pair of hiking trousers and a nice fitted parka that showed off her curves, maybe in a lovely shade of violet. They'd hike through the morning and have a romantic lunch of elk or something at a rustic lodge before climbing into a log bed to make crazy love all afternoon long under a puffy down comforter, until night fell and they watched the northern lights sparkle up the sky as snow fell around them, naked under a bearskin blanket, arms around each other.

Reverently, Stella placed the book in her cart. Not for Goat, of course. Not after that little display in his office. Unless maybe he came to his senses and . . . but no, Stella Hardesty did not wait around letting men walk all over her. The man on the book, why, he could be anyone. He could be the man around the next corner, someone she'd never even met yet, who would turn out to be rugged and hot and clever and funny and just a little devilish.

Just like Goat, the little voice in her mind whispered.

Not, she thought fiercely as she gazed down at Mr. Yukon— who was assuredly *not* Goat—and imagined how bear fur might feel on her behind as he rolled her on her back in order to take her to delicious new sensual heights.

And plowed her cart into a display stand of Windex Crystal Rain.

"Stella Hardesty, is that you?" a deep voice bellowed from down the aisle as the plastic bottles tipped and wobbled on their cardboard shelves. Stella looked up to see Big Johnson Brodersen rushing toward her just as the first bottle crashed to the ground.

Then things went a little slow-mo as BJ and Stella both attempted to forestall a Windex disaster and ended up crashing into each other and sending the display toppling over, Stella tripping on one of the bottles and causing it to burst and puddle on the floor. She scrambled to stay on her feet, but in the end there was nothing to do but clutch a handful of BJ's faded denim shirt and hold on for dear life as she fell.

BJ's generous frame softened the impact, and she found herself sprawled on his burly and surprisingly comfortable chest before they managed to disentangle themselves from each other and the litter of bottles and shelves.

"Sorry I wasn't quick enough," BJ said, getting to his feet and offering a hand. "I saw you wasn't lookin' where you was going—got your mind on something?"

Stella put her hand in BJ's and allowed herself to be helped up. "Nothing important." She gave him a big smile as she straightened her top and dusted herself off. "What are you shopping for?"

"Pickin' up a curtain rod. Doing a little fixin' up at the bar. Fact, you were on my list of people to call. You think you could find me someone might want to sew up some curtains? Nothin' fancy, I just got so sick of lookin' at them plaid things, I think they been there since they built the place."

Stella didn't doubt that was true. BJ's Bar was a homely place, a tavern favored by folks who liked to do their drinkin' and carryin' on in an austere environment, without any frippery or frills. You could get Bud or Miller or Michelob on tap, your basic well drinks—if someone ordered a Tequila Sunset or a White Russian, a riot would probably break out.

Stella found herself at BJ's on business from time to time, hunting down some ne'er-do-well or other who'd been abusing his relationship with a loved one. Over time, she'd become friendly with BJ himself. He was a good-sized, powerful man with scarred-up knuckles and a brush cut flecked with silver. He'd flirted with her a time or two, and while Stella had never followed that trail to see where it led, she snuck a glance at the man on the cover of the Yukon book and thought that he did, in fact, resemble BJ a little, if BJ were a bit more rugged and narrower and illuminated by the magical glow of a northern sun.

BJ had taken hold of her shopping cart and looked ready to steer it wherever he was told. Unlike that stubborn Goat, who did not strike Stella as the sort of man you could drag around on a shopping trip. Not to mention the fact that she couldn't exactly see Goat leaping to her aid when she was about to collide with cleaning products—he was more likely to stand back and laugh his ass off.

Suddenly an old-fashioned kind of gentleman didn't seem like the worst thing in the world.

"I might could find you someone," Stella said. "Chrissy's probably looking to make a little extra cash. Here, let me help you with your rod."

Then there was a long and horrifying moment when Stella realized what she had said. She could feel her face turning all kinds of pink as BJ suddenly got something stuck in his throat that seemed to require a fair amount of coughing to settle down. Stella grabbed the front of the cart and dragged it—and BJ, who was hanging on to the handle—to Home Fashions. By the time she grabbed the first rod she saw and thrust it into the cart, BJ had mostly recovered.

"Do you need anything else?" Stella asked with as much dignity as she could muster.

"Nope, that's it for today. I'm a man of simple needs," BJ said, wheeling the cart gallantly out of her way so Stella could precede him down the aisle. As she headed for the front of the store, Stella dug in her purse for a mint and popped it in her mouth and just generally appreciated BJ's nice manners.

"Ooh, you fixin' that chili cream cheese dip?" the checker asked, running her groceries over the scanner. "Havin' a party, are you?"

"I guess I am, even though I was the last to know," Stella said. "My daughter's done invited half the town already. Um, BJ, I'd sure be pleased if you could stop by."

"I'd like that," BJ said, helping pile her purchases on the checkout conveyor. An appealing flush stole over his cheeks. "What can I bring?"

"Not a thing. Once I get going, I'm usually good for quite a spread."

By the time Stella realized what she'd said, BJ was well on his way to another coughing fit.

Chapter Twenty-one

The house smelled strongly of chemicals mixed with something fruity, and the kitchen sink was tinged a faint green, but any other evidence of Noelle's beauty projects had been cleaned up and the girls were gone. Stella put the groceries away and put the frozen chili in a pot on the stove to start thawing, and then she spotted a note on the table.

Gone shopping for the party, it read in Noelle's loopy scrawl. *Will get beverages etc. Be home soon to help with dinner. Love you!*

It looked like the girl had done a little party prep on her own. The house was picked up and dusted and vacuumed, and the dining room chairs had been dragged into the living room for extra seating. Plates were stacked on the kitchen table, buffet style, and Noelle had wrapped silverware up festively in paper napkins and tied them with snips of silver ribbon and stacked them in a basket. Plastic cups were arranged in neat rows.

Things appeared to be under control. Stella glanced at the kitchen clock—barely two.

Plenty of time for one more errand.

She made a quick call to Chrissy and asked her to look something up for her. By the time she put the groceries away, the girl called back.

"That was no kind of challenge," she said, sounding miffed.

"Well, I pay you the same either way," Stella said. "Might as well enjoy your leisure."

Chrissy snorted. "Leisure? Tater and Evvie got into Mom's closet and unwrapped the boxes she was fixin' to send to the boys overseas with her church group. She got a hell of a deal on these NFL belt buckles on Overstock with the Rams logo—I tried to tell her, ain't nobody backin' the Rams these days, but they were dirt cheap so she bought 'em out. She and Aunt Busty boxed 'em all up the other night while they was drinkin' that nasty port someone brought, and it didn't look like much, I got to say—only now it's a hell of a mess and we got to get them all wrapped back up. Dad said just ship 'em out like that, and Mom pretty much told him he could go drag his communist ass out on the driveway and sleep there if he didn't want to get into the patriotic spirit and support the armed services. And now they're all bickering, and guess who's in charge?"

"You," Stella guessed.

"Yeah, as if I don't have enough to do with these lamb costumes for the twins for the Easter play. Do you have any *idea* how hard it is to sew on that fake fur? I probably won't even get to go over to the U-Pub tonight. Why, it's been weeks since I had any of that kind a fun." She sighed audibly over the phone. "Hippity Hop, my ass."

"All righty, then," Stella said, and hung up hastily. Maybe it was better to do the afternoon's outing solo, she thought as she headed back across town.

As she rounded the corner onto Salty Mingus's street, he

came barreling toward her in his truck. He didn't notice her, since he was busy checking out his hair in the rearview mirror. He was going at a good clip, but Stella managed a neat little U-turn and followed half a block behind.

He didn't go far, as it turned out, only to the strip mall by the Home Depot that housed a Baskin-Robbins as well as DumBelle's gym. Salty fussed with his gel-slicked hair the whole way, trying to get it to camouflage his bald spot was Stella's guess. She was surprised at his choice: there were two gyms in town, and this one tended to be favored by ladies. It featured pastel walls and carpet and a variety of equipment gathered in a friendly circle with peppy music playing so you could chat or shake your booty in a sassy fashion while you did your squats or lat presses.

Salty stepped out of the car carrying a tidy navy gym bag, but Stella was ready for him, having inserted herself between his car and the gym.

"Well, hey, Salty," she said. "Imagine meeting you here. Going to take one a them Pilates classes?"

He swallowed. "No, I just, uh. Your assistant ain't along with you, is she?"

"She was busy today. How's the project going?"

Salty shifted from one foot to the other, looking like he had to pee bad. "Fine, I guess. I mean I ain't done a whole lot more since the other day."

"Oh, you mean when we visited."

"Uh . . ."

"Back when you were telling all those tales. About Priss's *landscape* business."

Salty's eyes widened and he tried to step around her, but Stella nimbly blocked him. "Not so fast. I think we should have us a talk. I was hoping to get some construction tips from you. I hear it can be a bitch to get a permit for one of those sheds like you're putting in. I'd hate to get halfway in and then . . . bam, some concerned neighbor calls it in and shuts me down."

Salty's ruddy face took on a deeper shade. "That shed's none of your business, Stella."

"I'm not saying it is. Come on, take a walk with me, we can change the subject, I promise."

Salty wavered, looking longingly at the gym, through whose large picture window a variety of ladies in coordinated exercise outfits were lunging and hopping to some unheard beat.

"Ten minutes," he finally said.

They set out down the street, turning into a neighborhood of neat brick bungalows. "So you weren't completely honest with me," Stella scolded. "That wasn't any kind of *landscaping* you were doing up in Kansas City with our girl Priss."

"What'd she tell you?"

Stella noted with interest the sudden change in Salty's composure. The flush in his skin took on more of a blush-type quality.

"She, ah, has fond memories of your skills," Stella ad-libbed. "You were one of her favorite, um, gentlemen employees."

Salty didn't say anything for a few moments. Stella didn't push him, but she managed a few covert glances and watched the storm clouds build up in his expression.

"I *ought* to be her favorite," Salty fumed. "I was her *first*. The whole escort service? It was my idea, you know."

"Really? She didn't mention that." Stella didn't bother pointing out that Priss hadn't, in fact, confided any details at all about the call boy operation.

"Hell yes. I used to go up there and visit her while she was in business school, did she tell you that part? Guess those MBA-type guys didn't have what it took in the sack to keep her happy. She always was a, you know, passionate one."

"So you'd go up there for booty calls? She'd go a few rounds with you and send you home so she could get back to her studies?"

"It wasn't like that," Salty protested, but Stella could tell by his dismay that it was, indeed, exactly like that. "I could of gone to school up there myself. We used to talk about what she was studying, her classes, all that shit. I got an entrepreneurial mind, she always said. Only I got, you know, my roots here."

"Uh-huh. So why'd you move there?"

"We both wanted it," Salty said a little defensively. "To be together more. I was working construction down here, good money and all, but nothing that I was really, you know, *passionate* about. And things were getting serious between us."

Salty didn't look at her when he said that, and Stella figured there was more than a little wishful thinking going on. She murmured a gentle *mm-hmm* to keep him going.

"She did one a them things, from Harvard? Them case studies where you look at where some company screwed up and figure out what they should of done instead? And she had one on this escort service, a legit one, and we got to talking about how you could add just a few massage services on the side and there you go, profits through the roof. There's like hardly any setup costs."

"I don't know," Stella said dubiously. "I'm not sure if I'd call a full menu of sensual delights 'a little on the side,' Salty."

"But that wasn't how it was supposed to be," he said, getting frustrated. "My thing was, give 'em a *little* romance. A little kissing, hugging, maybe—*maybe*—just a friendly grope or two. Make it about the fantasy, you know? That's what women really want—just the *illusion* of romance."

186

"You really believe that, Salty?" Stella demanded, surprised. It sure as hell wasn't true for her—a bouquet and a Whitman's Sampler sure as shit wasn't about to scratch the itch she got when she thought about Goat.

"Yeah, it's scientific, women are just *wired* different, they wouldn't even *have* sex if it wasn't for procreating the species and all. It ain't their fault."

"Mmm," Stella said, aiming to keep her tone neutral. Violent disagreement had no place in a stealth interrogation.

"Anyway, we were building a client base, we got a few leads among the business women community, lonely-hearts gals who wanted to spend time with a good-looking guy who *understands* them." He kicked at a flattened can, sending it skittering down along a curb. Overhead, the sky had darkened to a gloomy slate. "If she would a just stuck with my thing, we would of had it made."

"Let me guess. Business wasn't picking up at a pace she could live with."

"Hah. She could be—well, you know. Priss always wanted everything all at once. And then *he* came along."

"Who?"

"*Walsingham.*" Salty practically spat the name out. "Addney fucking Walsingham, this queer-boy fairy she met at school."

"Another business school student?"

"No, a goddamn hippie ex-instructor or some shit. The only thing he had on me was he was *old.*"

"I'm lost."

"Priss and me, we're young, and believe it or not, that limits the client base. I mean how else do you explain the resistance we were meeting up with? And Addney, he's like forty, Priss gets it in his head they'll tell people he's *fifty,* you know, go after women in their fifties?"

"Oh, I think I see where you're going," Stella said. Not bad, really. Pretty darn brilliant. "You tell folks he's really well preserved, and the ladies believe they're with a man their age. Was he good looking?"

"I'm a *guy*," Salty said with a wounded tone. "How the hell should I know?"

Right. *Excellent* looking. "So the long and short is, Addney starts pulling in all kinds of business and suddenly Priss isn't so hot to have you around. Is that right?"

Salty didn't say anything, but his chin sank down and his lower lip jutted as they strolled along. "She asked me to move out," he finally muttered. "Told me Addney was moving in. Gave me twenty-four hours."

"Ouch. That's kind of harsh."

"She can have him. She can have that old wrinkle-dick poseur professor, for all the good he'll do her. I'm better off—I'm taking good care of myself these days, you know, valuing myself for who I am. I got a *family*—what's she got?"

"She, uh, appears to be living alone these days," Stella said gently, watching for a reaction. Could Salty be carrying around enough hurt to still have a grudge against his replacement? Could the man who died—Keller—have been the same person as this Walsingham?

But if Salty wanted to kill Keller, why would he wait all this time? "You left Kansas City three years ago. Have you kept in touch with Priss the whole time?"

Salty stared at the ground and didn't answer.

"Come on—construction permits aside, all I'm trying to do is find her," Stella prodded. "I've got nothing against you unless you get in my way."

"What do you care, anyway?" Salty said. "I don't guess this is in your usual area of expertise."

Like nearly every citizen of Sawyer County who lived in the murky depths below upright citizenship, Salty appeared to know a thing or two about her reputation.

"Favor for a friend. So what gives? You talked to her?"

"We talk. Sometimes."

"You call her."

"Mmm-hmm."

"You go up for quickies."

"No!"

Stella tried to gauge whether his adamant denial was genuine or not, and couldn't decide.

"Okay . . . she doesn't call you back."

"She does. Sometimes. Just to *talk*. Priss is sensitive—she needs a man who respects her, who's willing to go slow, listen, like that."

Doubt it, Stella thought. Oh, some men—when it came to love, their feelings were like tender little shoots under the snows of spring, so vulnerable. It certainly beat the angry, cocky, beat-the-crap-out-of-you brand of boyfriend, but Stella herself couldn't imagine putting up with a mooning sap like Salty.

Man up, she wanted to say.

She didn't think Salty had killed anyone. But she'd be the first to admit that some of the darker reaches of humanity were way beyond her understanding. There was just no telling what a man was capable of when he'd had his feelings hurt.

"When's the last you talked to her?"

"New Year's Eve," Salty said a little too quickly. "Got her on her cell. Called her from a bar—she thought I was someone else."

"And after that?"

"I've, you know, tried a few times."

"Leave messages?"

Salty shrugged. "I don't know, maybe one or two. I don't remember."

They had circled around through the neighborhood and were back at the strip mall. A few icy flakes blasted out of the sky with force, stinging Stella's cheeks.

"Well, I guess I shouldn't keep you from your workout," she said. She was beginning to think she understood why he came to this gym. Salty was the kind of guy who wanted to be admired—*needed*—by a woman. But at the same time, he wasn't strong himself, but he was attracted to strong—*bossy,* even—women.

He probably came here and watched attractive women working out, maybe chatted a little, maybe offered to spot them or adjust the machines for them. Maybe most of them didn't give him a second look, with his neat, pressed gym clothes and his bland combed-over hair and his hopeful expression.

Maybe he was even looking for Priss's replacement, another woman to fulfill his fantasies of helping out, of being useful. Doraleigh, Stella was willing to bet, didn't fit that bill. She seemed like she'd be great at the ordering-around part—not so good with the grateful part. Priss—no matter how calculating she was, no matter how ice-cold her heart—well, she was the kind of woman who'd pour on exactly the right amount of whatever it took to grease a fella's wheels: she'd simper, and sigh, and squeal with fake gratitude—and Salty would have been putty in her hands.

And the thing about that kind of a man was that the entire rest of the world could be standing around on the sidelines hollering at him to grow a pair, to stop being her poodle, and he'd just keep on defending her. Because once that type of man got himself smitten, it didn't get undone easy.

"Look," Salty said, twisting the handle of the gym bag in

his hands nervously. "I heard what everybody else did—that Liman disappeared while Priss was visiting. Tell you what I think."

"Okay."

"I think she came down to visit and maybe gave him a little bit of cash. Like, you know, maybe it was his birthday? And they got to drinkin' and all, and she didn't want to drive her car, so she called up and got a friend to come get her. On account of Liman would have got ugly with her, 'cause no matter what she did, it was never enough for them. Priss used to tell me about it, how her family was always hounding her for cash."

Stella found that hard to believe, since she'd often seen elderly Mrs. Porter in the FreshWay with her food stamps, still wearing that old housecoat. Oh, she and Liman may have asked Priss for money—but Stella would bet the answer was a big fat no.

"Wait," she said. "Back up. You're saying she would have called a friend from Kansas City to drive down and get her, over an hour each way, and she was going to just leave an eighty-thousand-dollar automobile sitting on the driveway?"

"Well, she would of come back for it." The effort of keeping his preposterous scenario going was causing Salty to bounce anxiously on his toes. "She didn't know you all were going to have it towed. And now she's got to figure out how to get it without the sheriff and them going up to the city and poking around her business. You know, the escort business—now that Walsingham went and took it down to the gutter level with all that illegal shit."

So Salty—and presumably the rest of the town—had no idea what had been found in the trunk. Stella was relieved that news of the blood evidence hadn't leaked.

"Go on," she said skeptically.

"So when Liman figures out she's leaving, he gets all pissed off, she won't give him any more money, right? And maybe he calls the cops, you know, to make out like it was some sort of abuse thing, his sister whaling on him or some such. Only her friend showed up and they left. And then I bet he got it in his head to cut his losses. Take the cash she already done give him, and left. He's probably on a bender now, down at the lake."

"Nice theory," Stella said after a few moments, once she'd processed all the layers of idiocy. "Only how do you suppose he went? Seein' as his vehicles are all still on the property."

Salty shrugged. "He could have had a friend come. Maybe a lady friend. You know, call her up—hey, honey, I got ahold of some cash, pack you a nice dress and we'll have us a weekend."

Stella resisted shaking her head in dismay at the level of dumbassery concentrated in Salty Mingus. Or maybe it was just the sheer power of lovelornity. Never mind that Liman was known to have no special lady friends. Or, for that matter, any friends.

"So both Priss and her brother, in your view, are off somewhere with friends, not bothering to check on their personal property or address the complaints made against them or check in with the authorities who have opened a case against them or, you know, return for a fresh change of underwear," Stella said. "And you're not concerned. That about it?"

A storm cloud to rival the ones scudding across the late afternoon sky passed over Salty's expression. "Uh. Yeah."

"Well, all right, then. You have a nice workout. I guess I'll be getting back home."

She made for her Jeep, holding her coat tight to her neck against the biting wind.

"Stella," Salty called, and Stella turned to see him standing rooted to the spot, one hand raised in a half wave.

"Yeah?"

"When you *do* find Priss . . . I was thinkin' . . . maybe you could tell her to give me a call?"

"Sure," Stella muttered. Like that was going to happen.

Chapter Twenty-two

On the drive home, Stella cranked up Steve Earle's "I Thought You Should Know" and thought about love.

I won't tell you I don't need you tonight
I won't pretend I ain't burning inside

Salty Mingus was a guy who lost the woman of his dreams to another man, and who did he blame? Himself? His poor conversational skills, his lack of ambition? No. It was the *other guy* at fault, for showing up and making a play for her—and it was Priss, for falling for him. Meanwhile, Salty was wining and dining and romancing, in theory, a whole string of ladies for profit, never stopping to consider how Priss might have felt about *that*. Sure, he claimed it was all part of his business model, but he was still the one drinking the champagne and encouraging all those heaving bosoms while Priss had only her spreadsheets for company.

A woman who got tossed out of her lover's life tended to have a different reaction. *Where did I go wrong?* she might wonder, and then answer herself with a whole list of failures. *Not pretty enough. Not entertaining enough. Not a good enough cook, a neat enough housekeeper, a sexy enough lover, a clever enough conversationalist.* Heck, give a woman enough time, and she could probably write you a whole catalog of her shortcomings.

That was clearly an area where men had gotten the better deal, evolution-wise. How had that happened? Stella wondered. Had some long-ago lady ape caught her mate banging the cute primate from the cave down the road and blamed herself? And how could that have possibly been an evolutionary advantage?

For the children, of course, she realized. Men got to get crazy, get stupid, get laid with abandon. Women got to get the kids picked up from school and get dinner on the table.

Stella let out a long, indulgent sigh and hummed along with Earle.

Speaking of children, what would Ollie have made of their daughter's new romantic direction? The thought brought an unexpected smile to Stella's face. Oh, that would have been rich, Ollie Hardesty contemplating having fathered a gay child. That would have thrown him for a hell of a loop. It almost would have been worth letting him live a few extra years to see the look on his face when Noelle made her announcement.

Almost. But not quite.

Who would have expected BJ Brodersen to be such a *punctual* man?

Stella was wearing only her Spanx Slim Cognito bodysuit when he came to the door, but at least Noelle had almost finished her hair and makeup. The girl had been a virtual whirlwind, fussing with the food and setting up an impromptu tabletop bar with a kettle of ice and a bowl full of lemons and limes sliced into wedges and a vase of pink and white carnations, which barely left room for the impressive variety of liquor bottles arrayed in a half circle.

"That must of set you back," Stella marveled.

"Well, like I said, I got that money put aside."

"Your rainy-day fund," Stella pointed out. After Ollie's death, she had purchased herself a few hours' time with a financial advisor, who had laid out a self-education plan that left Stella keenly aware of the paltriness of her resources but also better suited than most to manage them. "This don't strike me as a rainy day."

Noelle had just tutted and ignored her. Oh, the wild irresponsibility of youth, Stella thought, but she kept her mouth shut. Sometimes a mother's best strategy was silence.

When the doorbell rang, and Noelle peeked out and confirmed that it was BJ, Stella bolted for her bedroom, yelling at her daughter to keep him entertained. She shrugged into her old leopard-print jersey wrap dress and took a second to enjoy the fact that it fit far less snugly than it had a year ago, thanks to her stepped-up workouts and physical therapy. She swiped on her Avon Anew Youth-Awakening lipstick in Regal Red—a shade she reserved for special occasions. Noelle had put a good half hour into making up her eyes until they practically smoldered. All that was left to do was to pick up all the outfits she'd tried on and abandoned and shove them into the closet and shut the door. The she fluffed the pillows and straightened the towels in the bathroom.

Because you just never knew.

Out in the living room, Noelle was perched on the edge of a chair chattering away while BJ listened with a rather glazed look in his eyes.

"Them oxidative dye molecules are all well and good," Noelle was saying, "but if you don't follow up with a sulfate-free surfactant, why, you're just screwed."

When BJ noticed Stella, he leapt to his feet and grinned wide. "Ain't you a vision," he said, letting his gaze travel up and down her clingy dress.

"Thank you," Stella said modestly, jutting one foot in front of the other and setting her shoulders back to better show off her curves. "You're the first to arrive! Has Noelle offered to fix you a drink?"

"She, um, yeah," BJ said, rattling the ice in his plastic cup with a look of consternation on his face. "She's got a generous pour on her."

"Lemme taste that," Stella exclaimed, taking the drink from him and slurping the edge. Tasted like pure rum, though there was a faint orange tint and a few shreds of pulp floating in the cup among the ice. "Lordy, Noelle, you like to pickle the man?"

Noelle pouted. "I don't know how to make a drink, Mama. I don't hardly ever have anything but a beer myself."

"Well, sugar, you could of asked for help."

"It's no problem at all," BJ said. "It's tasty. Maybe I'll just add a little bit of orange juice—"

The doorbell rang again, and Noelle went to answer it. Stella grabbed BJ's cup and carried it to the sink, where she poured most of it down the drain. "She means well," she said, topping off the concoction with juice.

"She's a very nice young lady," BJ said, and Stella felt her insides warm up a few degrees. Now *that* was something they ought to teach in man school—compliment a woman's children, and you're halfway there.

"Oh my *God*!" Noelle shrieked as a trio of women came through the door, brushing snow out of their hair.

Stella hurried over to greet her daughter's guests and see

what the matter was. Noelle staggered back a couple of feet and clamped her hands to her face in horror, as though the three young ladies had fangs and claws and flames shooting out of their nostrils.

"What have you *done*," she wailed. She opened her eyes and stroked the ponytailed hair of the closest one almost tenderly, and only then did Stella realize it was Joy. Her brown hair had been dyed a pale blond with chestnut lowlights, which made her look almost Nordic, but other than that, she looked about like she had the other night, with her face scrubbed free of makeup and a shapeless fleece sweater over a turtleneck and jeans. On her feet were heavy black work boots, which she rubbed carefully on the rug by the door.

"Do you want me to take these off, Mrs. Hardesty?" she asked politely, ignoring Noelle. "I'd hate to drag in snow on your nice floors."

"No, no, dear, that's just fine. Please, let me get your coats. *Noelle,*" she added pointedly, "help me take your guests' things."

To her credit, her daughter snapped to attention then, though her face bore a stricken, wounded look. "This here's Pamela," she said, indicating a tall brunette. "I met her at Sidewinders, and I'm sorry, I don't remember your name—"

"Maxine Groat," the shorter girl said, shaking Stella's hand. "From up to Independence. It's nice to meet you."

"And this is my mother, Stella Hardesty, and this is Mama's friend Mr. Brodersen."

There were handshakes all around, and Stella managed to wrest the coats and scarves and mittens away from the little group. "BJ, I wonder if you would do the honors," she said, pointing to the array of bottles with her chin, "since you're the professional and all. Noelle and I won't be but a minute."

In the guest room, they laid the coats out on the bed and Stella shut the door. "Noelle Elizabeth Collier Hardesty," she scolded, "I'm delighted to have your friends in my home, and you know I am fond of Joy, but what in the name of Sam was that about? Why, you barely said hello to your guests!"

Stella was dimly aware that she sounded just like her own mother, who would have died of shame before she allowed an error of manners to be committed in her home. And Stella was also aware that she was being a terrible hypocrite.

Pat Hardesty had kept an immaculate home, dusted every Tuesday, never spoke ill of a soul, and, Stella was willing to bet, had never uttered anything more coarse than an occasional "oh, durn." Stella herself had managed to stay civilized and polite and soft-spoken—until Ollie was gone. Then all those years of frustration and irritation came bubbling up and gave voice to a whole new person who, she had been startled to discover, may well have been her authentic self all along. And, as it turned out, her authentic self was not terribly fettered by manners.

Still, Noelle managed to look suitably chastised. "I'm sorry, Mama. It was just such a shock, seeing what Joy done to herself—especially after all that work."

"What do you mean?"

"Well—" Noelle gestured helplessly. "Her *hair*? I did all these soft waves that took *forever.* The color's *perfect,* Mama, and she's got it up in that, that *thing*? That ain't even a proper elastic, Mama, it's just some old rubber band, she's gonna have *breakage*—"

Noelle looked like she might cry, and Stella's heart went out to her. "But with it up like that, you can see her pretty face—"

"Oh, and that. I mean, I did *evening* eyes on her, I rimmed them in *navy* and used three shades of shadow. It took fucking forever! And Mama, I loaned her my DKNY sweater, the

199

off-the-shoulder one? And my BCBG platform boots? I mean she looked so incredibly hot. I just don't know why she'd want to go and, and, *do* that."

"Oh, sweetheart." Stella held out her arms, and Noelle came into them and snuffled into her mother's shoulder and let herself be hugged. "I'm sure that's all true, and you know I love it when you do makeovers on me. I always feel so, so pretty and special. But not everyone's like that. Some folks really just don't care to go experimenting with their outsides. For whatever reason, they get into a rut and that's where they're comfortable and, really, they're not going to thank you for trying to change it. Now, it don't mean they don't like you," she said reassuringly as she rubbed small circles on her daughter's back. "Or that you can't be friends, even special friends. Only, you got to accept them for who they are, not who you want them to be."

Noelle hiccupped gently and drew back, wiping her eyes carefully so as not to smudge her own luminous violet eyeliner. "I know you're right, Mama. Only I'm just trying so hard to find the things that Joy and I have in common, that we can do together, you know? Since we're in a relationship and all, and I'm trying to honor that, I really am. I want us both to be givers, but I just don't know how to give what she needs."

"Mmm," Stella said. "Well, now, let's get back to your party."

What she wanted to say was that if you had to try that hard, it might not be the perfect match, but that was the sort of motherly wisdom that was almost never welcome.

BJ was standing behind the table looking just as comfortable as he did behind his own bar, but he had a big, pleased smile on his face and didn't appear to mind being on duty one bit. Several more guests had arrived, mostly women, and he was busy mixing drinks.

"These little gals remind me of my nieces," he confided

when Stella went over to pour her own generous splash of Johnnie. "Don't none of them got boyfriends, though? Them two there, hate to say it, but I believe they might just be battin' for the other team, you know what I'm saying?"

He gestured with an unopened bottle of Miller High Life at the lone male guests, who were scrutinizing the contents of Stella's china hutch, one of the few pieces of furniture she'd owned ever since getting married.

"Well," Stella hedged.

Here we go, she thought. This was what she had to look forward to, a life of educating all the local gay-bashers. There was another option, especially since Noelle was still in the tentative stage and had not, as far as Stella was aware, actually gotten herself firmly immersed in life as a gay woman—she could just say nothing, let BJ draw his own conclusions. The party guests seemed like a nice-mannered bunch, and with the exception of Joy, no different looks-wise from any other gathering of young people that Stella could tell. Well, there was a gal who had shaved the entire back half of her head, but the front was long and shaggy, and she had on some pretty dangle crystal earrings that Stella herself wouldn't have minded borrowing. And lots of the girls had tattoos. But wasn't that pretty much everywhere, nowadays?

So really, unless Noelle made a big thing of it, Stella could easily adopt a "don't ask, don't tell" policy in her own home. Let people wonder. It wasn't any of their business, after all. And if they did get a notion, pick up on some undercurrent of wanton same-sex pheromones flying around or something, well, weren't there plenty of flaws that Stella overlooked in her own friends all the time? Did she make mention of the crumbs that tended to get caught in Jelloman Nunn's beard? Did she let on that she noticed when Irene Dorsey got her eyebrows drawn on crooked? Did she fuss when Roseann Lu parked her car in Stella's favorite parking space in front of the store?

Of course not. In a small town, you overlooked things like that. You forgave people their minor sins, and hoped they did the same for you.

Only . . .

There was something very wrong with Stella's internal argument. She bolted the Johnnie back in one gulp and experimented with telling herself she'd examine her justification later. Tomorrow, for sure, when she could really think it through.

But that didn't fly with the little voice in her head.

Don't need to think it through, it chastised her. *Ain't nothin' to overlook. 'Cause it ain't no sin to be gay.*

Stella closed her eyes and tried to savor the burn going down her throat, the lovely spreading heat in her gut.

"Oh, hell," she muttered.

"Excuse me?" BJ gently took the empty cup from her and tipped her chin up with his fingers. "Are you all right, Stella?"

The sensation of his callused, rough thumb against the sensitive skin under her jaw was lovely. It went along extra-nicely with the whiskey puddle that was snaking along her nerve endings, and she couldn't much stop herself from leaning into his touch. BJ didn't seem to mind. He stepped a little closer and allowed his hand to close in on the nape of her neck, where he started doing something wonderful and vaguely wicked, his fingertips dipping down the collar of her top, grazing her hairline.

"BJ," Stella sighed, letting her eyes flutter closed, "I just got to tell you something . . .'fore we go any further. . . . I hope you're gonna keep an open mind here and all. . . . What it is, is just . . ."

There was a knocking at the front door, and somewhere through the haze of Stella's buzz and the lovely sensual delights of BJ's ministrations, she heard the happy chatter of her daughter and her guests, the laughter and clinking of glasses, and she gave herself one last chance to take the easy way out—

—and then, because she was Stella Hardesty, and she didn't take the easy way for anyone, she laid her forehead against BJ's overdeveloped pectorals and asked him what was, really, the only thing she could ask:

"What do you think of lesbians, anyway?"

But when she opened her eyes to find out the answer, she looked over BJ's shoulder right into the surprised face of Sheriff Goat Jones.

Chapter Twenty-three

After that, it got a little confusing. BJ made a sort of a hiccupping sound that launched into a coughing fit, bad enough that Stella felt obliged to give him a powerful wallop on the back. Goat, meanwhile, wavered in the doorway, half in and half out, while as if on cue, the music started thumping in earnest at high decibels, and a minor fracas broke out over the desserts.

"I *said* I didn't want no jam bar, Noelle," Joy exclaimed, and Stella turned to see her daughter holding cookies in both hands as though she intended to attack Joy with them. Her face was screwed up in a powerful fury.

"Might as well have a few," her daughter shot back. "Never mind they're messy. Hell, have some a this chocolate frosting and some spinach dip and a Jell-O shooter while you're at it. Don't matter none if it gets on you 'cause you're just wearing a old *rag* again anyway."

"You're mad I didn't wear that skirt you loaned me," Joy said with exaggerated patience, as though she were talking to a toddler. "I understand. And I really did plan on it. Only it was just so cold out and all, when I got out in the driveway I figured this wasn't the night to be doing any kind of fashion experiments, not when that wind was rushing up into my privates."

"You got to *suffer* for beauty," Noelle snapped. "That's, like, the basis of my whole career. It's my *passion*."

"Now, when you say lesbians," BJ said, evidently uninterested in the fight brewing a few feet away. "Are you talking, like, movie lesbians? Or regular ones?"

Stella bristled. "Why, would it make a difference?"

BJ seemed to pick up on her tone because he shook his head vigorously. "I've got no problems with it," he said. "Lovin's lovin', you know?"

"Excuse me," Stella said, giving BJ her best hostess smile and making for the door. Behind her, Noelle lit into Joy for scrubbing off the makeup she'd worked so hard to apply. The rest of the guests appeared to be trying to drown out the argument by singing along to the music and dancing in the little clearing Noelle had made in the living room.

"Goat," Stella said as matter-of-factly as she could manage. "Imagine, coming here on a night such as this. What an honor. I would think you'd be positively swamped, what with the demands of the Porter case."

Goat looked like he had half a mind to pick up the salami one of the guests had brought, and hit her over the head with it. Instead, he gritted his teeth and pushed past her to the bar.

"Don't mind me," he said to no one in particular. "I'll just fix me a little something, seeing as everyone else seems to have got a head start on me. Brodersen, don't you have a business to run somewhere?"

BJ bristled and pulled himself up to his full height, which was still an inch or two shy of Goat on a slouchy day. "I'm an invited guest," he said stiffly. *Unlike some people,* his tone implied.

"You didn't tell me this was going to be such a party," Goat said, ignoring the jab. His blue eyes went deep indigo with anger, and he leaned far into her personal space, putting his face inches from hers and glaring. "Good thing I happened to be in the neighborhood."

"It's just casual," Stella said. "Noelle and some of her friends. I didn't have time to call a lot of folks."

"And yet, there's BJ," Goat pointed out, stepping in between Stella and BJ as though the man didn't even exist. "Funny how he knew exactly where the party was tonight."

"It's my *calling*," Noelle's shrill voice cut through the conversations all around. "Making people look hot is just what I do. It's, like, a part of my *soul*. So when you do, do, do *this*—"

She gestured almost helplessly at Joy, taking in the canvas pants, the plaid overshirt.

"—and then your face!"

Joy frowned and paused with a Ritz cracker halfway to her lips. "If you find it so hard to look at my face when it ain't got anything on it, well, maybe you aren't as into me as you think you are."

Noelle dabbed at her eyes. "Do you always have to be draggin' out our personal little spats into public?" she stage-whispered, though no one but Stella appeared to be terribly interested. Someone had let Roxy in from the yard, and several of the guests were cooing over her. Roxy was submitting to their attentions amiably enough, but Stella knew the plump mutt was looking for a chance to snag the corner of a Fritos bag that sat perilously close to the edge of a TV tray.

Stella felt tugged in three different directions. Her hostess duties were overwhelming enough—corralling the dog, overseeing the snacks and drinks, all while keeping her hot evening look going. The face-off brewing between her suitors, which would probably be quite exciting if one of them wasn't capable of tossing her in the clink if she pissed him off. And the romantic travails of her only child, which somehow had gotten condensed into one ill-advised and stormy new relationship.

Add to that the very real threat that photos of her were about to surface somewhere in the murky underlayer of society, photos in which she was reducing a gibbering, bound man to a pile of weeping, bleeding, remorseful man-flesh.

When those photos came to the surface—and Stella was very much convinced that, with their owner out of commission and on the run, or possibly even kidnapped or dead, whoever's hands they fell into would find some advantage to making them public—Stella's options were going to close in on her fast. Her worst problem would go from choosing between two hot-for-her hunks to choosing which bunk she'd be using in her jail cell.

It was all too much pressure, especially when Roxy made a well-timed leap for freedom, breaking free of her admirers and launching herself into the TV tray with such force that it toppled over, so that dog and tray landed in a tangle of snacks and collapsible aluminum tubing and scrambling paws. Noelle surveyed the wreckage with a horrified expression before bursting into the tears that had been threatening, and bolted down the hall, slamming her bedroom door behind her.

"Yo, Stella," a familiar voice hailed from the living room. Stella whirled around to see Todd Groffe standing in a pair of frayed shorts that hung off his skinny butt, his mother's gardening clogs, and a puffy down coat, shaking snow out of his hair.

"What, what, *what*?" she demanded. "And where the hell are your *clothes*? Did you happen to notice that we are having a winter *storm*?"

Todd shrugged. "I'm not cold. I was skatin'."

Todd practiced his skateboard tricks all year long, flipping and careening up and down the street no matter what the weather, despite his mother's constant threats to back her car over the board or light a match to it. Following through on her threats often fell far down on Sherilee's to-do list, deprioritized by little things like going to work and cooking dinner.

"Your mom know you're here?" Stella asked, softening her tone only slightly.

Todd shrugged, but his shoulders slumped a little more than usual, and his bored frown was a bit more forlorn. "Yeah. I told her you was gonna help me with my math."

Stella looked at him closely; a little cloud of dejection seemed to have settled on his bony frame and angelic features, under his mop of badly cut hair. "That so."

She took a deep breath and looked around the room. The music had gotten even louder, if such a thing was possible, some girl singer belting out how she wanted to give someone "a taste of the sugar below my waist," and a couple of girls were playfully trying to drag Roxy back outside while her paws scrabbled for purchase and she clamped down on the chip bag in her jaws. Some of the other girls had climbed up on the sectional and were doing a sort of group bump and grind that was eye-poppingly suggestive, to Stella's mind, and Goat and BJ were glaring and circling each other like a pair of starved coyotes fighting over one turkey drumstick.

"Guess you better tell me about it," she said, grabbing a can of Fresca off the table and popping the top for him.

"Here?" Todd looked around in distaste. "This is just as bad as at home when the twins get loose. I cain't hear myself think. How about you and me cut out and go somewhere else?"

"Todd, this is a *party*. I can't just up and—"

"I got money," Todd said, jangling coins in the pocket of his shorts to illustrate. "I can buy us a slice. Long as you don't order a drink."

Stella took one last look around and figured the place wouldn't fall down if she left it alone for half an hour.

"Okay, Slick. Through the garage. Let's try for a clean getaway."

The Hut hadn't changed much since Stella was in high school. The pizza was still marginal, the booths were still sticky, the amber-shaded light fixtures were still grimy with years of accumulated grease, and the lighting was uniformly unflattering to everyone.

"So what's troubling you?" Stella asked after waiting for Todd to bolt down a quarter of a large pineapple, ham, and sausage pizza. She'd attempted a single piece, picking off all the pineapple, but it still tasted faintly fruity, which struck her as all wrong, so she contented herself with her beer.

Todd finished chewing and swallowed a hunk of pizza so huge that Stella figured she ought to be able to watch it go down, like those snakes that devoured entire rats at a time. Oh, to have a youthful digestive system again.

"Well," he said, and then seemed to be at an uncharacteristic loss for words. He cast his gaze at the middle of the table, where the remains of the pie were cooling in a puddle of orange grease.

"Is it grades?"

"Huh?"

No, of course it wasn't grades; Todd's were unspectacular, but only his mother seemed to find that upsetting.

"Your sisters?"

Todd scowled. "They're just the usual pain in the ass, I guess."

Stella felt a little spiral of hurt unroll in her gut. She knew what she had to ask next, but she sure didn't feel like going there. Todd's father, an unemployed pipe fitter living somewhere up near the Iowa border, had missed calling on Todd's birthday this year, and he hadn't been around in months. What with spring break coming up, the kids were bound to be wondering if he'd make one of his rare appearances. The girls were too young to care much one way or the other about the man, but Todd remembered just enough to make the wound fresh every time.

Stella sighed heavily. As usual, the women were left to clean up the mess. "Honey," she started gently, "Is it—?"

"It's that Chanelle!" Todd burst out, suddenly raking his greasy fingers through the shock of hair that hung in his face in a gesture so redolent with angst and despair that Stella's eyebrows shot up.

"Oh," she said carefully.

Well. That was a whole other brand of trouble.

Girl trouble.

Chanelle Tanaka was widely acknowledged to be the hottest girl in eighth grade, with perfectly straight silky hair and owlish eyeliner and a fetching little gap between her front teeth. Todd's crush on her went back years, but so, unfortunately, did the spell she'd apparently cast on nearly every boy at school.

"They're having this dance at school," Todd said miserably.

"And you want to ask her."

"What? *Hells* no, Stella, school dances are fuckin' lame, nobody goes."

"Uh . . . oh."

"But a bunch of kids tell their parents they're going and then instead they go over to the Arco, you know?"

Stella did know. It was a rare weekend night, any time of year, that you could drive by the Arco out on the east side of town without seeing a cluster of kids half hidden behind the car wash, the boys on skateboards, the girls in knots of two and three, hunched together like they were sharing state secrets.

"Todd," Stella said disapprovingly. "Ain't those the kids who're smoking pot and drinking vodka out of water bottles and having sex in the bathrooms and all that?"

She watched his reaction carefully and didn't miss the flicker of insecurity. Well, that never changed. The swagger that comes along with trying to hang out with the top dogs, it was a thin disguise for the staggering uncertainty underneath.

Stella knew that Todd was mostly a lone wolf among the eighth grade crowd. Part of it was that when the rest of the young hellions were out terrorizing the town, he frequently had to stay at home to help watch his sisters. Part of it was that his mother couldn't keep up with the material demands of the hip crowd. Todd's clothes came from the secondhand shop or, in flusher months, JCPenney. His haircuts were home jobs and his sneakers had to last an entire year before his mother could afford a new pair.

More than any of that, though, was the fact that Todd lacked the instincts to elevate his standing among his peers. Despite all his tough talk with her, she'd seen him a few times around other kids, and he became as shy and quiet as a blushing debutante.

Stella figured that Chanelle Tanaka barely knew who Todd was. And as much as she figured the girl was halfway to tramp city riding a river of trouble, her heart still broke a little for the boy.

"Ain't nobody having *sex* sex," he said uncertainly.

"What the hell does that mean?"

Even in the paltry restaurant light, Stella could see the boy's acne-dusted cheeks flush red with embarrassment. "Well, they're having, uh, the kind that don't count. Not the all-the-way shit."

"Whatever does that mean?"

Todd rolled his eyes so dramatically, Stella wouldn't have been surprised if they popped out of his skull and landed in the remains of his pizza. "Do I have to spell it out for you? You know, like, not . . . like one person, uh . . . you know, there's no, um, direct—"

"Todd," Stella said fiercely, "has your mother talked about this stuff with you? Prevention and safety and—"

"Jesus, Stella, it ain't nineteen-fucking-fifty. We get that shit every year in health. They spend more time making us stick our hands up condoms than we do eatin' lunch, and then we got to look at all those nasty pictures of people's parts. . . ." He gestured down around his belt buckle for emphasis.

"So I don't need to worry about you bringin' home any little Todd Juniors any time soon," Stella clarified.

"Damn it, Stella, I didn't bring you here for a damn lecture. I ain't talking about having sex with Chanelle, all I want to do is get her to *talk* to me!"

His voice had risen in frustration with each syllable, and Stella was suddenly aware of people at a few nearby tables looking over with interest.

"Hush now," she said, "let's not have the whole world in on your secrets, okay?"

Todd flushed even further and nodded.

Stella's phone, which she'd left faceup on the table so she'd be sure to hear it over the restaurant's din, started ringing. Todd reached for it, but Stella slapped his hand away and put it to her ear, jamming a finger in her other ear to try to drown out the noise.

"Hello?"

"Stella, this is Adriana Wolfort."

"Adriana!" Stella was genuinely pleased to hear the old lady's voice, though it seemed odd she'd be calling at this hour on a Monday night. A couple of years back, she'd met with the rich old lady to discuss measures to deal with her husband. It wasn't the usual case; her husband Milton's irascibility was a result of a stroke that had fried some key filter on his brain, so that he mostly sat on the couch and hollered strings of obscenities at nobody in particular all day long. Adriana, who'd never been all that fond of her husband and was very frank about having married him for his money five decades earlier, had suggested Stella could come up with some relatively painless but voice box–obliterating injury to keep the man quiet to give her a moment's peace, and Stella had been trying to get her to consider off-site care instead when Milt had obliged them both by having a second, massive stroke and pitching forward onto the carpet, dead before he hit the floor.

Adriana had wanted to pay Stella what she called a "consulting fee," but Stella had demurred. Now, given the state of her bank account, she wondered if she ought to have taken the old gal up on her offer.

"I'm desperately sorry to bother you," Adriana said breathily. She was a great fan of old movies and had adopted an oddly formal and dramatic way of speaking. "But there's a little matter here that needs your attention."

"What sort of little matter?"

"Oh, I don't want to say on the phone. Why don't you just buzz on over."

"I'm out to dinner," Stella said. "Can it wait an hour or so?"

"Oh, I certainly think not."

Stella raised her eyebrows. What kind of trouble could the widow have possibly gotten into? She had a gal that came around to help several days a week now, and her activities were generally limited to visiting with the very few spinsters in town she considered her social equals. Stella had often thought the old widow ought to join up with the Green Hat Ladies, but that would be a crossing of the social strata that, she was sure, would horrify the old biddy.

"Well, is it something, um . . . dire? Should you be calling 911?"

"No need for that," Adriana said crisply. "I'll put the coffee on."

Then she hung up.

"You done eatin'?" Stella asked, resigning herself to another fool's errand. Odds were that the old lady was just feeling lonely. "Call your mom and tell her you'll be a little while longer. You can come with me and do your civic duty."

Chapter Twenty-four

The once-proud iron gates at the Wolfort estate were propped permanently open, years of rust and corrosion having popped a hinge or two out of place. The road was not plowed, but lights burned from inside the big house. Stella pulled up the circular drive and gestured at Todd's feet. "Guess you wish you would have worn boots now," she said.

Todd jumped out of the Jeep and stomped around in a little circle, kicking up snow. Anything to prove an adult wrong. "I'm fine," he said through chattering teeth.

"Mind your manners," she cautioned as she rang the bell. "Mrs. Wolfort's old school. She won't put up with no sassin'."

Adriana opened the door with a grand, sweeping gesture. She was dressed in her country gentlewoman finest, a look she'd adopted years ago that was lost on most of the locals. Her Wellington boots were topped by a tweedy skirt and a sweater set that looked like it might have been picked out by the queen mother herself.

"Hello, young man," she said, holding out a gnarled, beringed hand.

Todd, to his credit, shook it with no hesitation and set to rubbing his shoes vigorously on the entry rug. "I'm Todd."

"Well, now," Adriana said briskly, leading them through the musty, once-grand foyer across threadbare carpets laid out all over the marble floor. Stella spotted cobwebs in the corners and a thick layer of dust on the furniture. She knew Adriana made a habit of firing housekeepers and had burned through every available cleaner in town.

In the sitting room, a tray was laid out with coffee cups and a china pot and a plate of what looked like stale Nilla Wafers. "Young man," Adriana said imperiously, "why don't you make yourself at home here for a few minutes while I confer with Mrs. Hardesty. Do help yourself to refreshments."

Todd looked around the room, which was stuffed with upholstered furniture and lined with breakfronts and cabinets and bookshelves, every surface piled with fussy knickknacks.

"Uh . . . ," he said, and Stella knew he was trying to figure out something to keep himself occupied.

"Oh, looky here," Stella said, seizing on a pile of magazines stashed on a bamboo tray. "*Saint Louis Town and Country*. Enrich yourself."

She thrust the magazines at Todd, and he sat down on a tufted settee and glared at her.

"This won't take long," Adriana promised, striding with surprising speed for an old gal toward the back of the house. She picked up a pair of flashlights on a table by the back door and handed one to Stella, and they went out onto a stone terrace. Stella offered a hand to Adriana to help her down the steps, which were dusted with fresh snow over evidence of recent foot traffic.

"I'm fine," Adriana snipped as a trio of sleek black Labradors came hurtling around the corner. They were handsome dogs, and well trained enough that they sniffed at her politely but didn't jump. "It's these three that alerted me to the problem. About an hour ago, they took to baying like the hounds of hell, and I came down here to take a look."

Stella followed the old lady along an overgrown path. The garden had once been a showplace, an English-style affair featuring benches and footbridges along the curved paths. At the bottom of the gentle incline, a few dozen yards from the house, was Milton's pride and joy, a large pond that he had once kept stocked with trout. Beyond it, a road led from the pond to what used to be the rest of the Wolfort estate, but had been sold off and planted with soybeans. Stella remembered that in her childhood there had been old-fashioned grass tennis courts and stables and an archery course.

The dogs grew increasingly agitated as they drew up to the edge of the pond, and one tried an experimental bark, but when Adriana scolded him, he immediately quieted down and skulked along at her heels.

"Well, there they are, then," Adriana said. "I know I said you could use the pond any time, but I think you need to work on your technique some. I'm quite certain you didn't expect them to come floating up to the surface so fast."

Stella flashed her own light on a trio of lumps that lay at the edge of the pond, their sodden shapes hard to make out but distinct enough that she knew without a doubt they were bodies.

"Liman and Priss," she guessed, a sinking feeling in her gut. "And the fella from the trunk."

"Well, now, it might be better if you didn't tell me the particulars," Adriana said. "In case the police decide to interrogate me vigorously. If I don't know any details, they won't be able to drag them out of me, even if they resort to that waterboarding like the last administration was so fond of."

Stella bent to the closest body, which was facedown with its limbs out at odd angles. She couldn't bring herself to touch it, and looked around for a stick. It took some doing to get the thing rolled over, and even then its features were waterlogged and swollen, and only when she recognized the second corpse's black cape did she feel confident she was looking at the drowned remains of Priss and her brother.

"How the heck did this happen?" she said, her gut twisting from both the ramifications to her personal situation as well as a general queasy feeling about the distasteful effects of their deaths.

"Well, now, my guess is that they were of insufficient weight or density to stay down. But then, I'm hardly qualified to put forth an opinion," Adriana said. "I'm no forensic scientist."

"You think *I* killed them?"

"Now, Stella, you don't need to be coy with me. When I offered you the use of the pond, I understood it entailed a certain measure of discretion, and I would never dream of breaching that."

Offered the use of the pond . . . Stella racked her brain and dredged up a conversation she'd once had with the old lady the summer that Milton had his strokes. They'd gone for a stroll to get away from the old gent's off-color screaming. By then he'd been at it so long that his voice had been permanently reduced to a scratchy, hoarse grating that still somehow managed to reach every corner of the house.

When they passed by the pond, Adriana had made a point of mentioning that it was built on the site of underground caverns and that it was a surprising thirty feet deep in some places. What was it she'd said? *Be a fine place to stash a body.* Which, at the time, Stella had taken as the eccentric ramblings of a bored old lady, or perhaps wishful thinking about the disposal of her harmless but irritating husband.

"Adriana," she said carefully, "I didn't murder these three."

"Now, now, dear, I really don't need to know," Adriana said. "Your business is your business. I just thought you'd want to get them returned to their watery graves as quickly as possible."

"But I didn't drown them in the first place. I swear to you, this isn't my doing."

Adriana, her features drawn and eerie in the light of the flashlights, pursed her lips. "Well, now, how else would these unfortunate people come to be in my pond? Especially since Priscilla hasn't been back to Prosper in years, and then one day she shows up unannounced to visit a brother for whom she's never had a shred of affection? I'm not one to gossip or speculate, but it does seem clear as day that the poor woman must have been having troubles of the sort that require specialized solutions." She leaned in for emphasis, her hooked nose inches away from Stella's face, and winked. "The sort of solution that *you,* if I may be forgiven, are known to provide."

Stella sputtered in exasperation. "Well, if that was the case, why would I kill *her*? Or Liman, for that matter?"

"Well, I'm sure I don't know," Adriana said. "*I'm* not the professional here. Perhaps things were not as they seemed . . . a double cross or a deal gone bad, really it could be anything. But honestly, Stella, I think I had better get inside with the boy while you do whatever it is that you need to do here. You're welcome to use anything you need from the potting shed."

"What I need to do," Stella said with dawning urgency, "is get the heck out of here. Adriana, I can't be seen anywhere near these bodies. Do you understand? You need to call the sheriff. Give me time to get back into town. You know what, take your car out and drive it around the lane a few times, if you don't mind, make it look like you were the one driving, cover up my tracks. Can you do that?"

A light glinted in the old lady's eyes. "Oh my, yes. How exciting."

This isn't a game, Stella was about to say, but she bit her tongue. She doubted she would convince the old lady of her innocence. The best she could hope for was cooperation, and if that meant playing to the lonely old gal's longing for a little adventure, then she'd have to go that route.

"It's very, very important that you do exactly as I say," she said carefully. "If, uh, justice is to be served. If the innocent are to be honored. Do you understand?"

As they reached the house, it seemed to Stella that there was a bit more of a spring in the old lady's step.

"You can count on me," Adriana said with conviction.

The door burst open and Todd, holding on to an antique-looking black umbrella with a wooden handle, came flying out. "Oh shit, thank God you aren't killed!"

Adriana looked from the boy to Stella and lifted one aristocratic eyebrow. "Me? Or Mrs. Hardesty?"

"Either one of you. How'm I supposed to know which one they was after?"

"Who?" Stella demanded, taking the umbrella from Todd when she noticed he was shaking slightly, and hurrying him back into the house with a glance around the terrace—there were no signs of anything amiss.

Adriana closed the door behind them and locked it firmly. "Now, young man, what are you talking about?"

"Someone knocked on the door after y'all went out the back, and it was this dude in like a hat pulled over his face with just the eyes cut out? You know, like in the movies when they rob banks and shit?"

"My *lands,*" Adriana said.

"And I kind of jumped out of the way, because I got to say he freaked me out, I mean the dude was wearing all black like a fuckin' ninja or something, I mean, sorry, Mrs. Wolfort—"

"Thank you," she said primly. "You know, coarse language makes the speaker coarse. It will serve you well to remember that. My Milton—"

"What happened then?" Stella demanded.

"Well, he kinda looked at me and looked around and I'm all backing up—"

"Was he *armed*?" Stella said, heart seizing with cold fear. Facing down attackers was one thing for a hardened criminal like herself, but Todd was a mere boy, a defenseless *child*. Instinctively, she grabbed his arm and dragged him into a half hug, which he didn't wriggle out of for at least a few seconds.

"Nah, not that I could see."

"And then—"

"So he starts running around, I guess looking for you-all or something, and I saw you had that thing full of umbrellas by the front door—"

"It's hand painted," Adriana said. "Milton brought it back from India. Quite valuable, really."

"—so I grabbed the biggest one and ran through that room with all them red curtains and he was coming past the stairs going the other way and I just kinda whaled on him and he fell down and after a minute he got up and went out the front again."

"You hit the guy with the umbrella," Stella clarified. "Whereabouts?"

"I guess around here," Todd said, pointing to his rib cage.

"And he didn't say anything?"

"Nope, nothing."

"How big was he, Todd?"

Todd frowned and looked from one of them to the other. "Maybe an inch taller than you, Stella. He weren't real big or nothing."

"Well, no matter what size he was, felling him was quite an accomplishment, young man," Adriana said warmly. "How about a nice cookie?"

"You're sure?" Stella asked. Salty probably cleared six feet, though not by much. "He couldn't have been a little taller?"

Todd shook his head. "I don't think so."

Stella rubbed her temples, which were beginning to throb with the aftereffects of the adrenaline. "Oh, Sherilee's gonna kill me," she muttered. "What was I thinking, getting you practically murdered, and on a school night, too."

"We don't have to tell her," Todd said. "I mean, maybe you could, like, buy my silence?"

Chapter Twenty-five

Stella didn't doubt Adriana's desire to help, but when the sheriff's car raced by going the other direction, lights flashing, she realized with a sinking feeling that in the excitement of finding bodies in her pond and nearly being attacked, the old lady hadn't managed to keep the plan straight.

For instance, the part about waiting half an hour to give Stella a chance to get clear of the scene and deliver Todd home had evidently been forgotten. She had only about five minutes' lead on Goat, who flashed her an openmouthed look of what might have been horror, or shock, or out-and-out fury through the window of his cruiser as he went tearing by.

When her phone rang a moment later, she wasn't the least bit surprised. She glanced at the caller ID and, seeing that it was Goat, turned up the music to drown him out. Catherine Britt was singing "Swingin' Door:"

I ain't your gas-up, rest-stop swingin' door

Stella and Todd sang along, belting out the high notes, until she got to the Groffes' driveway, trying hard not to notice the second and third time her phone rang.

"Remember our deal," she said sternly.

"Twenty bucks now, twenty bucks when they find the guy."

"No, I meant the part about keeping your mouth shut."

"Whatever."

"And being real, *real* careful to keep the house locked and stay out of trouble for a while."

Todd shot her a crooked grin and ran up the steps to his front door. Stella waited until Sherilee poked her head out and waved before driving a few doors down to her own house.

She felt a little guilty about not letting Sherilee know what had happened, but she figured she'd feel about ten times more guilty knowing she'd deprived the poor woman of the very little sleep she got before another long day at the office.

Inside, the party was still going, but it was considerably subdued. Four or five of the girls were clustered around the kitchen table playing Monopoly—or rather a variation of the game that apparently involved rolling the dice and drinking without advancing any of the playing pieces. Paper money was strewn all over the table and floor, and at Stella's arrival, an enthusiastic if slurred cheer went up.

"Hi, Mrs. Hardesty," one of the gals whose name she hadn't caught earlier said. "Sorry about the chili 'n all."

Stella followed her gaze to the corner of the kitchen, where Roxy had her head inside the big stew kettle, licking the last of the chili from the bottom of the pot.

"Oh, my," Stella said. "Did she eat the entire thing?"

"Oh, no, we ate most of it and then she knocked it off the stove, and we had to let it cool before we could mop it up, you know? Only she beat us to it."

"We was playin' *charades*," another guest clarified, as if that explained the lapse in attention. "You know how that gets."

"Uh-huh. Is, er, Mr. Brodersen still here?"

"Oh, no, he'n the sheriff left right quick after y'all did."

"We thought they was gonna go to it in the driveway. My, but they got it bad for you, Mrs. Hardesty," the tall brunette said with unmistakable admiration.

"Oh, I don't think that's the case," Stella demurred, secretly pleased. "Has anyone seen my daughter?"

Looks were exchanged, and the gal holding the dice dropped one on the floor. "Um. She left."

"With Joy?"

"Oh, no, ma'am. Joy's right over there," she said, pointing to the living room, where—sure enough—Joy had kicked off her sneakers and curled up under an afghan and gone to sleep. She wasn't the only one; one of the young men had conked out in a chair, head slung back, mouth slack. It reminded Stella of Noelle's high school days, when she would have her friends over and they'd stay up late watching TV and Stella would fix them popcorn and Rice Krispies Treats, and they'd all end up sleeping on the living room floor, Stella fluffing blankets over them when she got up in the middle of the night to go to the bathroom.

"Well, where did she go?"

More looks were exchanged. Finally the brunette sighed and shrugged her shoulders. "She left with Cinnamon Ferling-hetti."

Stella glanced from one to another of the guests and demanded, "Is that a *bad* thing? Had they been drinking?"

"Oh no, ma'am, Cinnamon don't *drink*. She's a teetotaler, is what she is."

"Well, then—"

"Tell her," a little freckled gal suggested in the delicate, exaggerated fashion of someone who was one Jell-O shooter away from sleeping on the bathroom floor. "She deserves to know."

"Just, Cinnamon's kinda a heartbreaker, a little bit."

"The catch-and-release *queen*," the freckly gal sighed, and there was general nodding and concurring. "Cinnamon can't much resist startin' up things, 'specially with someone smokin' hot like Noelle, but they never do seem to stick."

"Oh," Stella said, pinching the bridge of her nose up high in the place where headaches occasionally seemed to cluster. "I see."

There followed the sort of embarrassed silence that only drunk people are capable of, but by the time Stella decided she had done the best she could, and sent up a quick prayer asking the Big Guy to sort everything out as He saw fit, the festive Monopoly game was gathering momentum again.

In the morning, there were a few more revelers crashed in the living room. Since Hardesty Sewing Machine Repair & Sales was closed on Tuesdays, Stella didn't bother rushing as she got all the blankets and afghans she could find and covered them all up, and set a pot of coffee on.

For herself, she stopped at the Doughnette Diner and got herself a large Irish crème–flavored coffee and a couple of glazed chocolate cake doughnuts. That was the problem with having a doughnut—for days after, you couldn't stop thinking how darn good they sounded every morning. It was like getting a Journey song stuck in your head, a problem only the passing of time could heal.

She called Chrissy from the parking lot and apologized for talking with her mouth full as she related the events of the night before.

"Gee, Stella, way to go, dragging a young'un into your life of crime."

Stella bristled at the suggestion. "There wasn't any actual shootin' or anything—"

"Oh, well, that's all right, then."

"Well, what would you of done?" Stella sighed. "You know, Chrissy, I'm gonna be glad when all your mom's company's gone so she can watch Tucker again and you can come on these errands with me."

"Aw, that's sweet—you miss me!"

"Maybe a little. I guess you're too busy to come check out this Addney Walsingham guy with me."

"Oh, I promised Carmela we could do a craft project, since the shop's closed today."

Carmela was Chrissy's oldest niece. She stuck out like a sore thumb in the Lardner clan. Quiet, serious, and bookish, nine-year-old Carmela adored her aunt Chrissy. And since her own mom's interest in her had waned since she went to live with a guy she met at a revival the summer before, Chrissy had been trying to fill in some of the gaps.

"What are you doing, making pot holders?"

"No, it's the coolest thing—found it on the Internet. Did you know you can make a holster out of an old milk jug?"

"You're teaching Carmela to make a *holster*? What's next, you two gonna make a pistol out of office supplies?"

"Stella," Chrissy chided. "It's a *present*. For her dad. Pete's got a little .38, fits okay in the pocket of a pair of Dockers or what have you, but on the weekends he wants something he can tote if he's wearin' jeans."

Stella thought about that for a minute. "Okay. I'll bite. How do you make it?"

"Oh, this is so cool. You heat the milk jug with a hair dryer, see, it softens it right up. Then you staple all around the gun to get the shape right, cut it out, and wrap up the whole thing with duct tape—it's perfect, and you wouldn't believe how slick you can draw against that plastic."

"Huh. That's damn ingenious, I got to say."

"Hey, Stella, how's a gun better than a man?"

Stella smiled. She could think of a few ways—depending on the man. And the gun. "How?"

"If you admire a friend's gun, and tell her so, she'll probably let you try it out a few times."

Chapter Twenty-six

Addney Walsingham lived in a part of Kansas City that could only be described as past its prime, in a beat-down apartment building that shared a parking lot with a liquor store and an Everything for a Buck. Everything seemed to be broken—the asphalt parking lot was cracked and busted up; a rusting car sat on four flat tires in one of the garage stalls; the mailboxes lurched on a bent pole where some careless driver had taken a swipe at it. Even the numeral 6 on Walsingham's door had lost a nail and spun upside down, making it look like a 9.

Stella peered at the door, considering her options. She'd circled the lot slowly, determining that the apartments had no back exits, just smallish windows on what were probably the bedrooms. The only signs of activity were a gnarled old gentleman hosing off the sidewalk in front of the Triple-X Video store across the street, and a lady with a twin stroller full of bags of groceries but no twins, not even a single baby, who was rolling slowly and serenely down the street.

Stella unlocked the steel box bolted to the floor of the Jeep where she stashed her guns when they weren't in use, and considered her options. The Bersa was more suited to threatening amateurs, especially smallish ones, as it didn't have a whole lot of firepower. Not knowing what to expect from Walsingham, she chose the 9 mm Mak PA that she'd picked up used from a guy who was trading up. The thing had a sort of old-fashioned look to it, and it was a pain to find the surplus ammo, but it fit nicely in the hand and got the job done.

She folded a lacy crocheted sweater over her gun hand and headed for the door, swinging the Tupperware full of lock tools in the other. The sweater was strictly for show—Stella figured the day she started sporting pastel twin sets was the day they might as well put her out to pasture—but it was an amazingly effective bit of camouflage. Folks saw the sweater and just couldn't help their brains from forming a picture of a nice granny. Hell, outfit the Special Forces from the Tog Shop catalog, and you could probably send them right into the most dangerous hot spots on the planet without drawing any attention.

She knocked softly. No point interrupting Walsingham's neighbors' morning business, if any of them were home.

"What," a pleasant-enough male voice said after a few seconds. "Who's that, then?"

"Census Bureau," Stella said. It was an old standby, not terribly creative, but she hadn't been expecting to find anyone home.

After a longish pause and a curious scuffling sound, the voice spoke again, closer to the front door. "Cen-*what*?"

"I'm with the Census," Stella repeated. "Just need to ask you a few questions about the household. Won't take but a minute."

"I'm sorry, but I'm not interested."

"Oh, it's mandatory," Stella said, slipping a little extra sugar into her voice. "You mostly just have to sign it."

"Just leave it out there. I'm, um, I'm in my bathrobe."

"Oh, dear, I wish I could, but see, this is, like, federal property?" Stella improvised. She'd tried the ruse out a couple of times before when rousting was necessary, and as a rule she liked to use it only on her stupider victims; she doubted whether Walsingham would go for it. Damn—she'd have to find somewhere to hunker down until he came out and she could break in. "Leaving it unattended is a crime. I could lose my job. I could be prosecuted."

A string of expletives was muttered, but to Stella's happy surprise, the door jiggled and opened and a suspicious brown eye regarded her through the crack. She tucked the lockbox under her gun arm as a hand slipped out, fingers wiggling.

"Just let me have it, then," the voice demanded.

Stella seized the door handle with her free hand and yanked as hard as she could, crunching the man's fingers in the door-jamb. Then she plowed into the opening with her shoulder, ignoring the cursing and sounds of pain, taking advantage of the moment to send him staggering backwards into the apartment. The sweater and toolbox fell to the floor as Stella raised the gun and bumped the door closed with her butt.

"Just lay facedown on the floor with your arms out to the side," she said calmly, "and we'll get to collecting data."

"Now, that's just plain *rude*," a voice said off to the side. Stella's heart did a little skip as she swiveled her head slightly to see the source—an impossibly good-looking young man had leveled a pistol of his own in her direction.

"Well, shit," she sighed, and took a closer look at the man she'd shoved out of the way.

If he was Addney Walsingham, he was the most remarkably preserved forty-something gent she'd ever laid eyes on. He looked a lot more like a sleek and polished twenty-five. As she was processing that, a third hot hunk stepped out of the kitchen, drying a glass on a dish towel, and scowled at her.

"What the hell do you want?" the first one asked.

Stella slowly and carefully lowered her gun to the nearest surface, a battered brown sofa table stacked with books and papers. Nearly every surface in the apartment, she now noticed, held piles of paperbacks and dusty hardbacks and papers and notebooks. Dish Towel Boy picked up her gun between a thumb and forefinger with an expression of distaste and carried it into the kitchen.

"So what have I walked into here, anyway—y'all shootin' some kind of hard-luck beefcake calendar?"

The one with the gun grimaced. "We're trying to save *lives* here."

"Hah. Funny way of doing it, you ask me. What did you do to Walsingham?"

The three exchanged looks. "What do you want him for, anyway? And forget about that census bullshit—I don't believe a bit of it."

Stella rolled her eyes. "Darn, I guess my cover's blown. What was your first clue, anyway?"

"Don't be a smart-ass," the tallest of the three said. His dark good looks were only slightly marred, in Stella's opinion, by the ridiculous facial hair that he'd carefully sculpted into thin sideburns and a sort of chevron on his chin. "As for Addney, we've got him under control—don't you worry about that."

"Okay," Stella said. She could hear muffled thumping and what sounded like moans from the back of the apartment. "Um, this is awkward. Are you sure? Did you tie him up or something?"

"Yeah, we— What do you care?"

Stella cracked her knuckles and rolled her shoulders. The tension of the last few moments had seized up her muscles, and she had learned in physical therapy that she thought best if she took a deep breath or two and relaxed. "Look, boys, I realize this might be hard for you to absorb, but I'm kind of a professional. I got a stake in keeping Walsingham in one piece, and if you ain't tied him up right, he's gonna come busting out of there and somebody'll end up with a hole blown clear through him, and that's not going to look good for any of us."

She waited a moment for that to sink in, taking a more careful look at her three new friends while they cast all manner of anxious glances at one another. They truly were a fine-looking bunch, each with his own special look, kind of like the series of plastic suitors Noelle had for her Barbies when she was a little girl. There was the smooth-skinned Latino hottie with the odd and complicated facial hair . . . the densely built Nordic-looking fellow with the—

"Hey!" Stella exclaimed, realization dawning. "Y'all work for Priss, don't you?"

More glances and frowning. "How do you know her? Look, I think it's about time for us to ask questions."

Stella nodded and took a step toward the boy with the gun. "Yeah, okay, but how about if you hand me that thing so nobody gets hurt. It ain't any kind of toy. . . ."

She was counting on Pretty Boy being like so many other young men with their first gun, which was to say, barely aware of which was the business end. Stella herself had been in that position not so long ago, but her first year in the justice business, she had made a serious study of firearms. Not to mention the fact that she had the twin advantages of being a female—unhindered by any machismo action-hero urges—and middle aged, which meant old enough to know better.

She was about to close her hand on the barrel, when the boy

tipped it a fraction of an inch to the side and took a shot. Stella whipped around and saw that he'd nailed the wooden base of a lamp across the room dead center.

Huh.

She swallowed hard. "Okay, then. So you can handle a gun. Well, I'm still gonna go check on what you done to Walsingham, so you might as well shoot me if you got any objections."

She walked slowly down the hall, legs trembling until she arrived at the end of the hall unshot.

"Oh, fine," Pretty Boy said. He followed her down the hall and pushed the door open ahead of her, keeping his gun trained on her the whole time.

They both gaped: a sweating, balding middle-aged man with a fairly nice physique had got himself into an uncomfortable-looking pretzel, the leg of a desk chair hooked between his bound hands behind his back, his legs kicking furiously, lengths of electrical tape trailing on the ground. What appeared to be a handkerchief was stuffed in his mouth and secured with tape, but it, too, was loose and flapping free.

"Oh, for fuck's sake," Stella said. "You call this any kind of restraint? Honestly, ain't you ever seen *MacGyver*?"

"Mac-who?"

Stella glanced at him incredulously. Oh, youth today. "Look, just give me the tape and some rope, if you got any."

She plucked a corner of the tape from Walsingham's mouth and prepared to rip. "Don't you get to squawkin'," she warned him. "I ain't exactly here to rescue you or anything of that nature, despite any appearances to the contrary."

Then she pulled.

The exclamation of pain Walsingham blurted out quickly turned to the sort of yelling that was so unhelpful in these circumstances, so Stella gave him a quick and precise jab to the voice box that she had learned watching martial arts videos on YouTube, and the yelling turned to a gargling gasp for breath.

"Now, unless you especially enjoyed that, how about you tell me where you keep the rope," she suggested.

It took a bit of pantomiming and, once Walsingham got his voice partway back, strained whispering, but Stella found a length of nylon clothesline and a rubber ball of the sort used by weight lifters, as well as a few neckties and a handful of carabiners. Within ten minutes, Stella had Walsingham tied up nice and tight, sitting more or less comfortably on the living room couch. She sat next to him, and the eye candy trio moved enough books and papers off the kitchen chairs that they were able to form a ring around the couch, Pretty Boy in the middle with his gun and an expression that was getting more sour by the moment.

"Okeydoke," Stella said cheerfully. It was true what they said, a little good hard work could really lift your spirits. "I know you're kind of the party host here and all, but how about if I take the lead, and you can, you know, wave your little gun around if you don't like how it's going."

That got her nothing but a skeptical snort, but Stella barged ahead. She'd learned that—particularly if you were a middle-aged lady in this country—your best course was often to just keep on going until someone made you stop, rather than waiting around for anyone's approval.

"So how about if we start with introductions. I'm Stella, I'm pretty sure this here's Addney Walsingham, and—hey, are any of you by any chance Turk Hardpole?"

That got her a reaction: All three of them exchanged disgusted looks. "Hell no," the Nordic one said. "I got principles."

"Oh," Stella said, a little disappointed. Despite lecturing Chrissy, she was mighty curious about the mystery feat herself.

"I'm Rock," the boy with the gun said. He stuck a thumb out at the other two. "That's Maverick, and Jett."

"I suppose those are all your professional names," Stella said. Nobody disagreed. "Uh-huh. I don't guess it matters much to me. Well, tell you what. I don't suppose any of us is exactly squeaky clean from the law's point of view, so I guess we can drop any kind of holier-than-thou business. Why don't you all tell me why you're bothering this gentleman?"

"Hell no!" Maverick protested. "I don't see where we ought to tell you anything. What are you, some sort of union buster?"

"Do I *look* like a fuckin' union buster?" Stella demanded, incredulous. "And just how dumb do y'all breed around here, anyway? I just had to explain this to your buddy Beau Mandrake—what y'all do is *illegal,* so you can't *organize.*"

"You saw Beau?" Jett demanded. "Was he still alive?"

That caught Stella up short a bit. "Um . . . yeah," she said slowly. "Any particular reason he wouldn't be?"

"He didn't return our calls since yesterday," Maverick said.

"So you automatically assume he's *dead*?"

"What sort of business did *you* have with him, anyway?" Rock said, getting a little agitated with the gun again.

Stella gave the question a quick thought and came to a decision—she couldn't see any reason it would hurt to tell these boys what was going on, at least in broad strokes. "Priss has a flash drive I would dearly like to get my hands on."

"Oh *ho,*" Rock said, comprehension flooding his broad, handsome features. "You're on one of them tapes of Turk's."

"I didn't say—"

"How many of you did they get to anyway?" Maverick said, shaking his head sadly. "How many will be made to suffer? How many times are we going to let that bastard get away with that?"

"I'm not—"

"Lady, what I don't understand is why y'all line up to pay for that. It's not—not—well, it's not what nature intended," Maverick said, his face flushing a deep red, while his friends shuffled their feet and looked off in opposite directions.

They were just overcome with envy, Stella realized with astonishment. Whatever it was that Turk could do—and took video of to prove it—it was rare enough that none of his colleagues—trained professionals, every one—was up to the job.

She'd meant it when she told Chrissy she didn't need to know, but now her curiosity was starting to wear on her. "I don't know what you're talking about," she said carefully, "but maybe, in the interest of full disclosure, you could, um, *describe*—"

Rock raised the gun a few inches off his thigh, where he'd been resting it, and Stella was afraid he was going to put on another marksmanship display.

"Right," she said quickly, "forget I asked."

"Quit playing games here," Rock ordered. "Our friends are being killed. *Slaughtered*. Now, I'm sorry that there's embarrassing footage out there, but we have bigger things to worry about, like if we're gonna wake up dead tomorrow."

"Are you by any chance referring to a dead guy Priss might have been hauling around in her trunk?" Stella guessed. "Was he, uh, one of you?"

"Keller McManus—God rest his soul," Jett said, his voice breaking with emotion. "One of the *best*."

"And you think Priss killed him."

"Priss? Why would she kill him?" Maverick demanded. "She *loved* him—as much as that coldhearted woman could love anyone."

"Moved him in with her," Jett agreed.

"Kicked Walsy out," Rock sighed. "Which is why *he* killed him."

Stella's head was starting to spin. "Wait up here. You're saying Priss wasn't seeing Addney here anymore."

"Not in six months or so. And he never did get over it—did you, Walsy," Rock muttered, giving the man a sharp kick in the shin, which produced a sort of shriek, though it was considerably muffled due to the rubber ball in his mouth.

"Only where's it going to get you to come after us?" Jett demanded, sounding genuinely aggrieved. He shook his head sorrowfully. "Bloodshed ain't the answer to bloodshed."

"His daddy's a preacher," Maverick confided.

"Oh, Christ," Stella said. "I've just about had it with all of you. Look here, I'm gonna undo the man a little. You just hang on to that gun there, Junior. You can shoot me in half an hour if you're still itchy, but I think I can get things moving here a little quicker than the three of you."

She undid the knots holding the makeshift gag in place, but before she popped it out of Walsingham's mouth, she grabbed his hair and gave it a yank, forcing him to look at her. "You ain't gonna make any trouble now, are you?"

He shook his head as much as he could, given her grip on him.

"You're just going to answer my questions calmly and quietly."

Vigorous nodding.

"You got my permission to shoot him somewhere if he yells," Stella told Rock. "Somewhere nondeadly."

Rock assented grudgingly.

Stella hooked a little finger in Walsingham's mouth, grimacing at touching his saliva. She'd mastered removing gags without any danger of getting bitten, but she surely hated getting drooled on.

The ball popped free and rolled on the floor. As promised, Walsingham stayed mostly silent, except for a faint mewling.

"Here's what I got to ask," Stella said. "I mean, I want to know who-all you been killing and all, but before we get to that, what the hell is all this union shit about?"

"I never said *unions*," Walsingham said stiffly. He worked his jaw as though it had cramped up on him. "It's a matter of philosophy. I tried to explain it to Priss. You'd think with her training in economics, she'd realize the dangers of exploitation of the proletariat, but she just wouldn't listen."

"Prole-who?" Stella interrupted. "Is this some kind of Marxist bullshit?"

Walsingham glowered, while the boys nodded along. Whether they were agreeing with him or with her, Stella wasn't sure.

"Marxism can be a jumping-off point in the discussion, sure," Walsingham said, warming to his subject. "Why not? His labor theory of value applies—we workers have no choice but to produce more and more output under conditions we don't control. All's I ever did was, I was an advocate for collective self-liberation." He waved his hands in a semicircle to include himself and the other men.

"Now when you say output . . . ," Jett began, confusion knitting his brow.

"Figure of speech," Walsingham said, not unkindly.

"So what does all of this have to do with you killing Priss's boyfriend?" Stella asked. "I would think that with all that collective-thinking nonsense, you'd be into sharing."

"Damn commie," Maverick observed, glowering.

"I did not kill Keller," Walsingham said, looking wounded. Stella squinted and tried to figure out whether, if the man wasn't trussed up and sweating, she would find him attractive. He wasn't as muscular as his younger colleagues, and his grooming was a little less precise. Still, she supposed he had a sort of . . . professorial charm about him that some women might like.

The judge, for instance—Stella would have guessed a high-brow gal like that might have gone for the kind of guy who looked like he could spout Sartre while greasing your wheels. But that just went to show a person, didn't it—love, in all its infinite variety, was a mysterious thing. Who knew what lay behind the attraction of one person to another? Did it really come down to nothing but hormones, those pesky little phero-mones doing their best to stir up trouble everywhere they went? Was it the accumulation of small moments, long-forgotten ex-periences that set patterns into memory, so that a towheaded first crush led to a lifelong love of blonds, or a gone-wrong fling with a fellow with a Bronx accent permanently put a person off anyone else who talked that way?

"So what kind of woman takes a shine to you, generally, would you say?" she asked Addney thoughtfully.

"What—don't you want to know if I killed anybody?"

"You just said you didn't."

"Wait one damn minute," Rock said, gesturing back and forth between them with the gun. "You're gonna believe him, just because he *said* he didn't do it?"

"Not because he said it," Stella said. "But the *way* he said it."

"What the hell does that mean?"

Stella sighed. She knew she couldn't put it into words, be-cause she had tried before, when she was training Chrissy. Over time, her sense of whether a man was telling the truth had be-come fine-tuned, and as her confidence in herself grew, so did her perceptive skills. She figured it was some combination of facial expression and tone of voice and gestures, but when she tried to break it down and find the patterns, it all fell apart. It only worked when she let her mind empty out and just kind of put her brain on . . . *receive,* that was the only way to put it. Let it absorb what she was seeing and hearing, and then her brain mixed it all up and did its thing and she had a pretty clear idea of whether a guy was telling the truth or not.

She hadn't been wrong in a long while.

But trying to explain it like that wouldn't get her very far with these yokels.

She made a snap decision. "What I am, is a human polygraph," she fibbed. "I work for the cops, the feds, whoever—I'm an independent contractor. But under the radar, see? They can't pay me through the regular channels, the public wouldn't have it."

"They pay them police psychics," Maverick said. "They got 'em on Montel all the time."

"That's *PR,* is all," Stella lied patiently. "They got a whole budget for that. It's to make the public feel like they're doing something."

"They are doing something, lots of times it turns out they're right," Maverick said.

"Yeah," Jett agreed. "It's a real science. I get feelings sometime. You know? Déjà vu. Like when you just know something's gonna happen. Yesterday I had a feeling they'd have Mini-Wheats on sale. I don't ever buy them full price 'cause—"

"This is bullshit," Rock said. Stella had a feeling that he was the brightest of the three, not that that was saying much. "If you were working for the cops, they'd be keeping tabs on you, and I ain't exactly seen them busting in here helping you out."

Stella kept her features placid. "It's just reconnaissance so far. I got a few different directions I'm going. All I was planning was a casual chat with Mr. Walsingham here."

"Well, I still think he did it," Maverick said, pouting.

"One easy way to find out," Rock said, and leaned forward

and jammed the end of the barrel gently into Walsingham's crotch. "Don't go making any abrupt moves there, cowboy. I'm kinda nervous today."

"I didn't kill him, I didn't kill him!" Walsingham squeaked, trembling and staring down at the gun in horror. Stella felt almost sorry for him. "All I did was challenge him to a duel."

"A *what*?"

Walsingham swallowed hard. "Could you just stop—?"

"Ease up on him, pardner," Stella advised Rock, who reluctantly sat back in his chair, keeping the gun leveled on Walsingham, who looked both immensely relieved and ready to cry.

"What the hell do you mean, a duel?" she demanded.

"It was a common way to settle disagreements in the nineteenth century," Walsingham sniffed. "I am an experienced fencer, so I offered Keller a choice of sidearms."

"*Sidearms?* What, you all were just going to shoot it out?"

"A sidearm can refer to a sword or other dueling blade," Walsingham said, his tone getting all stuffy and academic. "I told him I'd let him use both my rapier and smallsword and I'd use my little dagger, to even things up."

"Now, this just makes me mad," Stella exclaimed. "How about letting the *woman* decide? A gal says she's moving on—what makes you think that stabbing the crap out of her new guy's gonna convince her any different? I mean, I'm no fan of Priss's, but she's got a right to pick who she wants to . . . um." *Had* a right, she meant, though maybe there was some advantage to keeping Priss's demise to herself. Besides, there was no telling what that bit of news would do to this already explosive situation.

"I was defending her honor," Walsingham said tightly. "No man has a right to speak openly of his private . . . consorting with a woman."

"You got to be kidding me," Stella said.

"Keller liked to talk quite a bit," Maverick explained. "You know, over a beer or whatnot."

"He was a technique man," Rock sighed. "Really dedicated."

"Hang on a sec, here," Stella said. "You're telling me y'all get together and . . . what, talk about the workday? Kind of like a bunch of, I don't know, phone company linemen or something?"

"You *learn* stuff," Jett said. "When I was new, they really taught me a lot, helped me figure out how to handle things."

"I'd think you'd be into that," Maverick said stonily to Walsingham. "You and your commie worker comrade shit. All for one and one for all, and so forth."

Stella was pretty sure that last bit was from *The Three Musketeers,* not Marx, but she let it slide.

"So, to summarize," she said, "Keller was telling everyone about how he was doing your ex-lover, who was also the boss, including all the juicy details, and that made you mad, so you dragged him out in the alley and told him to put his money where his mouth was, and you beat the shit out of him but didn't kill him—"

"Well," Walsingham said uncomfortably. "The duel was to be traditional. I mean, there's conventions one follows. And he wouldn't. I offered to explain it all to him but—I mean he was crazed, just utterly crazed, coming at me like a—like some kind of a thug, like a two-bit tough, he dropped all pretense of observing protocol and just took a swing at me—"

"Well, yeah," Stella said, "some idiot comes at you with a broadax I would *think* you'd get to defending yourself pretty quick—"

"Naturally, I defended myself but Priss was, ah, adamant that we stop—"

"Wait a minute, she was *there*?" Stella demanded.

"Priss thought she could talk us out of it. She never understood how fiery my passion for her is," Walsingham said regretfully, shaking his head.

"So you're going at each other on the street—"

"At the waterfowl sanctuary, actually, that the city put in down by Willow Lake. On account of it's usually deserted."

Stella guessed that made sense—not too many people were probably in the mood to tramp around looking at ducks in the middle of winter.

"Okay, you're beating the shit out of each other in some nature park. He swings at you, you retaliate, you cut him up some, Priss gets mad, and then what?"

"Well, she, um, made us stop."

"She *made* you stop."

"She yelled at us."

Stella let that settle for a moment. Thought of a couple of responses. Figured they'd be lost on the current company.

"Let me guess. You probably brought your own cars, and she told you to leave."

Walsingham nodded. "But look here, if you're thinking I killed Keller, I mean, all I did was cut him a little, only superficially, you know?"

"How much?" Stella demanded. "How much blood?"

When Walsingham hesitated, Rock encouraged him again, and he blurted out, "Those superficial wounds can bleed like crazy."

"A cup? A bucket? What? Get specific."

"He, ah . . . he was pretty bloody. His shirt, his pants, his, um, face . . ."

And then he'd somehow gone from alive and bloody to dead and bloody in Priss's trunk. Maybe Walsingham had hit some vein or artery and didn't know it, though that was doubtful—you'd think a person would notice arterial spray.

Walsingham was an idiot, and the rest of the Elegant Company team assembled in his apartment were a bunch of numbnuts, and Stella figured she wasn't much closer to figuring out who'd killed McManus or, for that matter, Priss and Liman. And she sure as hell wasn't any closer to getting her flash drive back.

"Look here," she said. "This has been fun and all, but I'm tired. I got family to get home to, I just want to put my feet up and watch the Charlie Brown Easter special. I'm leaving now, and I suggest y'all untie Mr. Walsingham here once you've finished having your fun with him and forget all about this. 'Kay?"

No one tried to stop her.

Chapter Twenty-seven

The drive home was surprisingly pleasant. The snow stopped swirling, and the weak sun warmed up the inside of the Jeep to a toasty yellow. Willie Nelson crooned "Uncloudy Day," and Stella caught up on her gratitude, which she'd neglected for a few days.

Dear Big Guy, she started, *Thanks for watching my back in there.* After that, she got stuck on specifics.

She was a person of interest in a murder case. Additional incriminating evidence was still in circulation somewhere on one of Priss's hard drives. Another entire year had passed without her getting laid. Her daughter seemed headed for an epic heartbreak. She could barely afford to keep Johnnie in the cupboard, much less fix everything that was broken around the house.

Still, there was plenty to be thankful for, wasn't there? As she drove past the winter-plowed fields, melting snow leaving the furrows looking like chocolate brown frosting stripes on a giant vanilla sheet cake, she thought about all the ways that this Easter was going to be better than any in recent history. There were the Easter-morning cinnamon rolls she would bake from her mother's recipe, and the biggest chocolate bunny she could find for Tucker. Noelle was too old for Stella to buy her a frilly hat, but maybe they could shop for something cute to wear to church. Church! Stella hadn't been in ages, and the thought was surprisingly inviting.

By the time she pulled into her driveway, her outlook had warmed considerably—but it was still somewhat startling to see Noelle holding a ladder up against the sugar maple while teetering near the top rung was a curvaceous gal with a pile of bleached-blond curls and a tight top and even tighter sweatpants with the word PRINCESS stitched on the rear.

"What on earth are you-all doing?" Stella demanded, leaping out of the car practically before it stopped rolling. Roxy bounded over and plowed into her with joyful abandon.

"We're putting up the eggs, Mama," Noelle said, and gave her a lovely big smile that showed off her dimples while holding tight to the ladder. Only then did Stella notice that her daughter was wearing a sassy little pair of fuzzy rabbit ears on her head, and looking happier than she had in weeks.

Well, she had a pretty good guess what *that* meant. At least someone was getting some attention around here.

Stella ran her hands through her hair and pinched her cheeks to get a little color in them as Noelle's new friend climbed carefully down the ladder, wiping her hands on her sweats. The Rubbermaid totes full of giant plastic eggs and pastel lights had indeed been brought down from the attic and were lined up on the lawn. The lights were spread out in a tangled mess on the thin layer of snow.

Stella suddenly remembered the way this task went in the old days, Ollie on the ladder hollering at her while she struggled to unknot the mess he'd made getting them down the previous year, and decided that having Noelle's new friend doing the job was a welcome change of pace.

"Well, hello," she said, "I'm Stella Hardesty, Noelle's mom, and you must be Cardamom."

"Cinnamon," the girl corrected her cheerfully, extending a hand to shake. "It's just real nice to meet you. I *love* your house."

"Oh . . . you do?" Stella looked at it doubtfully. In addition to the damaged roof, there were quite a few other aspects of the house that needed attention. Several of the shutters had come loose during a series of tornadoes earlier in the fall, and hung askew. Paint was beginning to flake near the bottom of the paneling, and the windows could do with a good wash.

But as she tried to see the place through fresh eyes, she had to admit that the place had a certain cozy charm. It wasn't a Park Avenue showplace, but it was home.

She squeezed her eyes shut and remembered the first Easter she spent in this house. She and Ollie had been married long enough for her to know that she hadn't bought her way into any kind of bed of roses, but not long enough for her to realize how terrible things could get. She had been pregnant with Noelle, and as she decorated the house with the pots of hyacinth and narcissus bulbs she forced in February and hung an old straw hat with a checkered bow on the front door, her heart had swelled with anticipation and joy.

"It's just so *cute*. I grew up in this big old modern thing my stepdad built. It just had no charm at all," Cinnamon said wistfully. "Noelle's so lucky."

Noelle gave Stella an impulsive little hug. "Once we get the lights up, I was thinking we could get the rest of the decorations down and maybe we can boil up some eggs, Mama. Only, neither me or Cinnamon was tall enough to get them boxes out from on top of the shelves and we couldn't get the ladder up there."

Long before Stella and Ollie had ever bought the house, someone had nailed up two-by-twelves to create makeshift shelves, and it had always been Ollie's job to put the decorations away, since Stella couldn't reach. "Oh, honey, maybe we can get Todd to come over and help."

"Todd ain't hardly any taller than us," Noelle said. Then she smiled conspiratorially. "Besides, I had a better idea—the sheriff's coming over, Mama!"

Stella's heart did a little slip-slide. She sincerely doubted Goat would be arriving any time soon, unless he was digging in his belt for his handcuffs to haul her off. "Uh, did you actually *talk* to him?"

"Well, sure, only he just had a minute or two on account of some trouble they've got. Dotty called about an hour ago, she saw that crime scene van heading through town. Mama, you don't know what's going on, do you?"

Noelle's lovely green eyes were wide and unsuspecting, and Stella realized that the near impossible had happened—the sheriff's department had managed to keep a lid at least partway on its business for something like twelve hours. Now that the Fayette crew had been called in, though, that wouldn't last. Folks would be following the county vehicles like a row of ducklings after their mama, and short of Mike and Ian taking potshots at the townsfolk, there was bound to be a whole gaggle of bystanders out at Adriana's pond in no time.

It was a wonder, really, that they'd managed to get the bodies out the night before without attracting more attention. They must have locked Adriana up in her butler's pantry to keep her from calling around town—and Goat and his deputies must have had a heck of a night as well, babysitting the soggy corpses until they could get backup.

She took a deep breath. "Why, no," she said as innocently as she could. She didn't like to lie to Noelle, as a rule, but this concerned Goat, a subject she didn't really care to discuss with anyone at all . . . and besides, they had company. "Noelle, sugar, what-all did the sheriff say? Did he sound especially, you know, *exhausted* or anything?"

Noelle shrugged, stooping to gather an armload of lights. "Not really. He was nice, like usual. He said he'd try to get free later today, but it might be tomorrow. I explained how I'm taking a little time off and told him any time was fine with me."

"So he specifically said he would, uh, come to *our* attic, here at the house? Did you tell him where I was?"

"Mama, I didn't *know* where you were. Remember? You didn't exactly leave me a note." Noelle didn't look impatient; she gave her mother a tolerant, affectionate little smile, her smooth skin rosy and pink in the winter chill. More evidence of young love, Stella thought wistfully—there was nothing for the complexion like the thrill ride of infatuation. "Where were you, anyway—care to share?"

Stella raised her eyebrows. "Maybe later, honey. Boring work stuff."

"Well, if you're done for the day, why don't you help us? Cinnamon's staying for dinner. When we get done, we can maybe fix brownies and watch a movie."

"Oh," said Stella, and she could feel the color creeping into her face. "That sounds real cozy and all, but I. There's. Um."

What there was, was a real chance that she'd come face-to-face with her baby girl snuggling on the couch with, well, another girl. Which Stella had absolutely no problem with, in theory. But in application . . . well, she might just need a little more time to get used to it.

As soon as the thought popped into her head, Stella felt

ashamed of herself. For one thing, Noelle wasn't really a little girl anymore—she was a grown woman of nearly thirty, old enough to make all her own decisions and hang out with whomever she wanted to.

Noelle was looking at her anxiously, a few stray twigs stuck in her magenta hair, which was back in its usual spiky style today.

"I'd love to," Stella amended as heartily as she could, just as her phone started ringing. "Excuse me, will you?"

She squinted at the phone and went to the front porch to take the call. Chrissy. She hit the answer button and eased down on the top step as Roxy bounded over and leaned into her knee, demanding attention.

"Hi, Chrissy."

"Hi, Stella, figure out who done it yet?"

"No, but I found you a few new boyfriends." She described the outing up to Walsingham's.

"Dang, you keep having all kinds of fun without me. Well, we got rid of most everyone around here, they've all gone home so everything ought to be back to normal tomorrow and I'll be back at the shop. Can you live without me until then?"

"I'll do my best." Stella grinned. "Find out anything new for me?"

"Just a little more on Priss's car. Nothing they won't already have up in Fayette, but I figured you'd want to know. You hear anything from Goat?"

"Naw . . . no news is probably good news from him right now." She told Chrissy about the crime scene van. "I guess with them all being back down here, they've probably left Priss and Liman and Keller on ice up there. The car's probably fallen pretty far down their priorities."

"Ewww, Stella, that's nasty," Chrissy objected. "You really think they got 'em in a freezer?"

"No, I think it's more like a fridge. I don't know, probably they keep it right above freezing or something."

"Anyway, that car of hers? She's only had it a month. Paid full sticker, too—the guy at the dealership said he told her she could take a silver one off the lot with all these dealer incentives and what not, and she told him she only drives black cars. It was kind of funny, he said she made it sound like anything else was the height of bad taste, you know?"

Stella grimaced. "I can just imagine. Why, she's probably got opinions on every last little thing—what toothpaste is worthy of her teeth, what brand of toilet cleaner is good enough for her toilets."

Was, she corrected herself silently. *Had.* Past tense.

"Yeah, well, this guy didn't seem to mind too much. Said she buys a new car from him every two years on the dot, but this was her first Mercedes, and I don't guess he's sold a whole shitload of those while the economy's been on vacation."

"Yeah." Something stirred in Stella's memory, something that didn't fit quite right. "When did you say she bought the car?"

"Let's see . . . she picked it up on February eighteenth."

"And when did Salty say he last talked to her?"

"Salty? What does that have to do with anything?"

"It was New Year's, didn't he say? He hasn't talked to her since January, so how do you figure he knew she was driving a Mercedes?"

There was silence on the line, and Stella could imagine Chrissy pinching her bottom lip, the way she always did when she was thinking.

"Huh. I guess he wouldn't."

"But there he was, sure as shoot, talking about how she had her uptown life now, with her Mercedes and her country club and everything, remember? Which makes me think he was lying to us."

"Yeah . . ."

"And why does a guy lie about a woman?"

"Why, Stella, that's your department, ain't it? I imagine there's as many reasons as there are men out there stretching the truth to suit them, which is practically all of them."

"I'm thinking I might ought to go see Salty again." Stella could feel the excitement building in her veins. She'd been lied to . . . and in her business that nearly always meant she was digging in the right direction.

"That's getting to be a regular thing," Chrissy exclaimed. "You been to his house, you waylaid him on his way to the gym—why, if that wife of his gets wind of you stalking him, she's liable to get jealous."

Stella hung up and managed to get to her feet without her knees making more than a token complaint, just as the girls were packing the leftover lights into the boxes.

"We're going to take a break, Mama," Noelle said as they came up the walk, Roxy bounding at their heels. "Could you make us some popcorn?"

"Why, sure, honey. Only then I'm going to have to run out on an errand after all." She had a thought. "I'll, um . . . call, when I'm close to home. So you know when to *expect me*." She was tempted to add a wink, just to make sure she got her point all the way across.

Inside, Cinnamon went to wash up in the powder room, and Noelle followed Stella into the kitchen.

"Mama, you don't have to do that," she said.

"Do what?"

"You know—that whole thing with the *I'll call first* and all. Honestly, you're embarrassing."

Stella gave her daughter a tentative smile. "Isn't that a mother's job? To embarrass you at every opportunity?"

"There ain't anything going on with me and Cinnamon, anyway," Noelle continued calmly. "So you can quit blushing and carrying on."

"Oh?"

"Nope. I've been thinking about what I learned from my relationship with Joy. I think what I didn't focus enough on was, when you try to make things go faster than they naturally would, why, you can just *ruin* the whole thing."

"Ah." Stella nodded and tried very hard to look like that thought had never occurred to her.

"So with Cinnamon, I'm going to take it nice and slow. Friends first, you know? If it turns into something else, fine. If it doesn't, I guess that's fine, too."

"Um . . . sure. Only . . . it's just, last night—when I got home and you weren't here—and I talked to your friends—well, the ones who were still up, anyway—I mean I just kind of figured you all were, you know, that you and Cinnamon were hitting it off."

"Mama, I was *drinkin',*" Noelle said, horrified. "Me and Cinnamon went for a drive, and I'm pretty sure we had a nice time, but she wouldn't take advantage of a situation where someone was out of their senses. Why, that would be just, just a breach of, of, *manners* and *courtesy* and doing what's right."

Stella nodded slowly. She considered warning Noelle that her new friend was rumored to be a heartbreaker, but then she figured maybe it wasn't really her business.

Cinnamon came out of the bathroom with a big smile on her face. "Oh, Mrs. Hardesty, I just love them little samplers you got in the bathroom. Did you stitch those yourself?"

"Yes, honey," Stella said, unaccountably pleased, though

she'd stopped noticing the cross-stitched samplers years ago. She really ought to take them down; they were part of the old life, the other life, the one from before, when Ollie ruled their home with his temper and his fists.

"'Every house where love abides'—why, that just made me smile. I love that quote. At my dad's place, the only thing they got on the wall is that nasty modern shit, big old splashes of paint and what-all that looks like a toddler done it in preschool class."

"Oh," Stella said, her misgivings melting away. Impulsively she gathered both girls in for a hug. "Let's put that corn on the stove and get poppin'."

Chapter Twenty-eight

S tella stuffed a generous serving of buttery popcorn into a jumbo Ziploc bag and had just tossed it on the passenger seat for later, when a familiar cruiser rolled slowly to a stop in front of the house. She briefly considered making a run for it, but she'd recently installed a fence in the backyard for Roxy, cutting off her own best escape route. Instead she took a deep breath and waited for the sheriff.

He unfolded himself from the driver's seat, a process that involved grabbing the top of the car's roof with one hand while he swiveled and wrangled his long legs out first. It was a fascinating thing to behold, kind of like seeing someone unfold a pair of nail scissors out of a pocketknife. They just didn't make a car that could properly contain a fine specimen of man like Goat.

"Heading for the border?" he asked dryly. "Without saying good-bye?"

"This is awkward," Stella said. A brisk wind gusted along the street, stirring the last of the fallen leaves into the drifts of snow that had refrozen here and there in the gutters. "I know you're probably figuring on a chat and all, but I'm just ever so late."

"I could insist," Goat said. He shut the door of the cruiser with an ominous thud and walked slowly toward her, hitching up his regulation khakis. He wore mirrored sunglasses even under the steely gray skies, and Stella got a crazy funhouse view of herself in their lenses as he came closer.

Damn that Goat Jones. Even as the working part of her brain was cooking up excuses just as fast as she could manage, the swampy feelings part was starting to bubble and burble.

"All's I'd have to do is mention to Daphne and them all about that one little bit of evidence I ain't logged yet," Goat continued. He took one extra step, and Stella found that she was staring squarely at his Adam's apple, not six inches away. Slowly, exquisite alarm shooting along her nerve endings, she let her gaze travel up, up, up . . . past his slightly stubbly and hard-edged jaw, over the ridge of his almost-too-generous bottom lip, along the planes of his cheeks, up to the sunglasses. At this distance, she could make out the shadow of his eyes behind the lenses, but then something—the wind maybe, or a bit of dust drifting by—obscured and blurred her vision and she blinked.

"I'm not *trying* to hold y'all up," she found herself mumbling. "Only it's got a little complicated."

What would Goat say about the flash drive, about the pictures of Ferg Rohossen, who not six months after Stella's vigorous session with him had got himself picked up by the Morgan county crew for jacking a load of cigarettes? The sheriff might be sympathetic. He might find his way to understanding the delicate balance between justice and vengeance. He might even understand that Stella had to use unorthodox methods to get there—after all, he'd saved her bacon several other times when the demands of her job had propelled her into the gray area.

Except for one thing: Goat was proud, and dedicated, and committed, and above all, he was a law man. He truly believed in the motto stitched on the pocket of his uniform, the one that said HONESTY—INTEGRITY—COURAGE in gold thread right above the state seal.

And damn if that didn't just charge her up that much more.

"Everything's complicated with you," Goat said, his voice going dusky and low and growly. He lifted one big strong hand and pulled off the glasses, so that Stella found herself staring up into a thousand megawatts of blue-eyed fire. "I'm pretty sure you ain't worth the trouble."

And then he took his free hand and gently pushed a flyaway chunk of Stella's hair off her forehead, tracing along the edge of her brow with a callused warm thumb. He followed a hot-blooded path along the curve of her ear, down the nape of her neck, across her collarbones, and dipped his fingertip into the hollow of her throat, at which point Stella figured Salty might as well keep on murdering all the ex-girlfriends he cared to, because she wasn't going anywhere.

"But then again, I might be," she managed to whisper. She stood up on her tiptoes and closed her eyes and aimed, and the next thing she knew, her lips found his and some crazy-assed energy went sparking off in every direction and there was tongue and there were teeth and there was more of that growling thing he did, and then she was somehow backed up against the Jeep and she wasn't even teetering on her toes anymore, because Goat had practically lifted her right off the ground with his strong hands on her ass, his sunglasses clattering to the street as he leaned in and let her know just how he felt about how much trouble she was.

"Oh," she gasped, because this new side of Goat was more than she dared to expect, and then he kissed her a little harder and lifted her legs right off the ground and she wrapped them around him before she remembered where she was, in front of Rolf Bayer, who had a habit of peering out his drapes and the Knowleses, who at any moment might come out the front door, and her brain sent a firm message to her feet to get right back on the ground where they belonged, only Goat picked that moment to wrap her hair around his hand and pull her head back so he could kiss her along the soft place under her jawbone and she wondered idly if he'd mind just taking all her clothes off right here or whether he might sling her over his shoulder and carry her into the house.

Instead he drew back and let her slide slowly to the ground, his expression both amused and irritated and smoldering. Stella was pretty sure she'd just keep sliding until her jelly legs collapsed on the ground, if Goat didn't grab her shoulders at the last minute and hold her up.

"Didn't plan on that," he said. "Ought to arrest you twice, making me behave like a damn fool in the middle of the street."

Stella sucked in sweet cold air and licked her bruised lips and tried to gather her wits. She didn't care about Bayer or the Knowleses or anyone else who might have seen what had just taken place; she didn't even care if Goat tossed her in the lockup—as long as she got to ride over in his car, and they took the long way.

But she was trembling. Chalk it up to some post-endorphin-rush effect—her teeth were a tick away from chattering out of her head, and her heart was thudding overtime. And a little blinky light was going off somewhere deep in her soul.

A warning light. A danger sign.

Because she was on the edge of giving it all away, of caring so much for Goat that she endangered everything else—the barriers she'd constructed, the side business she'd built up so carefully, the safe place she represented for the abused and helpless.

Reckless felt irresistible. In the moments that they touched, all that mattered was getting a little more of him, a *lot* more of him, and that wasn't right. They both had jobs to do, and even if they sometimes seemed to be at cross purposes, the work still had to be done.

So Stella bit the inside of her cheek just hard enough to shock her system back to attention. The feeling in her limbs tingled and returned, and she stood up on her own power and gave Goat a gentle little shove, pushing him back away from the Jeep. Then she tugged her top down over her jeans—it had somehow managed to ride up in a scandalous fashion—and patted her hair back into place.

"Arrest me all you want," she said, making her voice sound bored, "only it won't change the fact that *you* started that, not me. Now git on out of the way, I got to go. And before you head back to all your law duties, make sure you get them boxes down like you promised Noelle."

Then she edged past him and walked around the front of her Jeep to the driver's side and managed to get the door unlocked and her seat belt on and the engine started without looking back.

And that felt so good, so brazen, that Stella figured she'd push her luck and got her lipstick out of her purse. Oh, she loved that Regal Red. She applied it with care in the rearview mirror, mashing her lips together when she was done, and only then did she start driving slowly away from her house.

And she didn't look, not until she was safely past both Goat and his damn department-issue Charger, and then she peeked in the mirror just long enough to see that he was standing with his fists on his hips, shaking his head and laughing.

Guess I won that round, she thought happily as she put the pedal to the floor and left him in the dust.

Chapter Twenty-nine

By the time she got to the Mingus home, her heart had stopped hammering and her skin had stopped tingling, though the memory of Goat's hands on her ass was proving difficult to shake.

Still, she pushed those thoughts from her mind as she parked a couple of houses down the street, behind a mud-splattered Ford pickup. No sense alerting Salty that she was back to pay another visit. At least it looked like she might have him to herself, which would make things far simpler—the minivan was nowhere to be seen, and Salty's truck was parked neatly where it had been the last time.

She got her lightweight portable rig from the cargo hold, slinging the high-tech pack over her shoulder. She'd brought only the simplest gear along for this job, because even though Salty's innocence was looking far more dubious than before, she still didn't get the kind of vibe from him that warranted the heavy-duty treatment. And more and more these days, Stella was going with her gut.

Her luck continued. After getting no answer at the front

door, she slipped carefully around the side of the house and found him in the backyard, tinkering with the electrical that he was laying down in the half-finished shed. It clearly wasn't working the way he'd planned, since he had a work light strung on a fat yellow extension cord running from inside the house, and he was cussing a blue streak while he poked at a galvanized floor box. Stella was treated to a fine view of his mostly adequate rear end, but she leaned against the framed-out shed wall for a moment and considered how, once you get one nice man-butt stuck in your mind, you can look at all kinds of others and they don't do anything for you.

Finally she coughed delicately. Salty dropped the screwdriver he was holding, and it clanked on the poured concrete floor and rolled away.

On top of Salty's other problems, the shed wasn't level.

"I'd keep my day job," Stella suggested.

Salty managed a terse string of curses and got to his feet. "This ain't the best time, Miz Hardesty," he said. "My wife's taken the kids over to her sister's so I can get this fucking thing finished, and I want to take advantage of daylight."

"Dark's coming early today, I expect," Stella said mildly, setting her pack on the floor and unzipping it. She crouched down and sorted through the contents, and when she stood up again, she took the Bersa from the leg holster under her loose fleece pants, almost as an afterthought. The Mak was a loss at this point—she only hoped the boys babysitting Walsingham would have the good sense to wipe it, but otherwise, it was just another in a long line of unregistered weapons, one of the sunk costs of Stella's business.

Salty regarded the gun with resignation. "Well, hell. What now? I told you everything."

"You didn't tell me you talked to Priss last month," Stella

corrected him. "Probably more than once. Am I right? You know, I can look at your cell phone bills, if I want."

She wasn't 100 percent certain about that last bit, but she wouldn't be surprised; Chrissy had gotten so slick with her on-line poking around that Stella guessed she could probably get a hold of his baby pictures and first grade report card if she wanted, too.

Only, to her surprise, forty-five minutes later, Salty had admitted only to occasional drink-and-dial sessions where he tried to get Priss to indulge in phone shenanigans. Beyond that, he was still sticking to his story. Stella had got him rigged up to the foundation two-by-fours with a simple set of plastic restraints and some boot cuffs that she had recently treated herself to because they came in a rainbow of colors. For Salty, she used a vibrant purple, though he didn't seem to appreciate her thoughtfulness.

A little work with a suede flogger seemed to unsettle him more than causing him any real pain, but it did get him to admit that Priss had occasionally asked him to wear an Oasis Pool Maintenance uniform in the bedroom while she ordered him to check her filters . . . and a turn with a leather riding crop had him coughing up some rather dull details about tax reporting for his father-in-law's firm, but despite Stella's best efforts, he continue to maintain his innocence in the matter of knocking off his rival for Priss's attention, or Priss herself, or Liman.

And that was perplexing. It was exceedingly rare that Stella got this far in an interrogation without turning up the dirty little nuggets she'd been looking for. In fact, she didn't recall ever interrogating anyone who turned out to be innocent before, and she didn't care for it one bit. For one thing, it meant she would have subjected an innocent—well, relatively speaking—man to unnecessary pain. And for another, she did not care to be wrong.

That was why, when she felt the whoosh of something moving fast through the air behind her only a fraction of a second after hearing the snap of a footstep in the shed, it was almost a relief. She had been breathing hard from exertion, and Salty had been making various sounds of protestation, so she wasn't really surprised she'd been snuck up on, but just as something heavy crashed down on the top of her head with a distressing amount of force, Stella had the satisfaction of knowing that while she'd been wrong about Salty, she'd been barking up a tree that wasn't growing too far away from the right one.

Chapter Thirty

Stella had woken up from being beat unconscious a couple times in the past, and it had been a disorienting experience, involving grogginess and double vision and tingling in the extremities.

This time, however, Stella found that within seconds of waking up with a considerable headache, she had a crystal-clear memory of being beat at her own game. She also noticed that her mysterious bludgeoner had got into her supplies and secured her wrists with a pair of her own disposable black plastic riot cuffs. Something weighed uncomfortably against her midsection, but she couldn't see what it was over her bound wrists.

It took her all of half a second to figure out where she was: the backseat of a minivan that was clearly used more often for toting kids than captives, judging from the faint smells of Frostees left in a hot car, and diapers and spit-up and lost french fries. And there were visual clues, too, armless action figures and wild-haired dolls and Legos lodged in the corners and under the seats, and car seats bolted tight to the captain's chairs.

She couldn't make out much in the way of the driver, from

her vantage point in the backseat, other than a thin wrist fiddling with the radio.

Well, it wasn't Salty—that was for sure—since Salty was built bigger and wasn't wearing maroon nail polish or jangly silver bracelets the last time Stella saw him. No, it appeared that Stella's fate was in the hands of his wife. Interestingly, Doraleigh hadn't brought her husband along. Maybe she hadn't even bothered to take off his restraints. The more she thought about it, Stella figured that must be the case, or Doraleigh would have used the boot cuffs on her; as it was, her feet seemed to have been left free, which she confirmed by jiggling them.

Which was, in itself, a useful development. A woman who comes home and finds her husband tied up and being tortured, and then elects to leave him there, is a woman dealing with a complicated set of emotions. Something to be delved into, for sure, as soon as Stella was in a position to delve.

Which she would be in a matter of moments. Funny thing about those riot cuffs—you'd think all the rabble-rousers and protesters and demonstrators who ended up in them might have had the foresight to watch any of the dozens of YouTube videos showing exactly how to get out of them. Of course, real foresight would mean tucking a straight pin—preferably one of those nice .50-millimeter steel-shaft glass-head pins she sold at the shop—into the stretchy bit of lace covering the underwire of her bra, as she had trained herself to do before each and every mission.

Because preparation was one of those things that separated Stella from the amateurs. Which Doraleigh clearly was.

She slipped the pin from her bra and went to work on the cuffs' roller locking tension system. It took only a few minutes of fiddling to get the pin where she wanted it between the roller lock and the strap, and her left hand was free. Thirty seconds later, her right hand was, too. It was the sort of thing that took hours and hours of practice to master, but slow times in the shop were perfect for that sort of thing.

Stella dropped the plastic loops on the floor and flexed her wrists a few times. She couldn't see much out of the minivan's windows other than the occasional treetop or power line. With her hands free, she found she could focus a bit better, and she thought about the fact that it appeared to have been Doraleigh all along who'd been behind the killing spree.

All, presumably, over a man—and not just any man, but the spectacularly unimpressive Salty Mingus. Sure, it was bound to piss a woman off if her man kept mooning after his old girl-friend. And no doubt, it complicated things when you were staying home bringing up his children. But honestly, Stella couldn't quite get her mind around the idea of a woman taking a long look at Salty and finding herself stirred to passion strong enough to make a killer of her.

Stella twisted to get a better look at whatever was cinching her stomach and discovered with surprise that she was wearing a Home Depot giveaway canvas tool belt, the kind they handed out at vendor demos. The ends had been wrapped around twice and knotted securely, if a little snugly, at her waist. More inter-estingly, the handy tool pockets bulged with lumpy objects—heavy sons of bitches that were pressing down in the neighborhood of her bladder and her kidneys and whatever else was located at that latitude. The tops of the pockets had been clamped shut with big heavy-duty binder clips.

So it was another drowning that Doraleigh had in mind to keep Stella quiet. She nodded to herself: a beginner mistake. Novice criminals tended to find something that worked for them once, and stick to it, rarely thinking to branch out and expand their repertoire until they were a lot further down the criminal path. Just like a man who hit his wife with an open palm to reduce the risk of bruising was liable to do it to the next gal he hooked up with, and the next.

Still, she doubted Doraleigh would be using Adriana's pond again, and she made a quick mental inventory of likely ponds, lakes, and reservoirs in the county. Depending on how far Doraleigh felt like driving, there were lots of possibilities. If it was up to Stella—if it were she who was hoping to send a body to a watery and hopefully permanent grave, she'd probably go for one of the old limestone quarries up near Picot, which went nearly a hundred feet deep in some places.

Of course, a quarry was a funny place. With a stone bottom and walls, it wasn't as friendly to aquatic life, to plants rooting on the floor and critters eating algae and so on up the food chain, as was, say, a farm pond. Stella had gone swimming in the old quarries as a teen, and it was downright creepy how the bottom, as it sloped away from the walls to unknowable depths, was covered with only a thin layer of greenish brown slime, with not even a school of guppies for company. A body left in such a place would bump about the bottom, where the sun couldn't reach without even a catfish for company. The thought made her shudder.

"Are you wakin' up back there, Miz Hardesty?" a voice came from the front. A full head of striped curls leaned around to look at her.

"Doraleigh Wall," Stella said. "Or I suppose I should say Mingus, now. How long you and Salty been married, anyway?"

"Three years in June, not that you'd care."

"What do you mean? Why wouldn't I care?" Stella demanded, mystified. "I'm as big a supporter of matrimony as the next person."

"Yeah, well, the way you been chasing around trying to

figure out what happened to that no-good homewrecking stuck-up bitch Priss Porter, when *she's* the one gone and, and, and made a *mockery* of my marriage—so I can't even hold my head up high in the grocery store—"

"Are you saying folks knew about Salty seeing Priss? It was common knowledge?"

"What would you call it, when your husband doesn't bother to come home from his so-called business trip to the city until midnight even though he *knows* it's your bunco night? Oh, you can bet all the girls in the neighborhood know about that."

Because you told them, Stella thought. Doraleigh didn't strike her as the kind of woman who'd suffer in silence. "Did you kill her, Doraleigh?"

"Only 'cause she didn't leave me no choice! It was self-defense! I mean, it was self-defense of Salty, but that's like my own personal self-defense 'cause we're married and all." Doraleigh's voice had gone all high and thin and wobbly.

"Which is why he's still tied up to a two-by-four and you're driving the getaway car," Stella muttered.

There was a suspicious pause. "You making fun of me, Stella?"

Stella sighed. "No," she said tiredly. "Just trying to get the facts straight." She felt the lumpy objects tied to her waist through the canvas and figured them for river stones, the kind of rocks that people liked to line their driveways with. Had she seen them at the Mingus's place? She couldn't recall, but there had certainly been a bounty of building materials lying around in back.

"Well, you might as well quit that. I hate to say it, but you might want to stop worrying about mine and Salty's differences and start makin' your peace with Jesus with the time you got left."

"Me? What do *I* have to be confessin' over? Wouldn't that

be more on you, seein' as you're fixing to drown me like a bag of cats?"

"Only 'cause I was *provoked,*" Doraleigh insisted in that same thin and reedy voice, and Stella realized there would be no talking sense to the gal. Denial put folks in a weird state, one where you might as well let them just spin their wheels because nothing you said or did was going to reach them anyway.

"What about Keller? Did you kill him, too?"

"Who?"

"The guy in Priss's trunk?"

"Oh, *that.* Of course not. Why would I kill a perfect stranger? You'd have to ask Priss why she done it."

"Priss killed him? You're *sure?*"

"Well, I mean, she didn't say she did, exactly—but there she was sitting in *my* living room asking *my* husband to get rid of a body, I'd say it's pretty clear she done it."

"Wait. Priss came to your *house?*"

"Well, yeah." Doraleigh's voice trembled with bitterness. "She comes to *my* house and knocks on *my* door, and when I open it I know right away who she is, of *course* I knew from all those pictures Salty hides in the bottom of his sock drawer, and I couldn't even *believe* she had the nerve after I'd caught Salty sneaking up to the city last summer—"

"So you knew all about the affair."

"Yes, but I didn't know how far she'd go to hang on to Salty. She was an evil, scheming woman, Miz Hardesty, you got to see that."

"Yeah, that's pretty evil, forcing herself on Salty that way," Stella muttered under her breath.

"And I made him *promise* it was over, or I told him he could just stay up there and forget coming home."

Stella didn't say it, but she'd lay odds Salty would've taken

271

that deal, if Priss had been the one to offer it. He was one seriously smitten man. For the umpteenth time, she marveled at the hold Priss seemed to have on such a variety of men.

"So when she sat her skinny little ass down in *my* living room, and Salty told me to go to our room and give them time to *talk alone* . . ." Doraleigh's voice was finally cracking, sniffling hiccups punctuating her speech. "Well, I went down the hall but I was listening, of course I was listening to her and she wasn't even all that *nice* about it, Miz Hardesty. It was like she thought she could just waltz in and wind Salty around her little finger and get him to do whatever she wanted—with our own two *babies* sleeping down the hall from her—and she wanted him to help her get rid of a dead body in the trunk of that fancy car. I mean, of all the nerve, she says it won't take him but an hour out of his evening and he had all the equipment and tools and what-all and didn't he think he owed her after all the time they'd been together?"

"So that's when you decided to kill her?"

"No, not then, not quite I didn't. I waited until I just couldn't stand it no more, and then I came into the living room and I told her to get the hell off my property and then, and then—" Doraleigh's sniffles turned to choked sobs, and Stella felt almost a little bit sorry for her. "—and then Salty tells me she's in a hard place, couldn't we just help her this once, and I see that she won't quit until she's got every bit of him poisoned with her evil desires."

"Here's the thing I don't get, Doraleigh—you're not a real big gal. How the heck did you get all three of them bodies into Adriana's pond?"

Doraleigh made a sound of disgust that was half snort and half ragged cry. "I wasn't gonna kill anyone at all. That's the crazy thing. After Priss left, Salty had him a couple a tall boys and passed out in the living room and the whole time I was just getting madder and madder. The kids were down for the night and I just thought, well, I'll go and I'll reason with her, woman to woman. You know?"

"Uh . . . yeah. Sure. What time was this?"

"I don't know . . . maybe one thirty or so by the time I made up my mind. Anyway, when I got there Priss was so wound up, I couldn't get a word in, she told me *forget* Salty, she said we're a couple of *resourceful* women, we can take care of things ourselves, and the whole time I'm like whoa, wait, bitch, I'm here to call you out and then she's waving her checkbook around, saying if I just help her get this dead guy into the Wolforts' pond, she'll pay me five thousand dollars and if I don't, she'll make it look like Salty did it anyway."

It was almost refreshing to know that Priss's shamelessness knew no bounds, but Stella was perplexed. "How would she have done that? I mean, it wasn't like she had, you know, Salty's prints or DNA or anything to connect him to the body."

Doraleigh fixed her with a toxic gaze. "Stella. We're talking *Salty,* here. Who knows what she had of his?"

"Uh . . ." Stella considered trying to explain elementary forensics to the woman, and realized she was out of her depth. "Okay. So . . . you helped her?"

"I made her put the plastic in the van," Doraleigh said with a trace of satisfaction. "Them captain's chairs? Why, they just pop right out and we moved them back and made a nice big area back there. With two of us, it didn't take much work to get that—that *man* in here, and then we went in to have a stiff drink to get ready, which was *her* idea, Miz Hardesty, before we went over to the pond."

"Weren't you curious about why she had a dead guy in the first place?"

"Miz *Hardesty*," Doraleigh said with considerable dignity. "That was *not* my business. All I meant to do was come to an understanding and get home to my *family*."

"Er . . . okay. So you're having a drink . . ."

"And there's all this thumping around from the bedroom and we can hear Liman talking on the phone and Priss is like, *Oh shit, he's not supposed to be awake,* and she's all, *Don't worry, don't worry,* but then he comes busting out of there like I told you, like some kind of lunatic—"

"I think she drugged him," Stella said. "So he'd be asleep when you-all were doing the body disposing."

Or, more likely, she'd drugged him much earlier, before Stella herself had visited, and after Salty had turned her down. Priss was just full of contingency plans, Stella noted with grudging admiration.

"Well, maybe. All's I know is he tears out of his room all crazy like it's the Second Coming or something and Priss hits him with that thing—"

"Beer stein," Stella interrupted helpfully.

"That's what you keep saying, but have you ever in your life seen anyone drink a beer out of one a them things?"

"Uh . . ."

"No, ma'am, and you won't, either. Not when you can get a frosty mug, it ain't even a contest. Anyway, Priss hits him and he goes down all twitchy and then it got a little weird for a while because I'm like uh, *Maybe he needs a doctor,* and she's all, *Shit, shit, shit,* and by the time she made up her mind, he was kind of, like, you know, dead."

"*Kind of* dead? Did y'all check?"

"Hey, that was *her* thing, I figure *she* hit him and besides it was *her* brother, not mine, but she seemed sure, yeah. And she stares at him a minute and then she says, well, how about if I add a couple thousand bucks, we can get rid of two as easy as one, and what am I going to do? I mean I'm already toting around one body, what's another? And so we dragged Liman out there, too. And that was almost worse than the first one, Miz Hardesty. I mean on account of he was still kind of warm and all. And his head kept bumping on the ground when we dragged him."

Hysteria, definitely, Stella figured. "Just one little thing I don't get. Where, in all of this, did *Priss* end up dead?"

"Oh. *That.* So we get Liman out to the van and Priss is like, I'll take the hands and you get the feet and we'll just put him up on top of, you know, the other guy. And I'm like, are you sure, it's your *brother,* your kin, and that guy's not fresh, if you see what I'm saying. I say, just let's get some more plastic from the shed, because Liman had plenty in there, I think they were drop-cloths, they had paint on them. I said we'll put some plastic on the other guy and it'll be more, um, sanitary or whatever. Because I don't care what you say, at the end of the day, it's still your blood kin, you don't want to go disrespecting that."

Stella figured the *disrespecting* line had been crossed somewhere before Priss had actually killed her own brother, but she kept the thought to herself. "I take it she didn't agree."

"So get this," Doraleigh said, twisting in her seat to look Stella in the eye, momentarily oblivious of the road. "She tells me, why don't I leave the thinking to her. We haul Liman up into the van and she goes and gets some bungee cords from the shed and kind of wraps the plastic around them two and then I'm like, well, let's get this done so we head out to the Wolforts'. Only the whole time I'm just thinking about what a bitch she's always been. And not just to me, to everyone. *Leave the thinking to me*—don't that sound like something she would of said back in school?"

"Well, I don't . . ."

"I was a couple of years ahead of her, but everyone said it. Everyone."

"So you get to the pond," Stella prompted.

"Yeah, we parked on the far side and it wasn't too hard, we got Liman dumped in no trouble, he floated out a ways and just kind of sunk down real peaceful. That wasn't bad. And then we're dragging the other guy and we're, you know, trying not to breathe his smell and all, and Priss all of a sudden drops her end and flips her hair and says, *Look at us, a couple of women doing men's work,* and I'm all, *What the hell?* And she says men are dumb beasts, you can get them to do anything you want when it's all fun and games, but when you got trouble, it's women got to clean up the mess."

Stella couldn't help thinking that wasn't too far off of her own philosophy, but she could see where it was a delicate and subjective matter. "You didn't care for that," she guessed.

"I said, what do you mean, get them to do anything you want? And she gives me this look like she feels *sorry* for me, and she says, come on, I think we both know what I'm talking about. And I'm all, you have something to say to me, just *say* it, and she . . . she . . ."

Doraleigh was beginning to choke up again, which Stella had to believe wasn't great for her visibility. "It's okay," she said as soothingly as she could.

"It's *not* okay. She says, well, all I ever had to do to Salty was give him this one look and he'd do, he'd do anything I wanted."

"Oh."

"And she wasn't even *sorry.* It was like she thought I'd agree with her or something. My own *husband*? I couldn't get Salty to take out the trash if I offered to flash my tits at a Cards game."

"Okay, I think I—"

"Now you see where I'm going?" Doraleigh demanded, giving the road a cursory glance and tugging the wheel back into a roughly straight direction. "Now you understand? I just grabbed one of those bungees off those guys and I got her before she figured out what I was doing."

"You strangled Priss with a bungee cord."

"Well, yeah, Miz Hardesty, what do you think I been trying to tell you? I mean, Salty couldn't even help himself around her, she was *that* evil."

Poor Salty, Stella thought, getting tangled up with two such utterly reprehensible, unredeemable women. Only, he was the one who'd kept going back for more, wasn't he? Wasn't like there was anyone holding a gun to his head to make him keep pursuing Priss after she'd dumped him.

That gave Stella an idea. Of course, she didn't have an actual gun on her any longer—and if Doraleigh had an ounce of sense, the girl would have tucked it away someplace safe so she didn't hurt herself with it, but unfortunately she struck Stella as the kind of girl who'd run headlong into trouble, so it was probably sitting on the passenger seat nice and handy for Doraleigh to shoot her with if she got the hankering.

So one course of action was to simply barrel through the car's midsection, between the two captain's chairs with their child seats strapped firmly in place, and make a grab for it. But if she was wrong, if Doraleigh had the gun in her purse or pocket or, for that matter, in her hand, something was bound to get fucked up and they'd end up shooting and veering into oncoming traffic, which wouldn't be a good outcome for anyone.

So Stella rolled onto her side a bit farther, one of the river rocks squishing into her ribs, and reviewed the contents of the floor, considering and discarding food wrappers, empty juice boxes, a stuffed frog . . . until her gaze lighted on the remains of a plastic car that had once worn a jaunty grin painted on its hood but now, after apparently being stepped on by someone of considerable weight, sported a broken windshield with plastic shards poking out in several directions.

Stella palmed the car, keeping an eye on Doraleigh, who was back to fiddling with the radio, trying to tune out the persistent static. She worked one of the shards back and forth until it tore free from the toy, and regarded her makeshift weapon, a four-inch strip of soft plastic whose edges were soft and flexible, but which ended in a sharpish point.

It would have to do.

Stella closed her eyes and took three slow, deep breaths, the way she'd learned in physical therapy. She conjured up her peaceful vision, the one that Glynnis, her therapist, had suggested she choose to center herself before every session. Stella had told Glynnis that the vision was a tall sunflower bending softly in a breeze, but the truth was that what she saw when she closed her eyes and breathed deep was the very fine rear view of the sheriff, from the broad no-nonsense shoulders straining the limits of his uniform shirt, down to that sweet, tight ass, down those long, long legs to those polished black brogues.

She gave herself a moment to focus on her vision, letting it fill her senses with a feeling of peace and belonging in the universe, and then she sprang from the seat and through the car as fast as she could, slamming into the back of the driver's seat and hooking an arm around the headrest and Doraleigh's neck, jabbing her in the space behind her ear with the plastic shard with the other hand.

"What are you doing?" Doraleigh shrieked as the car wove dangerously into the other lane before she righted it at the very last moment.

"Don't talk," Stella said quickly. "Keep your eyes on the road and keep driving. What I have here is a *kris* knife. It's Javanese, and it's small, but it's engineered to be completely fucking deadly, and it's digging into your sternomastoid which is just *dangerously* close to your jugular. If I stick you just so, you'll bleed to death, and there won't be anything anyone can do to help you. Not many people know exactly how to get around all the nerves and tendons and whatnot, but an old army medic taught me and I guarantee you I won't miss if you give me reason."

It was a lot of tall-tale-telling to get done in one breath, and Stella was shaking with adrenaline and the sheer effort of the lie by the time she finished. She glanced at the passenger seat and, sure enough, there was her little gun glinting in the summer sun.

Doraleigh nodded slowly, straining away from the plastic shard. "Don't hurt me," she whispered. "I got kids that depend on me."

"I ain't going to do anything at all to you," Stella said. "Long as you do what I tell you."

"What happened to you, anyway?" Doraleigh asked in a plaintive voice. "You used to be such a nice lady. I remember when you used to volunteer in the school office."

Stella sighed. "I'm still a nice lady. Only, a different kind of nice."

She glanced out the window, checked the slant of the winter sun to get her bearings, and recognized a black ridge of cliffs that rose up out of the ground to the right a few miles away, and realized where Doraleigh had been planning to dump her.

"Homer Reservoir," she said admiringly. "Not bad. If you would a tipped me into the far end, I probably would have got all tangled up in the water weeds and shit, and they wouldn't of found me until the Second Coming."

"That was the idea," Doraleigh said glumly.

Stella dug a little deeper with the shard. "Well, better luck next time you decide to off somebody. Now, why don't you take a nice wide U-turn and head us back to town."

Chapter Thirty-one

She would have called ahead, but reaching for her phone would have meant letting loose her headlock on Doraleigh, plus even though she had Goat on speed dial, she was afraid she'd hit the wrong keys in all the excitement, and it seemed to her the situation had become plenty confusing enough.

When they pulled into the sheriff's department parking lot, she was relieved to see Goat's cruiser in its customary spot—and dismayed to see that the Fayette folks were still in town, the crime scene van and Daphne's unmarked Chevy Lumina parked in the guest spaces.

"Pull right up to the front door," Stella suggested, and Doraleigh sighed mightily and eased the minivan's front bumper within a few feet of the glass double doors that were a holdover from the Hardee's days. "Now, lay on the horn."

It took a couple more applications of the "knife," but Doraleigh finally set to honking. Irene was the first out, squinting in a burst of weak late-afternoon sunlight, and Stella reached past Doraleigh and poked the window button. When it slid halfway down, she hollered, "Get the sheriff, please, Irene!" and the old gal ducked back inside without a word.

But it wasn't just Goat who emerged from the building a few minutes later. He was followed by Mike Kutzler and Ian Sloat; Detective Simmons, who was running her hands furiously through her feathered '70s-style shag; as well as Officers Hewson and Long, the two crime scene techs that Stella knew slightly from the last time the team had come to town. It was a wonder any of them still had their jobs, after the debacle they'd shunted onto Goat and his deputies, but it was a sad truth of law enforcement that often it wasn't the cream that rose to the top, but the dregs.

Stella had an inspiration. "Tell 'em you'll only make a full confession to Sheriff Jones," she whispered quickly into Doraleigh's ear. "The way you want to play this is, keep it local. The minute you get into county hands, why, you'll fry for sure. Ask for a private audience with Goat, and you've got a chance."

The knot of lawmen and -women circled the minivan. There was a bit of excitement when the Bersa was spotted on the passenger seat, but Mike dug a wrinkled hankie out of his pocket and opened the passenger door and picked it up gingerly.

Goat, meanwhile, stared in the open driver window, ducking down to get eye level with Stella. "What have you got for us today, Miz Hardesty?" he asked politely, giving away nothing in his clipped, cool tones.

"Only a double murderer," Stella said. "This here's the Porters' killer, in the flesh."

"I ain't talkin' to no one but you, Sheriff," Doraleigh said with conviction. "Now, can you take that knife outta my neck, Stella?"

Daphne had her gun drawn and trained somewhere around the headrest. Stella figured the woman would be just as happy to shoot her as Doraleigh, so she decided to play it by the book.

"I'd, uh, like to surrender my weapon to you, Sheriff Jones," she said. "Maybe if you could open the slider—"

"I advise you not to," Daphne barked.

"Oh, can it, Simmons," Goat said without giving her a glance. He slid the door open and regarded Stella—and her makeshift weapon—with surprise, and then amusement.

"My, my," he said softly.

"What's she got?" Ian called from the other side of the car. Daphne's gun was unmistakably aimed at her now, Stella thought, so she moved very slowly as she handed the plastic shard over to Goat.

"Never you mind that," Goat rumbled, never taking his eyes off Stella as he slipped the plastic into his pocket. "All you need to know is, Miz Hardesty certainly knows how to handle a weapon."

Chapter Thirty-two

Two weeks into April, the house was decorated top to bottom. Goat had come around as promised and brought every single Easter box down from the attic, including some that hadn't been opened in a decade.

Goat also brought the surprising news that Keller McManus had managed to die all on his own, without any intervention by would-be killers, when he mixed Viagra and Ecstasy in an effort to give Priss an evening she'd never forget after the duel—despite the poor showing he'd made against Addney Walsingham—and surprised her with a spectacular coronary event instead. "Blew out his pipes but good," was the way Goat interpreted the autopsy report.

Stella spent a few minutes thinking it was a damn shame that Priss hadn't just called the cops like a rational person, but then she realized that all that mattered to Priss was her own coldhearted self, and she'd never jeopardize her business just to give a guy an orderly exit from the world. If she'd called the law the minute Keller dropped dead, Elegant Company might have gotten itself investigated and Priss might have had to find herself a new occupation, but at least she'd still be alive. As it was, half the town showed up at the Porters' funeral, giving it an almost festival air, but few tears were shed.

A more exhaustive search than the one Stella and Chrissy made failed to turn up a will, and with Priss's only close relative dead right along with her, her extensive estate reverted to the state, where it would spend eons tied up in probate, being piddled away in legal fees.

Stella figured it might be a fitting end to the Priss Porter empire.

On a cold but clear Friday evening, Goat stopped by with takeout from China Paradise. Noelle and Cinnamon were doing laundry and playing checkers in the living room—the pair seemed to have become friends with, as far as Stella could tell, no benefits at all other than those of companionship and a bounty of shared interests. Everyone seemed content to let Noelle's sexual orientation remain an ongoing mystery.

After a thoroughly mediocre meal, Noelle and Cinnamon cleaned the kitchen and Stella and Goat stole a private moment in the living room.

"Got a couple of presents for you," Goat said. "Sorry I didn't wrap 'em."

He handed her an evidence bag containing a blurry, cracked piece of paper. Only after Stella slipped on her reading glasses did she finally make out that it might or might not have once been a photo of a woman standing over a man. She glanced up quickly at Goat, who was polishing his own reading specs on his soft chamois shirt.

"Found that in a pond," he said. Then he handed her a second plastic bag.

The items inside—four of them—were small and gray and oblong with metal thingies that stuck out the ends. Flash drives,

Stella was willing to bet. She could feel the blood flooding her face. Now Goat wasn't looking anywhere near her vicinity.

"Oh, damn," he said, hand going to his pocket. "Called out again. And on a cold night like tonight."

"I didn't hear your phone," Stella said in a shaky voice, clutching the bag of drives tightly in her suddenly clammy hand.

"Got it on vibrate. Well, sorry I couldn't stay."

Stella was sorry, too, in a *you can never get enough of Goat Jones* sort of way, but she was also very glad to have time to process the fact that he'd just saved her ass eight ways to Sunday.

The unseasonably cold and snowy spring kept Goat and his deputies hopping with fender benders and icy-road pileups and the usual bar fights and domestic calls that cabin fever seem to bring out in some folks, but he promised to take Stella out for a proper dinner as soon as things calmed down. Meanwhile, BJ called and invited her to the movies.

Stella felt a little funny about accepting a date with BJ when things with Goat were simmering and sparking, but Noelle gave her a thumbs-up. "No sense trying to control love," she said dramatically. "You got to just let it come in its own time." Stella did her best to pretend she hadn't given her daughter pretty much that very same advice herself.

Dear Big Guy, just let her be happy, she prayed.

Noelle's boss called in a panic, begging her to come back to help with the backlog of beauty-starved customers, and she went back to work. But she took a day off to go shopping with Stella one Tuesday when the shop was closed. She helped Stella pick out a fuchsia dress with an eye-popping V-neckline to wear to Easter services and a darling little suit with a bow tie for Tucker, which, along with a pretty set of amethyst earrings she'd picked out earlier as a surprise for Noelle, pretty much cleaned out her share of the holdup money.

They were having lunch at the food court of the Fayette mall when Noelle put down her fork and set her chin in her hand and got a thinkin' kind of look on her face.

"Joy'n me had a talk," she said.

"Mmm?" Stella was grateful to be chewing at that moment, so she wouldn't be expected to make a more thorough reply.

"I guess I shouldn't have ought to gone fixing her up when she was fine with how she was," Noelle continued.

"You *did* make her look awfully pretty," Stella said after she took her time swallowing.

"Yeah, I know. It's hard to believe, Mama, but I guess not everyone wants to look their hottest."

She looked so full of wonder and amazement at the notion that Stella merely nodded along sympathetically.

"And I got to respect that. Only, that got me thinking. Sometimes there's folks that *would* like to look their best, only they just don't have the means. And that seems like such an awful shame."

And then she told Stella the plan she had cooked up.

That Saturday, the night before Easter, Noelle drove over after work and everyone enjoyed an early supper of scrambled eggs and frozen waffles, since nobody felt like going out to the store. As Stella did the dishes, Chrissy helped Tucker fill his basket with the eggs they had dyed earlier in the day.

"What do you think's keeping that boy?" Noelle asked, handing her mother a fresh beer and reaching one across the table to Chrissy.

"I don't—," Stella began, but then there was a clattering from the hall and they all turned to look.

"Holy Mother of God," Stella breathed.

Noelle had made them all wait to see the finished product. She'd done her work in the hall bathroom, and laid out her purchases in the guest room. For the last couple of hours, there had been a lot of mysterious sounds and the occasional hoot of laughter from that end of the house.

"Damn, I'm good," Noelle said, clapping her hands together.

Todd Groffe was standing in the hallway looking like he didn't know what to do with his hands. He could have put them in the pockets of his baggy jeans—there were pockets to spare. He was wearing a plaid shirt that looked like something her dad would have kept for working on cars, over a T-shirt that she was pretty sure had a bad word emblazoned across the front in some sort of Gothic script. His shoes weren't much of a change from his old ones—still giant and puffy, still unlaced with the tongue sticking out the top—but they were brand new.

Most amazing was his hair. Considering how long Noelle had been working on it, Stella had expected it to be a little shorter, but she'd kept nearly all the length, the ends now faded from his natural brown to a nice blond to pure white at the tips, and half of it stuck straight up and half sort of clumped around his face.

It wasn't like anything she would have picked out, but she had to admit that Todd looked just like all the fellas she saw on the celebrity rags at the checkout.

"What's in that shit you made me put on my face," he said, glowering at the floor—but trying hard not to smile, Stella was nearly certain. "Smells gay. Uh, I mean, sorry, Noelle."

"That's okay," Noelle said serenely. "But that *shit* costs thirty-five bucks a jar and it'll clear that skin of yours right up, so I wouldn't be disrespecting it."

There was a brief silence, during which Todd looked as uncomfortable as if Noelle had dressed him in a ball gown, and then Noelle got her purse off the counter and swung her car keys around her finger. "Okay, then, might as well go."

"You're sure it's okay to meet at the Arco?" Stella asked one more time, though Sherilee had reassured her in an earlier phone call that she and a couple of other moms were planning to cruise by in fifteen-minute intervals, just to check things out.

"Mom," Noelle protested at the same moment that Todd muttered, "I'm sure."

After ducking out of would-be hugs, Todd refused to have his picture taken and then they were gone. Stella and Chrissy and Tucker stood in the picture window and watched them pull out of the driveway in Noelle's little blue Prius, waving to beat the band.

"That Chanelle better treat him good," Chrissy said fiercely, swinging Tucker up into a bear hug.

"Oh, I expect he'll get his heart broken a time or two," Stella said. "It's only natural."

"Bye bye, Todd," Tucker said. "Bye bye, Null."

After that, there was a fire to build and hot cocoa for Tucker and a stack of quilts to snuggle under, and *The Sound of Music* to watch, just as Stella had with her own parents so many years before. When it got to the scene where the Reverend Mother tells Maria to find out how God wants her to spend her love, Stella got a little teary and reached for a Kleenex, and noticed that both Chrissy and Tucker had fallen asleep.

"Sweet dreams," she said softly, and carefully disentangled herself from the quilts and snuck down to her sewing room, where Tucker's giant chocolate Easter bunny was hidden in a drawer in her sewing cabinet. She nestled it into his basket, where he'd see it first thing when he got up in the morning.

Then she went back for the other three.

She propped two of the chocolate bunnies on the fireplace mantel as surprises for Noelle and Chrissy, and then she snuggled back in front of the fire and sighed contentedly, unwrapping the foil from the last one. She started with a big bite of the ears, just like she had when she was a little girl. Only this time, she didn't plan to stop there. Life was too short to save a single sweet moment for later.

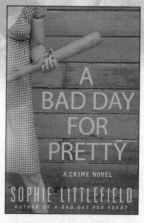
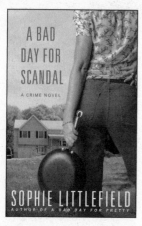